THE PERFECT ST[...]

It seemed too good to be [...] that the man she had wed in haste, then lost in battle, was alive. All too soon, however, she found that it *was* true—but not necessarily good.

Viscount Lucian Morley was very much alive, as he stood beside the beautiful Lady Barbara Barrington and stared at Alicia with dead, blank eyes. His life had been spared, but his memory had been destroyed, and there was no way for Alicia to escape the terrible truth that her perfect husband had become a perfect stranger.

An even more dreadful discovery soon followed, when the Viscount made Alicia a proposal as different from his first one as night from day. The only thing that this man who once had wanted only her now wanted was his freedom—his freedom to wed another. . . .

THE
FORGOTTEN
MARRIAGE

More Delightful Regency Romances from SIGNET

THE FORGOTTEN MARRIAGE

Ellen Fitzgerald

A SIGNET BOOK

NEW AMERICAN LIBRARY

SIGNET TRADEMARK REG. U.S. PAT. OFF. AND FOREIGN COUNTRIES
REGISTERED TRADEMARK—MARCA REGISTRADA
HECHO EN CHICAGO, U.S.A.

SIGNET, SIGNET CLASSIC, MENTOR, PLUME, MERIDIAN AND NAL BOOKS
are published by New American Library,
1633 Broadway, New York, New York 10019

First Printing, April, 1986

1 2 3 4 5 6 7 8 9

PRINTED IN THE UNITED STATES OF AMERICA

1

The Honorable Barbara Barrington sat at her dressing table while Jane, her abigail, put the finishing touches on her coiffure. Her hair was newly cut and the effect, she thought, extremely becoming. She stifled a small sigh. Lucian would no doubt admire it. Poor Lucian. She was feeling very sorry for her old playmate and erstwhile lover. He could not help but notice how incredibly beautiful she was looking. The horrid freckles she had acquired last summer were nearly gone. Her skin was once more alabaster white, and the slight darkness she had applied to eyebrows and eyelashes, which were, alas, the same shade as her red-gold locks, was also becoming, though Lucian might not approve of that. He was amazingly old-fashioned when it came to the use of what he insisted on calling "unnatural aids." and equally old-fashioned in other ways, too. However, she reminded herself, his approval, or the lack of it, had ceased to matter. She stifled another sigh. It would have been easier had she not felt it incumbent upon herself to see him. Her mama had wanted her to write him a note.

"Poor lad, he'll be much cast down," Lady Barrington had said. "I am sure 'twill be a painful experience for both of you, my love."

Barbara was quite in agreement. She had known Lucian nearly all of her life and she had been affianced to him for

5

two years—or, more precisely, one year, eleven months, and five days. However, as her mother had said, she had been a mere child when the understanding had been reached—not quite eighteen—and Lucian ought to understand that he had not been at home in either Yorkshire or London for the last two years, save for some very brief leaves . . . and on one of these, she had not even seen him! And absence, as she had recently learned, does not always make the heart grow fonder.

In the beginning she had loved him; she had, in fact, loved him since they had been respectively fourteen and nineteen, or thought she had until the Duke of Pryde had come calling. They had met at a rout and discovered that they both came from Yorkshire—of course, she had known that beforehand but he had not. He had been agreeably surprised and had asked her to come driving with him. Lucian, being away, she had consented; she had also accepted an invitation to a ball at Carlton House and had waltzed with him at Almack's. By a surprising coincidence, they had met at the country estate of a friend, and as they walked through a maze in the Italian garden, she had agreed to let him kiss her, once they had reached its center. It was a sort of victory kiss for having accomplished their goal, but it had lasted longer than she had anticipated. Once they were back in London, he had taken her driving again—and her parents, naturally, were delighted. If there were a coronation in the near future—which there must be, because George III was old and ill and insane, she would have a place very near the front of the abbey. As the Duchess of Pryde, she could expect no less. Lucian's father was only a viscount and he was not even dead yet, though he had been in poor health for years. The Duke of Pryde, on the other hand, had been in possession of his title since he was a lad of eleven. But supposing he did not come up to scratch? Barbara shivered. Though he had certainly given every indication that he might, or rather would, he had yet to speak. However, the *on-dit* (from unimpeachable sources) was that he was entirely infatuated with the Incomparable Barbara Barrington.

Her mama had not approved of her being voted an "Incomparable" by the dandies of White's, but that had not been her fault. One could not help being beautiful, nor could one help exciting admiration in the breasts of Lord Alvanley and Beau Brummell. And she had certainly not solicited the honor. She did not even know Brummell! Lady Barrington, however, did not think it an honor, and furthermore she had given it as her opinion that the Duchess of Pryde (soon to be the Dowager Duchess of Pryde) would not approve either. Barbara grimaced. She had heard that the duke's mother was very top-lofty and not an ideal choice for a mother-in-law, but she would cross that bridge when she came to it.

"There," Jane said. " 'Tis done."

The Incomparable Barbara started slightly. "Oh, Jane," she said pettishly, "you are so abrupt."

"I am sure I did not mean to be," Jane said. "But your 'air, it be done, ma'am."

"I see it is." Barbara rose and cast a martyred look at the door. "I expect I had best go down."

" 'E's been coolin' 'is 'eels for the last twenty minutes or more, poor young gentleman," Jane remarked.

"That need not concern you," Miss Barrington reproved.

"No ma'am, but—"

"You may go, Jane," her mistress interrupted coldly.

"Yes, ma'am."

As the abigail went out, Barbara cast a frowning look after her. Jane had been with her ever since her thirteenth birthday. Another saying arose in her mind: "Familiarity breeds contempt."

Jane was far too familiar. All too often she said exactly what she meant. Indeed, she presumed on her position and she would be sorry when, rather than calling her "ma'am," her new abigail, the one she would hire directly after Pryde offered for her, would be addressing her as "your Grace." Jane would regret her insolence, then. She might be standing in the street one day and see the ducal equipage go past carrying her Grace, the beautiful young Duchess of Pryde, and her new abigail on her way to a fitting at some mantua maker's or to have her portrait painted for the Long Gallery at Pryde House. And Jane, watching, would wonder why she was out on the street without the references that would enable her to seek another position . . . However, she ought not to be dwelling on such matters at a time like this—not when there was poor, poor Lucian to be considered! She would have to dispose of him very tactfully, but undoubtedly, no matter what she were to tell him, his poor heart would be broken.

She visited another lingering look upon the lovely countenance that regarded her from the depths of her glass. Her green eyes were dancing, and that would never do! And she must certainly obliterate the pleased smile that curved her perfect mouth. Or ought she to smile on Lucian . . . No, not when she must needs speak about cruel parents and a forced marriage and days and nights of agonized pleading on her part and Papa being adamant and Mama too. And what had Mama said? Ah, yes, "An alliance contracted in childhood before either of you knew your own minds." But, of course, she must needs assure him that she, Barbara Barrington, *knew* her own mind—it was only the terrible, terrible pressure that Papa and Mama had exerted upon her, with Mama sending her into gales of tears by saying that one never knew whether Lucian would even come home. It would have been easier, certainly, if he had not been so very fortunate—going through two engagements in which so many, many poor young men had made the ultimate sacrifice. Lucian, it appeared, had a charmed life. She ought not to regret that, she did *not* regret it. She did wish him well, but it would have been better had she not been called upon to deal him what must surely be a mortal wound.

She rose, admiring the lines of her green muslin. Pryde, too, had admired the gown. What had he said? "A dryad, ma'am. You do look like a dryad."

THE FORGOTTEN MARRIAGE 9

One would never have thought the duke to have so poetic a turn of phrase. He did not look poetic. Barbara frowned. In looks, he was not a patch on Lucian, being short, plump, and no more than an inch or two taller than herself. His eyes were good—small but vividly blue. However, his nose and mouth were almost undistinguished, while Lucian, tall and dark . . . dearest Lucian . . . was almost too beautiful for a man. Fate was certainly cruel. Lucian ought to have been born a duke and Pryde a viscount with a living father and only the smallest chance of inheriting the title in the near future, though Lucian's father was a martyr to the rheumatics and could not live forever. If only . . . But still, compared to a duke, a viscount must needs be put in the shade. With another glance at her speaking countenance, now properly downcast, the Incomparable Barbara Barrington glided gracefully from the room.

Brussels. The city was well enough, Lucian Morley thought as he rode back to his quarters. There were a great many British thronging the streets and more arriving each day now that Napoleon was, amazingly, gaining strength in France. However, not all his countrymen were in uniform. Some, in common with the Delacre family, were here because in Brussels one could live quite well on very little money.

He had received that information from Mr. Timothy Delacre, the son of the house where he was billeted. Young Mr. Delacre had described his father's losses on the gaming tables of White's, Brooks, Boodles, and a score of less distinguished hells with some bitterness. Lucian did not blame him—especially since Sir Anthony Delacre evidenced no disposition to change his profligate ways. On the few occasions he had seen the genial baronet, he was either returning from a late night at a Brussels hell or faring forth of a morning to "take the air," which air, his daughter Alicia said bitterly, was to be found only in those heated salons frequented by cardsharps and ivory turners.

At the thought of Miss Alicia Delacre, Lucian smiled and then frowned. He was very glad that her days of hurrying around seeing to his needs and those of Lt. Richard Seeley, his friend, also quartered in their house, was nearly at an end. He remembered the moment when he had first seen her. She had been hurrying up the stairs to the front door, carrying bundles that appeared far too heavy for her slender form—and they had been, he recalled angrily. On relieving her of them, he had found them weighty even for himself. Yet, she had actually protested his helping her, which, he discovered, was her way.

"I am very strong, sir," she had assured him. Her voice was beautifully modulated and surprisingly deep for one who was no more than an inch or two over five feet. She would not have even reached Barbara's shoulder, he remembered thinking. In those days, Barbara had still dominated his thoughts. He had compared every female he met to her, and much to their detriment, this despite the cruel blow she had dealt him. However, oddly enough, aside from her lack of inches, he had found nothing in Miss Delacre's appearance to make him wish that Barbara were standing in her place. In fact, even given his gloomy state of mind, he had been able to appreciate her bright golden hair, her startling brown eyes, her exquisite features, and her lovely shape. In fact, he had actually committed the solecism of staring at her in an amazement that had brought a blush to her face and a belated apology to his lips. The following day, he had wanted to call Dick Seeley out because he had found him laughing and talking with her.

Now, five weeks later, he still had difficulty curtailing a tendency to stare at her, to drink in beauty that was combined with intelligence and sweetness. Indeed, to his further amazement, Miss Alicia Delacre had succeeded in banishing the Incomparable Barbara Barrington from his heart and his head as well. If he thought of her and of that moment when he had been sure she had shattered his heart and ruined his life, it was to laugh loudly at so ridiculous a notion. That his heart and head were both totally intact was emphasized by the fact that he had fallen deeply and irrevocably in love with Miss Alicia Delacre; and much to his surprise and happiness, she, listening to his halting offer of marriage, had shyly confessed that she, too, had been smitten at that first moment on the steps and, unlike him, it had also been the first time in her life that she had experienced that tender passion called love.

His happy laughter rang out, startling a lady in a passing coach and causing Bellerophon, his own horse, to rear. In his mind's eye, he pictured himself in Barbara's house. He would be toasting her good fortune in snaring the Duke of Pryde and he would also be thanking her for freeing him from his long-standing obligation to herself—so that he might be married to Miss Delacre on Sunday, June 11, 1815. And Dick Seeley had agreed to be his best man. He had also agreed to say nothing about the forthcoming nuptials. "For," as he had confided to his friend, "I want to spend every possible moment with her, and then, when the war is at an end, I will take her back to England and introduce her to everyone."

"Marry in haste, repent at leisure," Timothy Delacre, broad-shouldered and a head taller than his sister, smiled at her teasingly. He added with an affection tempered by concern and a touch of regret, "I shall miss you, Licia." He fastened eyes that were much the same shade as her own on her face.

"I could never repent marrying Lucian," Alicia said softly, "but I will miss you and Papa, also. I love you both so much, you know that. And you will be returning to England one day. Papa was lucky last week and at least two of our creditors are satisfied."

"And the good Lord knows when he will be so fortunate again," Timothy said bitterly. "You ought to have marriage settlements instead of going dowerless to Lucian." He strode across the small parlor and stared out of the window, a habit of his when he did not want his distress to be viewed.

"I wish so, too," Alicia said regretfully. "But Lucian has laughed at the idea of 'paying for a bride,' as he calls it. Oh, Timothy, I never imagined I could be so happy. There are times when I think 'tis all a dream from which I will awaken and find myself . . ."

"Here with us," her brother finished dryly.

"Not that at all," she cried indignantly. "Yet, I did think 'twould be difficult . . ." Her voice dropped and she said a little gruffly, "Portions, you know."

"Any man who gets you can consider himself far richer than he deserves to be." Timothy crossed back to her and smiled down at her fondly.

"You were just mentioning marriage settlements," his sister reminded him.

"Only because of the convention. My damnable family pride, you understand." Timothy flushed. "I expect I ought not always to be looking backward to a tree that has ceased to flourish. But a Delacre did fight at the Battle of Hastings and another followed Henry the Fifth to—"

"Agincourt," Alicia finished. "The fact that we no longer possess a fortune cannot dim those exploits, my love, and once your books are published, you will add new luster to our crown or rather greener leaves to the tree."

"If they are ever published," he said gloomily.

"They must be," Alicia declared. "I vow they are as good as Mr. Walter Scott's *Guy Mannering*, which made such a stir in February."

"You are my sister," Timothy sighed.

"Mr. Creevey has said that they have literary merit, and sure he ought to know," she insisted. "Furthermore, he has promised that when he returns to England, he will take some of your manuscripts with him. But I need hardly remind you of that."

"Again, my love, you are my sister."

"And Mr. Thomas Creevey is no relation to you at all. He is a very important man. He knows everybody in London *and* everybody knows him. That does not always follow, as I am sure you are aware. I am also sure that you can believe him when he says he will help you, and if he does not, I will, once we are settled in London." Her eyes gleamed. "Oh, Timothy, I do wish Sunday would hurry up and arrive."

He looked down into her lovely face and kissed her lightly on the cheek. "It should for you, Alicia. You will make a most beautiful bride." He frowned. "Lucian's damned fortunate, to my way of thinking."

Alicia raised concerned brown eyes to his face. "There are times when I feel you do not quite like Lucian," she said unhappily.

"I do. I swear I do. Only . . ."

"Only!" she pounced. "There! You see, you do have . . . may I call them qualms?"

"I expect you may." He nodded. " 'Tis the swiftness with which everything happened, I expect. And the fact that the ceremony will be conducted in such secrecy."

"You know his reasons for that, and they are mine as well. As for the swiftness of our nuptials. Kitty Valant, for instance, was wed within—"

"I know," he interrupted. "That was because of the war."

Alicia flushed. "I do not think it is only the war, Timothy. Lucian says that until he met me, he did not know what love was, and sure 'twas the same with me."

A sound of trumpets caused Alicia to clap her hand over both ears. "Oh, dear," she murmured. "If only . . ."

Her brother turned troubled eyes on her face. "I beg you will not think of it, my love."

"That Napoleon," Alicia murmured resentfully. "I wonder that he can be called a man like other men. Remember Papa describing that idol they have in India, the Juggernaut with its cart, which they roll out for the faithful to cast themselves under it, to crush themselves to death? Five hundred and thirty thousand French soldiers perished in Russia alone. And how many more thousands and thousands have died because of Napoleon's passion for conquest? He is a juggernaut!''

"Oh, my dear." Timothy regarded her concernedly and, at the same time, helplessly. Words of comfort were of little value when faced with the reality of soldiers pouring into Brussels at a rate that far exceeded that of the *ton*, who had come to enjoy a limited version of that grand tour denied the sprigs of fashion since Napoleon had had himself invested with an imperial crown.

There was a knock on the door.

"Yes, Wilmot?" Timothy called.

But it was not the elderly manservant that entered but Lucian Morley, his eyes alight with happiness. He had a nod and a brief greeting for Timothy, but on turning to Alicia, he exclaimed, "Oh, my dearest love, I have missed you."

She laughed up at him. "You speak as if it had been days rather than hours since we parted."

"And has it not been?" he demanded.

Feeling himself *de trop*, Timothy, muttering an excuse, left hastily. Immediately upon his departure, Lucian swept Alicia into his arms, kissing her passionately. Upon releasing her, he said, "Why cannot we be wed immediately, my angel?"

"I—I wish we might be," she replied breathlessly.

"Then, why do we not—" he began eagerly.

"No, no, no." She moved away from him. "We cannot. Old Mr. de Jong, the vicar, would never, never forgive me."

He gave her a fond but exasperated look. "Are we marrying to please the vicar?"

"Oh, Lucian," she chided gently. "Our wedding is all arranged. Mr. de Jong has spoken to me about decorations for the church. He is a friend of the family, you know, and any change would upset him dreadfully. Papa would not like it, either, nor Timothy—and my bridal garments are not finished.

"I would marry you in your shift."

"That would start a new fashion," she teased. "And," she added, "Lady Octavia is to be my bridesmaid. You know her."

"Do I?" Lucian looked blank.

"You do!" Alicia exclaimed. "You met her last Tuesday."

"I am afraid that no one makes an impression on me anymore, not when you are in the same room." Lucian kissed her again.

"Oh, you!" Alicia laughed. "Well, Octavia is my very best friend and she is remaining here in Brussels just for the wedding. She was due to go back to London three days ago, but you certainly know all the reasons why we must wait until June eleventh."

"Of course, I do," Lucian relented. "And it will be as you wish, my angel. But afterward, we will spend our whole life together."

There was a flourish of trumpets outside.

Alicia winced but said steadily, "Of course we will, my Lucian."

2

Lady Alicia Morley, sitting at her dressing table, put on her earrings with fingers that trembled slightly. Behind her, Effie, her abigail, said admiringly, "You do look lovely, Miss Alicia . . ." She reddened. "I mean milady!"

"Do I?" Alicia asked anxiously.

"Won't be another at that ball'll be 'alf so beautiful," Effie said, opening her round blue eyes wider as if to give added emphasis to her statement. "Not 'er Grace of Richmond, either."

"How you do go on, Effie." Alicia managed a smile. "I'll warrant you've not seen her Grace."

"I 'aven't, but I know 'er girl wot works for 'er an' she says as 'ow she needs a good two hours afore she be fit to be seen in public."

"Oh," Alicia laughed, but added, "that is unkind, Effie." She put her hand to her heart as Lucian, in his scarlet uniform, suddenly entered. He was looking spectacularly handsome, she thought. The bright hue was flattering to his dark coloring. He had told her that he had often been taken for a Spaniard while he was on the Peninsula and she could believe it. In addition to his blue-black hair, his skin had an olive cast, all of which he attributed to one Doña Dolores, who had married his great-great-grandfather on the occasion of that gentleman's visit to Madrid in the train of Charles I, who had

16

been seeking to wed the Infanta María, daughter of Philip III. He had said whimsically, "Charles was not successful in his wooing, but my great-great-great-grandfather was wed within a month of meeting her."

"You must have your grandfather's eyes," she had said, loving the contrast of his silvery gray eyes under his ink-black eyebrows.

"No," he had demurred. "I inherited those from my late mother. I wish you might have known her, but you will meet my father after we have trounced Napoleon and sent him back to Elba or, I hope, some less felicitous spot."

She regretted that memory. She did not like to dwell upon the imminent conflict. Rumors were rife, however, but no one really knew anything. She could only hope that it would not take place for another month . . . she would have preferred forever. With an effort, she dismissed these thoughts and smiled up at him. "I am ready, my Lord," she said.

His eyes widened. "My angel, I've not seen that gown. Is it new?"

"Yes." She rose. "Do you like it?" She whirled about so that he might get the full effect of blue crepe over white satin, edged with white lace and crepe rosettes. It was cut low across her bosom and the sleeves were puffed.

"It is lovely and you are exquisite," he said warmly. "But must you wear that turban?"

"It is *de rigueur* with this ensemble. So insists Madame Van Slyke, the mantua maker."

"She cannot appreciate the full glory of your golden hair, my angel. And I charge you, you must dance every dance with me!"

"Can you imagine that I would not, my husband?" she demanded, savoring the word and wishing suddenly that he had not been honored by an invitation from her Grace of Richmond. The lady would wonder why she was there, since, in common with the rest of the *ton*, she did not even know that Alicia Delacre was alive! Possibly her attitude would have been different if their marriage had been announced. However, she did not blame Lucian for wanting to keep it secret. They would have been feted by his friends, many of whom had brought their wives with them. In common with Lucian, she wished they might have been able to take a wedding trip—only she longed for one that would bring them as far from Brussels as China!

Once more, thoughts of the emperor arose in her mind. His strength had been miraculously restored. One might compare him to those giants who had only to step on earth to regain their power, and Napoleon, escaping from Elba, had put his small feet on French soil—but he was no giant! He was a little man whose dreams of glory had proved deadly for the last two decades. Resentment flared in her mind as she gazed on the handsome young man in the becoming scarlet and gold uniform, every thread of which she hated. If only Lucian had resisted the call to arms! If only he, like Timothy, had been unable to afford a commission or, again like Timothy, thought a pen mightier than a sword—but then, of course, they would never have met. It was the war that had brought them together, and would it . . . But she refused to entertain that fear.

"A sixpence for your thoughts, my love?"

She started and, finding her husband staring at her quizzically, answered lightly, "They are not worth so much as a groat."

He said reassuringly, "You must not worry, my dear. I am known to possess a charmed life, something that has been demonstrated many times, as I think I have already told you."

"But I am sure of that," she said quickly, wishing that he had not guessed what she was thinking and remembering ruefully that Timothy had often commented that her face mirrored her mind.

"Then, let us go, that we may return soon," Lucian said ardently, and dropped a kiss on the little hollow at the base of her throat. "Oh, my dearest," he added with a sudden urgency, and then stepped back. "No, I will not keep you here. I want everyone to see you. And when this action is over, I will give a reception and introduce you. Do you mind being a secret for the nonce?"

"Of course, I do not mind. 'Tis what I want, also," she murmured. Her pulses were stirred and a need she had not known existed before her marriage moved her, but since she could not, out of shyness, tell that she would have preferred to have stayed away from the ball, she started to gather up her cloak—but was forestalled by his lingering kiss.

The Duke of Richmond's house lay down the hill, a walk, not a carriage ride away from their own dwelling. They would be arriving late, and hopefully, they would manage the early departure Lucian had mentioned, Alicia prayed. As they neared the great mansion, they found it ablaze with light.

"I am glad we were able to come here on foot," Lucian commented. "We would have been hard put to get through that mass of vehicles in a post-chaise."

"Indeed, we would," she agreed, staring at the many elegant equipages that lined the street. As they came nearer, they were nearly deafened by the sounds of horses neighing, the rattling of wheels, the metallic clash of harnesses, the din of coachmen blowing horns or yelling imprecations as they vainly tried to find a place to discharge their passengers. The passengers themselves added their voices to this cacophonous medley, and Alicia was thankful when Lucian, expertly skirting the crowds, managed to escort her into the house. Yet, as they entered, she was conscious that her throat had become dry and that her heart appeared to have risen to throb in that same area. She had no explanation for her qualms. It was only that there were so many young men in uniform milling about her, but she had seen uniformed gallants on the streets of Brussels for months and years! Consequently, she could not understand why she was so disturbed by their presence in the hallway. Perhaps it was only those rumors that had been circulating about town that caused fear to march foot-by-foot with love. She did not want it to be anything more. She did not want it to be one of her very occasional but frightening hunches concerning the future. She could only think of one or two of these incidents, but both had carried with them the sense of impending doom that she was experiencing now. Perhaps it was only her imagination! She forced a smile as she looked up at Lucian. "It will be a gala evening," she commented.

"Any evening where you are present is gala," he said lovingly.

Her worries were, for the moment, dispelled. It was wonderful to have him as much in love with her as she was with him. It was also unusual. Octavia had told her that. Out of her superior wisdom where men were concerned and fresh from a recent disappointment, she had said, "Lucian does not mind expressing his love—even before me. Usually gentlemen are much more reticent."

Taxed with criticizing him, Octavia had indignantly refuted that accusation. "I could wish only that more of the men I have known were like him. 'Tis certainly preferable than to be eternally trying to divine their thinking and, generally, to be completely wrong!"

Remembering that conversation, Alicia had a moment of feeling sorry for Octavia and wishing the worst for Sir Ivan Rutherford, who had hurt her. He was the reason for her abrupt departure for England. She could not dwell on Octavia's disillusionment now—not when she was so very happy.

"Captain Morley and Miss Alicia Delacre," bawled the majordomo as Lucian and Alicia came toward the receiving line in the immense ballroom. Subsequently, Alicia exchanged greetings with her Grace of Richmond, who hardly noticed her, and then they were inside. There was music and lights and the floor crowded with dancers, many of whom were in uniform, a plethora of uniforms, a mass of color—green, black, white, scarlet, light and dark blue—and there were the

Scottish officers in their plaid kilts, and the Austrian grena-
diers in white with bright gold sashes, and the Brunswickers
in black. The women with them were in pastels—white, or
pink, or blue like her own ensemble—but occasionally there
were flashes of scarlet satin, or yellow crepe, or black . . .
Did that signify mourning? No, 'twas not possible. Widows
did not dance. She wished she had not thought of widows.

Glancing about her, Alicia noted that the chairs that ranged
along the sides of the ballroom were empty. No languishing,
ill-favored young girls sat there yearning for partners and
looking enviously or wistfully at the gay company. Tonight
everyone was on the floor and the musicians were playing a
waltz—so much more satisfying than a country dance, since
it enabled one to remain with a preferred partner. Her thoughts
ceased as her husband took her in his arms and whirled her
onto the floor. One dance followed the next, and in the
middle of one of these she was aware of a distant sound—a
booming.

Lucian had heard it, too; he halted midstep, frowning.

"What is it?" she asked.

"It sounds like gunfire," he muttered.

"Oh, no," she breathed. She paused, straining to hear
more, but the sound in the ballroom, the laughter and the
music, drowned out that distant ominous boom.

"We will be able to go home soon, my love," Lucian said
then.

"Now, please." she whispered.

"Not yet," he sighed. "Sir Hartley Manners, my commanding officer, has insisted we join his table."

Dutifully they took their places and dined on cold chicken
and drank champagne. Though the food was delicious, she
wished they could leave. She glanced at Sir Hartley Manners
and was surprised and a little indignant to find he was no
longer in his chair. *He* had left early, then. She turned back
to Lucian and stiffened as she saw that Sir Hartley was
standing behind him. Her tension increased as she noted the

gravity of his expression and, out of the corner of her eye, noticed other men in uniform rising. She put her hand on Lucian's arm, silently mouthing the words that stuck in her throat—"No, please . . ."—for she dared not utter such a protest out loud. She was a soldier's wife, a position she had occupied only seven days, but it was enough to force a smile to her lips as Lucian turned a grim face in her direction.

"My own darling," he began, and swallowed.

She caught his hand. "You must go?" she said steadily.

"Yes . . . we have been summoned."

"I will walk with you to the door."

He bent to kiss her on the cheek. "No, I am allowed to accompany you back to the house. I have explained that 'tis only a step away. Come."

"I am glad," she told him, and not trusting herself to say anything more, she rose swiftly and, taking his arm, moved from the dining room. They walked across a ballroom that was emptying out even though the orchestra had not yet stopped playing. Then they were into the hall and down the stairs. Emerging into the warm June night, she heard a rumble and tensed.

"Thunder," Lucian said reassuringly. "There will be rain soon. Can you not smell it in the air?"

"Yes," she said, looking about her in surprise and wondering how she had come there.

Some ten minutes later, Alicia stood watching as Lucian walked quickly down the street. There was the sound of trumpets and drums in her ears now—and also in her ears was his smiling assurance: "I would have you remember, my love, that I am known to possess a charmed life, and when this is over, I shall come back to you, never doubt it."

What had she said in response? Words of agreement of course, though, again, she could not remember what they had been. He was gone now, he had waved and turned the corner and she had waved back, had she not? She stood there another moment and then went inside and was met by her father. He looked at her face and then put his arms around her and held her against him for a long moment. Moving away from her, he closed the door, and waiting until she had gained the stairs, he extinguished all the candles.

3

On a warm day in early September, the Honorable Barbara Barrington and her mother were seated in the cozy back parlor of their London house, a place to which they generally repaired when not entertaining guests.

Barbara, looking her Incomparable best in a round gown of nile-green washing silk, put down a letter she had just finished reading out loud to her mother, who, as usual, was wearing the half-mourning she had donned for her husband's death some six years earlier. Though she could easily be out of mourning by now, she found the color, a soft violet, very much to her liking, as well as flattering. Her countenance, generally wistful in repose, reflected surprise and a fugitive hope as her daughter said, "But it is entirely incredible . . . and after two months of believing him dead!"

"Entirely, my love," Lady Barrington affirmed. "His memory, though . . . poor lad."

"And his leg," the Honorable Barbara said. "I am glad 'twas not amputated. Surgeons in those field hospitals are often so careless."

"They are," her mother agreed. "I am indeed thankful that they discovered 'twas only a break. He was fortunate. A loss of memory is certainly not as bad as the loss of a limb. Those artificial legs cannot suffice. Will you go to see him, my dear?"

"How could I not, Mama?" Barbara said reasonably. "This Mr. Gerald Jenkins, physician, who penned the letter, says that Lucian is calling for me."

"That is certainly proof that he cannot remember," her mother said dryly.

"Indeed, he cannot, since he seems to believe that we are yet plighted."

Lady Barrington visited a long look on her daughter. "And what do you intend to tell him when you see him?"

She received an equally long look from the Honorable Barbara. "I would not like to cause him unnecessary pain at such a time, especially since there is now nothing standing in the way of our betrothal and"—her voice hardened—"his Grace of Pryde has returned to his country seat outside of Richmond to stay with his mama." Her sigh was duplicated by her mother. "And," Barbara continued, "since the shock of his being missing and presumed dead felled his father, Lucian is now the Viscount of Dorne."

"Very true, my love, but what if this loss of memory proves to be of a temporary nature, which can happen, you know." Lady Barrington regarded Barbara quizzically.

"I pray you will not borrow trouble, Mama. I will deal with that when and if the problem arises. Meanwhile, he *has* asked for me. Certainly, as one of his oldest and, I need not add, dearest friends, I could not refuse such a request."

In spite of her brave words, the Honorable Barbara was less than confident when, a week after receiving Mr. Jenkins' missive, her post-chaise drew up in front of the Morley mansion on Portman Street, to which, Lucian's identity having been discovered, he had been moved some four days earlier. A memory of their last encounter caused her to shiver as, accompanied by her mother, she mounted the three steps leading to the pillared portico.

"It *is* a charming house . . . one tends to forget how charming," Lady Barrington commented, evidently deciding to eschew any unwelcome comparisons with the ducal palace of the Prydes.

"Yes," Barbara agreed. "Quite a lot of money was expended on its rebuilding, Lucian told me. And there is the hunting seat in Leicestershire and, of course, the abbey." She grimaced. "But we need not count that."

"No," her mother agreed distastefully. "It has not been opened for years and I believe that Lord Dorne had it in mind to tear it down—at least the house if not the abbey ruins."

"I am quite in agreement about the house." Barbara grimaced a second time. "It is a moldy old place to be sure and always cold, but"—she achieved a sentimental sigh—"Lucian and I did meet in the ruins."

"Yes, I well remember that." Lady Barrington thinned her lips. " 'Twas when you were ten and slipped away from Mrs. Pope. What a fright you did give that poor woman, and myself as well. You were a very naughty child, willful and spoiled!" Lady Barrington sounded unusually stern.

"You cannot scold me for it now," her unrepentant daughter said with a smile that faded as her mother, reaching the paneled front door, lifted the knocker and slammed it forcefully against its plate. "He did ask for me, Mama," Barbara said in a small defensive tone of voice.

"Most assuredly he did, my love. I am sure . . . "Lady Barrington broke off as the door opened and Church, a heavyset man in his late fifties, appeared on the threshold. He had been looking very gloomy, but at the sight of the fair visitors he brightened.

"Yer Ladyship," he said obsequiously. He had a broad smile for Barbara. " 'Is Lordship'll be that glad to see ye," he continued. " 'E's been 'opin ye'd come."

Barbara bestowed a small smile on him. "One prays that he is on the road to recovery, Church."

" 'E will be now," the butler remarked with a touch of familiarity that, Barbara reflected, must be allowed a man who had long served the family and had known her since she was a child. In fact, she was considerably heartend by his attitude. Obviously Church knew nothing of that last fateful meeting when she had summarily broken her long-standing engagement to Lucian and broken his heart as well, as he had not scrupled to inform her. However, the butler's lack of knowledge was not surprising, for he had been at Tunbridge Wells with the late viscount during Lucian's last leave. Lucian had come to London from the watering place, and directly he had left her, he had gone to Belgium. Given his father's state of health, it was doubtful that he had written him concerning that disappointment. No, she decided, he could not have written, else Church would have known. Servants had a way of knowing everything. Pryde's failure to come up to scratch would have been blabbed all over London had she not given Jane a cameo brooch and three gowns she had not even worn yet, as well as the most delightful bonnet adorned with three ostrich plumes, all of which were very dear.

" 'Is Lordship's in the library," the butler said. He added, "Ye'll find 'im a mite confused as yet. 'E don't remember naught past Vitoria, an 'e 'as been 'ard put to realize that 'e were wounded at Waterloo."

"We are acquainted with his condition, thank you, Church," Lady Barrington said graciously. " 'Tis a great pity."

"It is that." Church nodded. He fastened a penetrating stare on Barbara's face. " 'E were in a rare takin' for fear you'd not waited, Miss Barbara."

The smile with which Barbara now favored the butler was beatific. "But I have," she said unblushingly. "And will lose no time in informing him of that fact."

Her smile broadened as she and her mother followed Church up the stairs to the first floor and down the hall to the library. She had quite forgotten the luxuries of the mansion. The late viscount's father had been an art lover and he had collected a number of fine paintings, including a splendid Rembrandt and, what was much more to her taste, a Botticelli that quite

rivaled the master's *Birth of Venus*. There was also a charming Romney that might be, she thought disapprovingly, an
early likeness of that depraved Irish doxy, Lady Hamilton
and, she also remembered, there was the famous Reynolds
portrait of Lady Morley, Lucian's grandmother, which hung
in the first drawing room.

That Lucian was in his library rather than his bedchamber
did not surprise her. He enjoyed reading and had been a
collector of books. He possessed a signed *Childe Harold*, she
recalled, and probably he would be much shocked to hear
about Byron's hinted incestuous relationship with his half-
sister Augusta Leigh, this despite his connection with Annabella
Milbanke. For one who served with the armed forces, Lucian
was surprisingly stiff-necked about extramarital relationships.
He had always decried the fact that even before his mother's
early death, his father had not scrupled to take as his mistress
Miss Violetta, an opera dancer at Covent Garden. Her thoughts
came to an abrupt end as they reached the library.

Church knocked on the door and she heard Lucian call
weakly, "Come."

Opening the door, the butler announced, "Lady Barrington
an' Miss Barrington, yer Lordship."

"Please have them come in, Church." There was a lilt to
Lucian's tone now.

As Lady Barrington entered, Barbara, following her, cast a
quick look at her gown—in her favorite green, as usual, and
part of that unofficial trousseau she had been collecting until
the miserable Duchess of Pryde had summarily put a period
to her dearest hopes. Though the Grecian look was not as
popular as it had been a few Seasons ago, it had always been
vastly becoming to her really beautiful figure and consequently she had had no qualms about having it made. She
was sure that it must meet with Lucian's approval. As for her
bonnet, high-crowned and ornamented with bronzed cock-
feathers, nothing could have been more becoming, she was
positive. Lifting her head, she stepped into the library. Her

eyes widened as she saw Lucian lying on his long leather sofa. Though he was thinner and much paler than when last they had met, he had lost nothing in looks. She moved forward, impulsively saying softly, "Lucian, my own love, oh, thank God, thank God . . . after all these weeks and weeks of uncertainty, to see you alive! 'Tis a miracle, indeed. If you but knew how very much I have suffered . . ." Her voice broke and she brought her gloved hand to her eye to wipe away a nonexistent tear.

He looked up at her and it seemed to Barbara that his heart was in his eyes as he replied haltingly, "My Barbara . . . my beautiful, beautiful Barbara. Then n-nothing has—has changed between us?"

"My dearest." She glided to his side and sank to her knees. "Oh, my poor, poor Lucian—all that has changed is that I know you are here in the world, and I can put my mourning aside, as you see I have. Oh, my dearest darling, have you suffered much?"

" 'Tis nothing," he said, looking at her as if he could not believe she was real. He put a hand to his head. "You know . . . Mr. Jenkins told you, I think, that I have received a blow that has wiped out two years of my life." He regarded her anxiously. "Are you sure that does not matter?"

"My love, nothing matters save that you have returned to me and we can be married at last," she dared to say.

He stared into her eyes. "We are still betrothed, then?"

"How could you think otherwise, my own? Have you ever known me to be unfaithful?"

"Barbara, my love," he exclaimed. He added with that impulsiveness that had always been an integral part of his nature, "When can we be married?"

She knew that he wanted an immediate wedding, but thinking about mantua makers, fittings, announcements, and the dinners, teas, routs, and balls given to celebrate this most felicitous and, she thought happily, triumphant occasion, Barbara said softly, "We will be married as soon as you can walk to the altar."

"Ah"—he expelled a deep breath that he must have been holding—"I will see that that will be very, very soon, my dearest Barbara."

In another household, another letter was received, read, and re-read with mounting incredulity by Lady Alicia Morley. Turning to Timothy, who was sitting at the edge of the couch on which she was lying, Alicia said faintly, "But—but it is not p-possible."

Timothy said in some surprise, "What is not possible, my dear?"

"Octavia writes . . . she writes . . ." Alicia shook her head and handed him the letter. "In the *Morning Post*," she said incomprehensibly, and leaning back against the cushions, she closed her eyes.

Her father, who had been standing near the fireplace, crossed the small parlor in two strides. "My dearest," he cried, "you'll not swoon!" He looked about for the vinaigrette, which had been in use more than once in the past three and a half months. He could not find it and, a second later, decided that this time it would not be needed. Alicia had opened her eyes again. He regarded his daughter with a mixture of sorrow and something perilously close to an agony he had not experienced since the death of his wife. She had had much the look of Alicia at the last, thin and pale, all her vivid coloring dimmed, but it had been a wasting illness, not grief, that had finished her. Still, of late, he had feared that Alicia too must succumb as the weeks turned into months and her anguish over the death of her young husband remained unabated.

He shuddered, remembering her terrible walk over the corpse-strewn field of Waterloo and her agonized wail that she had not found him during that desperate search. Nor had she found him in the many, many houses and hospitals she had visited in Brussels and environs. It was not until then that she had resigned herself to the fact that he was dead.

"If he were not dead, he would have come back to me," she had finally admitted.

Neither he nor Timothy, though they had discussed the possibility often enough, had dared to put forth the theory that if he were alive, he might not want to see her. There was always the chance that he had been terribly wounded or disfigured or both.

"Good God!" Timothy's explosive exclamation scattered his father's thoughts. He added, "We must go to London!"

Alicia's thin hand flew to her throat. "No, it—it cannot be true."

"Yet, supposing it is?" Timothy frowned.

"What is?" Sir Anthony demanded testily. "Where are my spectacles? No, better yet—what is in the letter, my boy?"

"Shall I read it to you?" Timothy said with a grimness that reminded Sir Anthony of those nights when he, coming penniless from the gaming house, was met at the door by his son, candle in hand. Yet this letter, which had come from London, more specifically from Lady Octavia Winterbourne, could have had no connection with his gambling debts. He said, "Please, dear boy."

"I cannot believe it," Alicia cried. "I cannot believe it." Slipping from the couch, she ran out of the room. For once her brother made no effort to follow and comfort her. He picked up the letter and began to read:

My dear Alicia,
I have news for you which I almost hesitate to set down, but feel that I must. Yesterday, (12 September) there was a notice in the *Morning Post*. I herewith enclose it. Read it and I will continue with what I have found out which is, unfortunately, very little.

"Read the notice," Sir Anthony prompted as Timothy paused.

"I was just about to do so," his son said. "Marriage to take place: Lucian Morley, Lord Dorne, to the Honorable Barbara Barrington, daughter of the late, etc. at St. James's Church, 12 October."

"No! I cannot believe it," Sir Anthony said explosively.

"May I please continue with the letter, sir?" Timothy inquired with strained patience.

Sir Anthony, who was well-acquainted with his son's moods, guessed that he was on the verge of exploding into one of his rare rages. He said pacifically, "Please do, dear boy. I am most anxious to hear the rest of it."

"Lady Octavia writes:

I have made as many inquiries as I may, given the fact that I, unfortunately, have no friends in common with the Honorable Barbara Barrington. And upon calling on Lord Morley, I was informed by his butler, a most officious individual, that his lordship was not at home to any but his closest friends—these the butler knows and is most protective and, I might add, suspicious of strangers, male or female. Why, I cannot know, but in the circumstances could not pursue my inquiries concerning his Lordship any further. However, my dearest Alicia, I have discovered that before his elevation to the title, the said Lord Dorne bore the courtesy title of Lord Lucian Morley, that he was in the Light Company, 33rd Regiment from Yorkshire. He had the rank of captain. He fought at Waterloo and was subsequently invalided home with a broken leg and sundry other injuries, the nature of which I could not discover. Still, I must conclude that the Lord Dorne whose engagement was announced in the *Morning Post* is, indeed, your husband.

With that in mind, I made a great effort and it met with success. I have obtained four cards to a ball given by Lord

Barrington, the uncle of the bride. It will take place on 30 September and I herewith enclose two cards for you. My fiancé (more about him in another letter) and I will make use of the other two and give you the support you need, should you wish to make any revelations and/or accusations at that time. I wish I could have garnered more information, but unfortunately my efforts have proved unsuccessful.

Please, Alicia, my love, whatever your feelings are, I pray that you and Timothy will attend that ball. If he, by some wild circumstance, is not your Lucian, then you will have set your mind at rest. If he is, you will be able to prevent a serious crime: that of bigamy. I remain, etc.

Timothy looked up from the letter. ''What have you to say to that, sir?''

Sir Anthony loosed a long sigh. ''I wish I could go with you, dear boy, but unfortunately my debts are not entirely settled and I stand in danger of being packed off to the Marshalsea or another of those poisonous dens. However, it being the nineteenth of September, I suggest that you begin immediate preparations for the journey. I have enough of the ready to send you across the Channel and subsequently to London, where you may stay at Grillons. It is a trifle dear, but I won a goodly sum last night and have quite changed my plans about trying to increase it tonight. If Alicia says she does not want to accompany you, she must be persuaded to change her mind.''

''I have changed my mind, Papa,'' Alicia said from the doorway. She ran to him and threw her arms around him. ''I—I cannot believe that it—it is Lucian, but . . .''

Sir Anthony looked down into her pale, sad little face. ''But, my dearest child, you owe it to yourself to find out one way or the other,'' he told her lovingly. ''I can see that you agree.''

"Yes, sir, I do," she said more strongly than he had heard her speak in the last three months.

He looked from Alicia to Timothy and said proudly but with a catch to his voice and an unusual wetness in eyes that were the exact color of his daughter's, "It may be premature, but I wish you *bon voyage*, my dear children, and good luck. May you arrive safely and find what you seek."

4

Lady Octavia Winterbourne, standing in the small parlor, part of the suite of rooms Sir Anthony had booked at Grillons Hotel, looked concernedly at Alicia. Tall and commanding, she towered over her friend. And, as usual, Alicia was reminded of a statue of Pallas Athena she had once seen in a Brussels museum. Octavia had the same wide brow, serene gaze, and large noble features, and that she, also, was aware of that likeness was borne out by the way she dressed her hair—pulled back in loose waves from her forehead and arranged in a Grecian knot. However, her tone, generally as serene as her appearance, was unexpectedly tart this afternoon.

Fixing an accusing stare on Alicia's face, she said, "You are being stubborn and—and ridiculous, to boot. You cannot appear at that ball in your widow's weeds!"

"But I am a widow," Alicia stated.

"We are not at all sure of that," Lady Octavia retorted, rolling her gray eyes in the direction of Timothy Delacre, whose hazel glance reflected her annoyance. She was positive that they were of the same opinion. Alicia was not daring to let herself hope that the man she would see that night was her lost husband. She continued, "Frankly, Licia, black does not become you. It blots you out. Lucian loved you in colors—I remember you telling me."

"Lucian is dead," Alicia said baldly.

35

"As I just told you, we are not sure that he is. That is why you are here, if you will remember."

"You have made me sure," Alicia retorted. "You just said 'Lucian loved you in colors'; *loved* is in the past. Lucian is in the past. I am in the past. I do not know why I was persuaded to come here. I should never have come, never, never, never." Alicia's tone was half-woeful, half-accusing.

"But," Lady Octavia, by dint of remembering her friend's misery, managed to control her impatience, "you are here, my dear, and widows, as you know full well, do not generally attend balls. You will only draw unnecessary attention to yourself."

"Then I will not go!"

"But you will go, my dearest sister," Timothy spoke for the first time since the argument had commenced. "And if Octavia does not think you should wear black—and I am in complete agreement with her—you can wear half-mourning. Gray or white or violet!"

"Violet would be the thing."

"White," Timothy contradicted.

"Gray," Alicia said firmly.

"Gray, it is." Looking over Alicia's head, Lady Octavia directed a grateful glance at Timothy. "And fortunately," she continued decisively, "my mantua maker will be able to provide the gown by tomorrow night. She is awaiting only my instructions. She has your measurements—though I must advise her to make it a trifle narrower, you have lost weight, I see. Now, my love, you must rest and, Timothy, I charge you, let your luggage be taken from here to my house. I have all the room in the world."

"No," Timothy said firmly. "I think we must stay here, Octavia. Alicia, as you say, must rest, and immediately. I do not think she should stir another step until then."

"Very well, as you choose. But remember, my dear, my house is yours."

"You are too kind. May I escort you downstairs?"

"Please." Lady Octavia kissed Alicia, and coming into the hall with Timothy, she waited until they had reached the head of the stairs before saying worriedly, "I would hardly have known her! She has lost much in looks. Has she starved herself for these last three months?"

Timothy's face darkened. "It has been a matter of forcing her to eat. Until your letter arrived, we feared that she would fall into a decline."

"Oh, dear, oh, dear, I guessed as much."

"It was a terrible shock," he said grimly. "Alicia has an intense nature and does nothing by halves, as I am sure you know."

"I am," Lady Octavia commented. "I have been extremely worried about her. She was so deeply in love with that young man."

He nodded. "And he with her—or so it appeared, but I need hardly refine upon that. You also saw them together."

"I did, and I agree with you. He had eyes only for her. Oh, dear, it is all such a puzzle."

"A puzzle, indeed," Timothy said harshly. "And if it turns out that this man is really Lucian Morley, the Lucian Morley we knew—"

"But he must be," Lady Octavia interrupted. "Charles, my fiancé, knows someone who knows Lord Dorne and he described his appearance. Dorne is tall, dark, and has gray eyes. He is known to be exceptionally handsome. He served with Wellington on the Peninsula, was subsequently posted to France and then to Brussels. This Lord Dorne was engaged to a Miss Barbara Barrington, whom Charles' friend also knows. He said that she was voted an Incomparable and that the so-called honor had gone to her head. He also said that she had cast out lures for Pryde."

"Pryde?" Timothy questioned.

"The Duke of Pryde," Lady Octavia amplified. "Nothing

came of it, of course. The present duchess lives up to her title. Indeed, she would frown on anyone the duke chose as consort. She, it is said, can trace her lineage back to Queen Bodicea, so it seems, but never mind that bit of nonsense. I have also heard that Barbara Barrington was almost a match for her, which says something about her character, or rather, lack of it.''

''But evidently she was not a match for her son,'' Timothy commented dryly.

Lady Octavia laughed. ''Oh, the duchess won, as she always does, but the fact that she was almost outfoxed is a point for la Barrington. I would imagine that they are two of a kind and . . .'' She sighed. ''Oh, dear, I cannot see such a creature with Lucian, who was so very much in love with Alicia.''

''But evidently on the rebound?''

''Possibly,'' Lady Octavia agreed. ''Oh, God, Timothy, what is to come of all this?''

''If it is, indeed, the same Lucian Morely, he will answer to me with the weapon of his choice,'' Timothy said grimly.

''I pray you'll not rattle your sabre yet,'' Lady Octavia begged. ''In talking about this it suddenly strikes me that there may be a perfectly reasonable explanation.''

''You are more perceptive than I.''

''I think I told you that the butler would not let me see him, something I found very peculiar. There is a condition known as amnesia . . .''

''Loss of memory?'' Timothy nodded. ''But that is very rare.''

''Yet, it is a possibility,'' she said. ''Timothy, I met Lucian Morley, and though I did not see him more than once or twice, he was so entirely in love with Licia and, at the same time, so frank and honest in that adoration that I cannot believe that I . . . that all of us were deceived.''

"I pray we were not. Indeed, I pray you are right. I, too, formed an impression similar to yours. I should not like to be totally mistaken in my estimate of Lucian Morley if, indeed, this is the man we knew. It would mean that I have less judgment when it comes to character than I imagined and my poor sister is the sufferer for that." Timothy loosed a long sigh.

She gave him a compassionate look. "I think you must not blame yourself, Timothy, my dear, not until we see what transpires tomorrow night."

"Tomorrow night, yes," he said grimly. "Then at least we will have an answer."

"I hope," she said, looking worriedly up into his set face, "that mine is the correct one."

Alicia, sitting at the large dressing table in her bedroom while Effie, looking concerned, arranged her hair, stared regretfully into a glass that was much clearer than the one at home. Though she had yielded to Octavia's order that she rest most of the day, she could not see that the fitful slumber of the afternoon had helped her. Indeed, she was much distressed by her appearance. In the three months of her widowhood, she had paid little attention to her looks, and now it was with a shock that she realized that the color Lucian had praised had fled. Furthermore, she had lost a great deal of weight so that there were hollows in her cheeks and her eyes were actually sunken. The dark circles beneath them resulted from a combination of weeping and lack of sleep. The gray muslin gown that Octavia had given her was stylishly cut, but she could not call it becoming. In fact, she thought, it made her appear almost wraithlike, and this is how he would see her, this man who might be Lucian Morley, arisen from the dead. Was he alive? She could hardly believe that—even though, as Timothy had said, the indications were that he very well might be.

Lucian alive!

How could that be? It could not be. The young man who had so joyously wed her and with whom she had spent the happiest moments of her life could not have coldly turned from her to another and offered for her . . .

"No, no, no," she whispered. In common with poor Richard Seeley, his best man, Lucian was dead. But he must be buried with others who had fallen there on that vast field over which she had walked, searching, searching, searching for him. There were many bodies that defied identification, she recalled . . . But she must not recall those scenes, which were like nightmares and had subsequently become nightmares during which she relived her travail upon the battlefield, walking and looking . . .

"Oh," she moaned. Tears filled her eyes.

"Milady." Effie put her arms around Alicia's shoulders, holding her against her bosom. "Do not take on, yet. 'E might be alive. It's 'appened before an' ye'll soon know."

Alicia blinked back her tears and attempted to smile at Effie. "I am becoming dreadfully tearful," she apologized.

"An' 'oo 'as a better right to be," Effie said hotly. "Oh, milady, I do 'ope . . ."

"So do I," Alicia said, realizing that no matter what the circumstances were, she wanted Lucian alive. Yet she felt cold and alone, even more alone than she had in the terrible days of waiting for the husband who, in spite of his assurance concerning his "charmed life," had not returned from the wars. He *had* returned in dreams, happy dreams that made her wish she had never awakened, but she could not think of that now. Soon it would be time to go, and she, who had vowed never to dance again, would be present at a ball to see a man named Lucian Morley, who might be her husband, and if so . . .

"No, no, no," she whispered a second time. He could not be her Lucian; it was unfair to her husband's memory to even entertain such a suspicion! She ought not to be going. She was half-inclined to divest herself of her gown and remain behind, but she could not. Her shameful curiosity kept her from giving in to that impulse. She had not traveled all this way to turn tail and flee before possibilities she feared to confront. She rose from the dressing table and let Effie drape her gray cloak about her, thinking, as she saw her image in the mirror, that she looked more like a ghost than ever: a ghost going to meet another ghost, for he could not be alive, not Lucian! At least, she amended, he could not be *her* Lucian!

"I should not insist that Lucian go through the paces of a waltz, my love," Lady Barrington advised Barbara as they came into the ballroom at Barrington House.

"Of course, I shall not, Mama, I . . ." Barbara paused on passing a tall mirror. Coming to a complete stop, she stared at herself with considerable satisfaction. Her hair, arranged in a Psyche knot, was ornamented with a diamond and emerald half-moon. She longed to wear that same combination of stones in a tiara, and once she wed Lucian, he would give it to her. She knew she had only to say the word. It was a mite dear but he could afford it. He was not as wealthy as Pryde, of course, but he was very well-off, and so handsome. Pryde could not hold a candle to him in looks. She had always been aware of that, and now that he had the title and the lands, she did not give a fig for the duke or his horrid mama. They would have read the announcement and she could imagine Pryde's chagrin. Had he expected her to wear the willow forever?

"My love," her mother prompted, "do come away from that mirror. Let others do the admiring."

Barbara flushed and stepped back quickly. "I was *not* admiring myself, Mama. I was *thinking*," she emphasized. She looked about her. "Where has Lucian gone?"

"He must be still in the garderobe. You know it's difficult

for him to move quickly—that is why I do not want you to insist on more than one waltz.''

"I will not, Mama. I am quite cognizant of the state of his health," Barbara said testily.

"Good," her mother commented. She frowned. "But do you know, my dear, I still find myself most concerned over—"

Barbara raised an impatient hand. "Even if he should regain his memory, I cannot think he will suffer unduly." With a touch of asperity, she added, "Not when he finds himself wed to me, Mama."

"No, I expect not," Lady Barrington agreed. "He was much in love with you—but you heard nothing from him once he had gone to Brussels."

"I did not *expect* to hear anything from him, Mama. He was much cast down. He said I had blighted his life." Barbara frowned. "Furthermore," she continued impatiently, "I cannot understand why you should raise these cavils to-night. Supposing Lucian should suddenly come upon us?"

Thus adjured, Lady Barrington cast a glance over her shoulder and was pleased to note that the bridegroom-to-be was not approaching. "You are quite right, my dear," she said apologetically. "Come, let us go and join dearest Frederick." She took her daughter's arm and in another moment was being welcomed by her brother-in-law and his lady. If Lady Barrington entertained qualms, Barbara's uncle was beaming.

"My dear," he said to his niece, "I have never seen you in such looks. Your Lucian is, indeed, a most fortunate young man."

Across the room, Alicia was standing with Timothy, Lady Octavia, and her fiancé, Sir Charles Graves, a pleasant-looking young man who seemed very much in love with Octavia. It was Sir Charles who had pointed out the Honorable Barbara. "But," Alicia breathed, "she is very beautiful."

"Is she not?" Timothy agreed.

"She is," Lady Octavia said shortly. "However, beauty is as beauty does."

"Quite right, my love," Sir Charles agreed.

"She is so tall and stately. She carries herself like a princess," Alicia said.

"And imagines herself a queen," Lady Octavia snapped.

Alicia, her eyes lingering on the Honorable Barbara, had, she realized, hoped to find her less attractive than Octavia had suggested. However, there was no denying that she deserved the designation "Incomparable." And with her crown of red-gold hair, her green eyes, her oval face, and her excellent figure, set off by a green silk gown that bore the stamp of Paris, she caught and held the eyes of many gentlemen in that large room. Yet, with all her beauty, there seemed to be something cold about her, Alicia decided—cold and proud. Her speculations came to a sudden end as a young man in black evening clothes and walking with a slightly halting step joined the Honorable Barbara. Seeing him, all the sound in the room—the talking, the laughter, and the music— suddenly ceased, for, of course, it was Lucian!

"Licia." Timothy's arm was around her shoulders for comfort and support. There was urgency in his tone, an urgency tinged with anger. "I beg you will not swoon."

"No," she mouthed, the while a plethora of emotions arose in her—anger, pain, amazement, more than mere amazement, incredulity—as she watched Lucian, *her* husband, smiling at the redhaired beauty as once he had smiled at her. It was obvious, even from this distance, that he adored her, even worshiped her, and Miss Barrington was looking at him lovingly, no, *not* lovingly, triumphantly! And tonight their engagement would be announced.

"No," she said. "No!" She moved forward.

"Licia, my love, are you all right?" Timothy muttered.

She did not answer. She continued to move forward, pushing past people who stood in her way, unaware of their

surprised and affronted exclamations. Timothy kept pace with
her and then they had reached the receiving line and there
were other guests arriving, but Alicia eluded them and came
to stand in front of Lucian, who was accepting a couple's
congratulations and smiling and thanking them. Barbara was
also thanking them.

"Lucian!" Alicia cried.

He looked at her in surprise, but before he could respond,
Timothy confronted him. "Lucian," he rasped, "what is the
meaning of—of this travesty?"

"Travesty?" the Honorable Barbara repeated. "Lucian, do
you know these—these people?"

Lady Barrington, her eyes wide and filled with concern,
moved to her daughter's side. "My dear, be calm," she
warned.

Lucian was shaking his head. "I cannot say that I do know
them." He looked from Alicia to Timothy. "You have the
advantage of me, I fear."

"The advantage!" Timothy roared. "If you are trying—"

"Sir"—Lord Barrington glared at them—"I do not remember inviting either of you. Will you please explain—"

"Wait, milord," Lucian interposed. "I might have known
them during that time. I—I cannot remember."

"You cannot remember?" Alicia said faintly.

"Of course." Lady Octavia had followed them, arriving in
time to hear Lucian's response. "Did I not tell you, Timothy,
this is what must have happened? You have lost your memory, Lucian?"

He regarded her concernedly. "Yes, I fear I have. The late
conflict at Waterloo . . . I am told I was there, but"—he
shook his head—"I remember only Vitoria. Two years have
been blotted out of my mind."

"Two years . . ." Alicia gasped.

Lucian turned to her. "I pray, ma'am, that you will help
shed some light on this darkness. Please tell me who you
are."

"And why you found it necessary to make such a scene at this time," Barbara added. She continued witheringly, "We seem to have gained the attention of everyone present."

"Better now than later, Miss Barrington," Lady Octavia said coldly. "I am told that this ball is in honor of your forthcoming marriage."

"My marriage?" Barbara echoed. "And what, pray, has that to do with—"

"Barbara," her mother muttered, "be silent."

Alicia was trembling. "You do not know me, sir? Not at all?"

He said regretfully, "I fear I do not, but again"—a slight touch of anger crept into his voice—"I hope you will help alleviate my ignorance."

"She is—" Timothy began.

"No," Alicia interrupted. "That question was addressed to me." She fastened her eyes on Lucian's face. "I am Alicia Morley, your wife."

"My—my—" He turned pale. "No!" he cried loudly.

"Yes, milord," Lady Octavia said. "I was present at your wedding. I was Lady Alicia's maid-of-honor and your friend Lieutenant Richard Seeley was your best man."

"Richard . . ." Lucian said. "Richard is dead."

"Conveniently dead," Barbara cried. "The dead tell no tales, they cannot say that all of you are lying!" Shaking off her mother's restraining hand, she glared at Lady Octavia and then at Alicia. "I do not believe you. 'Tis some sort of plot. We are to be wed, Lucian and I. It is a matter of long standing. Years." She glared at Alicia. "You heard of his infirmity, did you not? And recruited poor Dick Seeley to substantiate your tale and you have come here to confound him and to—"

Alicia was trembling but she drew herself up as far as she might, given her slight stature. "I am here because I was sent an announcement in the *Morning Post*. One I could scarce believe and—"

"You see!" Barbara shrilled. "She read the item and decided to press her fraudulent claim. She must have had some sort of a friendship with you. And do not tell me that you knew nothing of his loss of memory, you conniving little trollop."

"Barbara!" Lucian's exclamation topped protests from Timothy and Lady Octavia. "You must not speak so. One can see that she is no—"

"I see that she is a scheming harpy," Barbara cried.

"Barbara, please control yourself." Lady Barrington's fingers dug into her daughter's arm.

Her sister-in-law moved forward, saying pacifically, "Please, I think we must adjourn to the library, where this situation can be better discussed."

"Yes, you are right, my love," agreed his Lordship in a shaken voice. He put his hand on his niece's arm. "Come, Barbara, my dear."

She remained where she was, her eyes blazing, "I cannot see that there is anything to discuss. Would Lucian have wed a woman of her stamp when he was betrothed to me?"

"Barbara!" Lucian protested. "This young woman, whoever she is—"

Timothy spoke over him, "I will thank you not to refer to my sister in this disparaging manner."

"Please," Lord Barrington said. "We will go to the library." He put a compelling hand on Barbara's arm, saying in a voice that brooked no refusal. "Come, my dear."

"Very well!" Barbara's face was flushed and her green eyes were narrowed, giving her something of the look of an angry cat. "We might as well get to the bottom of this sorry intrigue."

"Barbara"—Lucian gave her a quelling glance—"let us hear what they have to say before we reach any conclusions, please."

"You may need to reach a conclusion," she retorted, "but

not I. You cannot believe you were wed to this—this—to her, can you?''

''I do not know what to believe,'' he responded unhappily. ''Save that, if I am, I have acted dishonorably.''

''Dishonorably?'' Alicia put a thin hand to her bosom. ''You . . .'' Tears filled her eyes and she closed them quickly, unwilling to let this stranger view her anguish.

''And where did you learn to act so convincingly? On the stage perhaps?'' Barbara glared at Alicia.

''Barbara! Anyone can see that this girl is sincere,'' Lucian said.

''Because she can produce a tear or two? Any Covent Garden whore can equal that feat and raise her price by the doing of it.''

''*Barbara!*'' Lucian and Lord Barrington spoke in unison.

Barbara, her head held high, turned on her heel and stalked into the hall. She was followed by her mother and, after a second's hesitation, Lucian.

''My God,'' Timthy muttered, ''if . . .''

''You will come with me, please.'' Lord Barrington turned his cold gaze on Timothy and Alicia.

Motioning to an aghast Sir Charles to remain behind, Octavia moved to Alicia's other side and amid curious stares and muttered comments from the assembled guests, they followed Lord Barrington. ''My dearest Alicia,'' Octavia murmured, ''I beg you'll not let anything that creature says disturb you. You can see what she is.''

''If I were in her position—'' Alicia began unhappily.

''If you were, I'll warrant you'd listen before you delivered yourself of all those gratuitous insults.''

''But did you hear her?'' Alicia whispered. ''She said she was—was betrothed to Lucian when—''

''I do not believe it,'' Octavia interrupted. ''There might have been such an understanding at one time, but I find it impossible to believe that Lucian would have acted so dishonorably. Do not forget what I told you about the Duke of

Pryde, whom she lost. It might well be that when Lucian came back in this unfortunate condition . . .'' She paused as a servant held open the library door and, coming inside, added in a low voice, ''I will tell you what I think later.''

The library was large and comfortable but dimly lit. At Lord Barrington's order, the servant lighted candles in several candelabra, including a pair on the mantelpiece, where a long mirror caught their light.

Indicating a group of chairs, Lord Barrington said, ''I suggest we all sit down and discuss this most unfortunate matter.''

Barbara moved to a couch and said to Lucian, ''Sit by me, my love.''

He shook his head. ''I think I—I should prefer to stand.''

''Your leg, my dear,'' Lady Barrington said quickly. ''You must not put any undue strain upon it.''

''Your leg?'' Alicia echoed, and might have said more had not her brother pressed her arm. She flushed, realizing that her inadvertent expression of concern was ill-timed. The man she had once called husband would not be in need of her pity. Her head was beginning to throb and she felt . . . But she was not sure what she felt. Her thoughts were in a turmoil. The happiness she ought to have been experiencing was in abeyance. Lucian was not dead, but in a sense, the man she had known and loved might as well have been dead. And had he proposed to her while he was still engaged to this proud, chill young woman—is that why he had insisted on keeping their nuptials a secret? No, she could not believe that. Dick Seeley had known and he would not have lent himself to anything so dishonorable. She could not imagine Lucian acting in such a manner, either, and judging from his shock and, she thought wryly, his horror, nor could he! She stole a look at his face and flushed as she found him staring at her.

''My leg, 'twas broken. I received a ball through it. It grazed but did not shatter the bone and—''

Barbara's eyes were flashing again. ''I beg you'll not

vouchsafe any more explanations, Lucian. I'll warrant that one knows all about your wounds—leg and head. I'll warrant she has done copious research on your condition.'' She glared at Alicia. "And where is your proof that you were wed to my fiancé? Did you bring your marriage lines? But those are easy enough to have made and—''

"Barbara,'' her uncle interrupted at the same time that Timothy stepped forward to confront her. "These exclamations only impede the explanation that we all wish to hear.''

"Yes, my dear,'' her mother said. "Please listen to what this young woman has to say.''

"Very well,'' Barbara flashed. "But I warn you, I'll not believe a word of it. Coming here at a time like this . . . 'tis outrageous!''

Alicia confronted her. She was trembling, but she said steadily enough, "I agree that our arrival is ill-timed but my friend''—she cast a look at Lady Octavia—"did make an effort to see Lucian and was turned away by his butler. And—''

"I wonder why!'' Barbara interrupted.

"The why of it''—Lady Octavia moved toward her—"is that Lucian's butler probably did not count me among his friends, since we had met in Brussels and the man did not know my face. Given Lucian's condition, I quite understand his reasoning. He did not want him confused.''

"And,'' Alicia said with a grateful look at her friend, "I had learned that an announcement concerning your betrothal was to be made at this ball, supplementing that which appeared in the *Morning Post*. I thought to save you both further embarrassment.''

"And consequently used this means so that all the *ton* has witnessed our meeting and is whsipering and speculating? I fear, Miss Whoever-you-are, that you have failed in your objective.'' Barbara glared at her.

Alicia lifted her chin. "I am not Miss Whoever-you-are.

My legal name is Alicia, Lady Morley. My maiden name is Alicia Delacre.'' Turning away from Barbara, she moved to Lucian and thrust out her left hand. ''I am sure you will recognize this ring, my betrothal ring.''

He stared at it and paled. ''Yes, my c-crest. I thought it was lost upon the battlefield.''

''And could it not have been lost?'' Barbara shrilled. ''We have all heard about those human vultures that comb the battlefields searching for what they can pilfer from the corpses.''

''Barbara!'' Lucian's shocked cry topped similar protests from everyone present. ''I must ask you not to level these cruel charges at this young woman.''

''Madame,'' Timothy said through clenched teeth, ''if you were a man, you would answer for this slander.''

''Please, sir.'' Lord Barrington, visibly shaken, stepped forward. ''I must crave your indulgence for my niece. She has, you must understand, suffered a cruel disappointment.''

Lucian had taken Alicia's hand and was staring at the ring. ''I gave you this?'' he questioned.

''Yes, and this one as well,'' she affirmed through trembling lips. ''My betrothal and my wedding ring.'' She touched the wide gold band, trying not to remember his words at that time, trying not to look at this concerned and obviously distressed, even horrified stranger.

''When did these happy nuptials take place?'' Barbara demanded.

''On June eleventh,'' Alicia said.

''You can prove that?''

''She can prove it and I, too, can prove it, since I was maid-of-honor at the wedding.'' Lady Octavia said. With a glacial look at Barbara, she added, ''I trust you will not dispute my word, Miss Barrington.''

''I do not—'' Barbara began.

''Barbara,'' Lucian said, ''though I cannot remember her,

I do not believe that this young woman is lying. I must have known her once—and well.''

"Well?" Barbara inquired coldly. "I am inclined to doubt that, Lucian. Everyone knows the manner of women with whom lonely soldiers consort when they are a long distance from home.''

"Good God, Barbara!" Lucian stared at her in an amazement mixed with horror while Timothy, his fists clenched, moved forward again, only to have Lady Octavia catch his arm as Lucian continued, "I scarcely know you!"

Lady Barrington put a hand on Lucian's arm. "I am afraid my daughter is so greatly shocked and so deeply disappointed that she is not aware of what she is saying.''

"I do know what I am saying," Barbara said. She glared at her uncle, who had directed a quelling look at her. "I am quite sure that poor Lucian was trapped into this—this sham of a marriage. How could he not have been? Our understanding was a matter of years. We were children together and fell in love even before we knew what the word meant.'' She moved to Lucian's side. "Is that not true, my dearest?''

"Yes, it is true," he said miserably. "It is entirely true. I have no excuse.'' He shifted his weight and an expression of pain crossed his face.

"Sir," Alicia said swiftly, "I think you must sit down. If your leg has been hurt, it is essential that you rest it.''

"Very wifely!" Barbara commented sarcastically.

"Barbara," Lady Barrington muttered, "that is enough.''

"I think," Lord Barrington said, "that we must have further discussion on this matter, but not this evening. My niece is understandably upset as you, too, must be.'' He bent a not unfriendly glance on Alicia. "May I name a time when we might all meet again?" His gaze shifted to Timothy.

"Why must we have a second meeting?" Barbara demanded. She turned on Alicia. "Why may we not settle matters now? How much do you want? Whatever the price for an annulment, we'll pay it and have done.''

Alicia turned white, but before she could respond, Timothy confronted Barbara. "You think—you dare to imply that my sister wants money."

"No!" Lucian turned to Barbara. "You cannot mean what you just said, my dear. This girl—I must have had a great regard for her, else I would not have married her."

"I have told you what I think about that."

"And I will tell you, Barbara, I have been in many battles. I have been lonely and far from home and I have not been minded to marry any of the women who have comforted me at such times, nor have they been of the caliber of this girl," Lucian said hotly. "I am sorry to be so frank, but it seems I have no choice. Anyone can see that she is no schemer."

Barbara flushed and looked down. "I—I am sorry, too," she managed to say. "You do speak reason, Lucian." She turned toward Alicia. "I pray you will accept my apologies, Miss, er, Lady Morley. My uncle was quite right. We must meet on the morrow when we are all calmer and have had more time to reflect upon this matter. I hope you will agree to that?"

"Yes, I will agree to it," Alicia affirmed.

"And I." Lucian sounded even more weary.

"Tomorrow it is," Lord Barrington said on a note of relief. "May we say at three? You may come here. Is that agreeable with both of you?" His glance took in Alicia and her brother.

Timothy, receiving an almost imperceptible nod from Alicia, said, "Yes, my Lord, it is agreeable."

"Lucian?" Lord Barrington looked at him.

"It is agreeable with me, also," he said in a low voice.

"Very good." Lord Barrington had another glance for Timothy, "Might I know where you can be reached, sir, in case of any change in our plans?"

"We are at Grillons Hotel, my Lord," Timothy responded.

"Ah, yes, well, I suggest we part company now." Lord Barrington turned to Lucian. "You'd best go home, my boy.

I will say that you have been taken ill—a happenstance that will, of course, delay the announcement.''

"The announcement," Barbara whispered. "Oh, Lucian!" She gave him an anguished, yearning look and, rising swiftly, hurried from the room.

"Barbara!" he exclaimed. He took a step toward the door and stopped, looking about him uncertainly.

Tears rose in Alicia's eyes. However, she managed to say calmly enough, "I think 'tis time we also left. Come, Timothy and Octavia.''

Making their requisite farewells, they too left the room.

5

The small china clock on the mantelshelf in Alicia's bedroom struck nine times. She counted the tings automatically as she had counted eight, seven, and six. And, as before, she paced the floor, wondering what to do and what to answer the man she had called husband when he asked the inevitable question. Undoubtedly, the answer he craved to hear was succinct, a matter of a few words, an agreement to an annulment. And if she were to agree, what, then, would she do with the rest of her life?

"You are young, my dear; you have yet to see your twentieth birthday," Timothy had said last night at the end of a discussion in which he had practically assented or consented to an annulment. " 'Twill not carry with it the stigma of a divorce, my love, and you'll have all your life before you. Furthermore, there will be a settlement."

A settlement! Alicia shuddered. If she were to relinquish her husband, she would be well paid for that act—well-paid and well-fixed, able to marry again. She did not want to marry again! She could not marry again, for who would want someone whose heart had been given away? And yet, were she to remain stubborn and insist on Lucian honoring his vows, he, too, would be miserable. Still, would he be any happier with Barbara Barrington?

With the thought of Barbara came the memory of their

days in Brussels. She remembered the first time she had seen him. He had come up the stairs to relieve her of her bundles. She could see his eyes, full of pleasure. And he had been laughing, too. Had he been secretly brooding over his lost love?

His *lost* love? The girl must have been lost to him. There must have been some manner of altercation—her intelligence told her so. That Lucian was an honorable man went without saying. It had been very evident last night. He had been in agony over his possible perfidy, his betrayal of Barbara and herself. Also, Alicia thought, there was the Duke of Pryde. Octavia had mentioned that situation again last night after they left. Barbara had been involved with the duke while Lucian was in Brussels. Had they quarreled because of that involvement? Very probably, and Lucian had found her while his heart was still sore from that rejection. She wished that Octavia knew more about the situation. Her friend had had much to say about the encounter of the previous night, but much of it had been vituperative. At the last, she had begged Alicia not to give an inch. "If not for yourself, my love, for Lucian's sake. Inevitably, he must come to his senses!"

But would he?

And what were his senses?

He seemed to be deeply in love with Barbara Barrington— but that love was two years in the past. What about the present? Dared she assume that the man she had seen last night was not the man she had known in Brussels? She ran her hands through her hair. The situation was becoming more and more complicated. She . . . She paused in her ruminations. She had heard a tap at the outer door. She tensed. Could it be Lucian?

"Yes?" she called.

Effie came in. "If you please, milady, it's 'er. She be downstairs, an' wants to know if you'll see 'er. 'Tis Miss Barrington, milady."

Alicia tensed. "Is my brother still out?"

"Yes, milady."

"I . . ." She paused and came to a decision. "I will see her, Effie. Have her shown into the parlor, please."

" 'Adn't ye better . . ." Effie began, and meeting Alicia's eyes, she flushed. "Yes, milady." She hurried out.

Alicia paused by her dressing table, and looking into the glass, she sighed. The effects of a partially sleepless night were all too evident. There were darker circles under her eyes and her face was even paler than last night, and since she had donned her black garments upon rising, she looked sadly washed out. She grimaced, remembering her refusal to discard her weeds or to take with her any of the garments she had worn before Lucian's "death." In effect, she had refused to accept the possibility that he might be alive and she knew the reason for that. She had been so very certain of his love that she could not imagine that he, if alive, would not have gotten word to her. But to dwell on that would do no good. She came into the parlor. She wished that Timothy were there. No, on second thought, she did not wish anything of the sort. It would be better to meet Barbara alone.

Barbara Barrington came into the parlor looking so vibrantly beautiful that she almost took Alicia's breath away. Everything about her seemed to glow—hair, eyes, and complexion. Tall and willowy, her figure, in a riding habit that fitted her to perfection, was superb. If she had not already earned the encomium of "Incomparable," she must surely have warranted it at this moment. Beside that incandescent presence, Alicia felt herself dwindling like a spent candle. And most surprising of all, Barbara was not looking upon her with anger or disdain. She was actually smiling and she almost caroled her greeting, "Good morning, Lady Morley."

Faced with this disarming attitude, Alicia tensed and figuratively girded herself for what, she realized, was a most formidable enemy and, alas, a most uneven contest. She could imagine that if Lucian were here, he would have no more interest in her than a fly on the wall. Yet, not so long ago he had reveled in her beauty, a beauty sadly diminished by her agony over his supposed demise. It was with considerable constraint that she said, "Good morning, Miss Barrington. Will you sit down?"

"Thank you." Barbara chose a leather chair, leaving the sofa for Alicia, who sat down in a corner, glad of the padded armrest that seemed to lend her strength.

Meeting those glorious green eyes, Alicia said, "You wanted to speak to me?"

"Yes, first I must apologize for my regrettable behavior last night. You see, I was taken unawares. I had not dreamed that dearest Lucian would be so cast-down by a slight altercation we had last spring. Never, never try to make a man jealous, Lady Morely, but I am sure you have much more sense than that. I did not.

"Having known Lucian for such a long time—since we were children, in fact—I thought I knew him through and through, from his eyebrows to his toes. Indeed, I was far too confident of his reactions, and so, to tease him, I tried to make him jealous by encouraging the Duke of Pryde. It was all in fun but"—Barbara sighed and looked down—"I fear that my head was briefly turned by his solicitations. They were so ardent, you understand, and he was a duke. That excited me—and I admit that I was also a tiny bit flattered—but I soon found out that he was a dead bore. And meanwhile, Lucian had gone off in a huff. You can imagine my horror when I learned that he had left for Brussels without even attempting to see me!

"I was devastated. I did not even know where to write to him, and I expect it was during this period that he met you." She sighed. "Oh, my dear Lady Morley, I am so sorry for you. I do hate to see you suffer in this farrago, and, of course, you have. Lucian and I have loved each other for such a long time and many have tried to come between us, but they've never succeeded and, of course, they never will. I should have told you that last night instead of saying such

horrid things to you, but it did come as such a shock. Here
we were—so ecstatically happy and about to announce our
engagement, something all our friends knew, and then to
have you come and tell us that Lucian was already wed,
something he could not remember, poor dear. You do understand, I hope?''

Alicia nodded, the while her heart beat faster and little air
bubbles rose in her throat, causing her to swallow convulsively. Barbara's statement seemed terribly logical and yet
there was something about the girl that gave her pause. She
was so very self-assured, and while she was pleading for the
man she loved, there was no softness about her. Indeed, she
seemed to glitter like a many-faceted diamond, and last night,
save for one last moment when that bright facade had seemed
to crack, she had also glittered and her words had been cruel,
taunting. Could Lucian really be happy with a woman like
that?

"I am glad you understand." Barbara leaned forward.
"Now last night, I know I was insulting, and in those circumstances, I cannot blame you for taking the stand you did. You
could do no less with Lucian present. However, he is not here
now, Lady Morley, and I will tell you that I am—or, rather,
my family is wealthy and we are prepared to give you the
sum of three thousand pounds to relinquish your claim on
Lucian. He, no doubt, will also give you a substantial amount
of money that will enable you to marry again, and marry
well, to someone who, unlike Lucian, will want you. What
do you say to that? Is that not a fair offer? I do hope that you
will be sensible."

How might one answer an insult of that caliber? Words
piled in Alicia's throat and swept to her tongue, but resolutely, she swallowed them, saying only, "I do not wish to,
er, sell Lucian to you, Miss Barrington. I want only to have
him at my side once more."

Barbara had been smiling, but at the word "sell" her smile
vanished and her eyes glittered with anger. "Does the fact
that he loathes you mean nothing to you?" she inquired icily.

"I do not believe that he loathes me, Miss Barrington."

"Do you not?" Barbara rose and walked to the mantel-piece and back, staring down at Alicia. "Well. *Lady* Morley, I had an opportunity to speak to him last night, late, when after walking the streets for several hours he came to me. And I might tell you that you are mistaken. Furthermore, he is sure that he married you to spite me. That is the conclusion he has reached, and I am in total agreement with him. You need only to look in this glass to prove my point." She gestured at the mirror that hung over the mantelshelf.

Cruel as that taunt had been, Alicia was glad of it. It suggested that her opponent was less confident than she appeared. She said calmly, "Neither you nor Lucian is in a position to reach any conclusions regarding the reason why he asked for my hand in marriage, Miss Barrington. You may think as you choose, if it makes you happy. However, have you given any thought to what would happen if Lucian were to regain his memory and found himself married to you rather than to me?"

Barbara glared at Alicia. "I would think, my dear Lady Morley, that he must consider himself the happiest of men. Lucian and I, as you were assured last night, have been in love since we were children, and if he wed you, it was because he was desperately unhappy."

"He did not seem desperately unhappy," Alicia retorted. "Quite the contrary, in fact. And I might add that he never mentioned your name, not once, Miss Barrington."

"That is totally understandable. The wound was too deep. Believe me, Lady Morley, I know him as you could never know him."

"I know that he loved me, Miss Barrington," Alicia said gently.

"When did he love you, Lady Morley? When he was about to go off to war and when he thought *I* was lost to him forever, that is when he turned to you—as a drowning man tries to clutch at any piece of flotsam that he might."

Her insults were succeeding only in giving Alicia further strength. "You hinted at something of that kind last night, Miss Barrington, and Lucian immediately denied it, if you will remember."

"He denied it because of his innate chivalry to all women, however undeserving, and not because he believed it to be true. You should have been a party to our conversation later in the evening." Barbara moved toward the door. "And if you are determined to try to retain your hold on him, you will soon find out that I am right. I do not envy you that revelation, *Lady* Morley!" Whirling about, she pulled open the door and went out, nearly bumping into Timothy. With an extra glare for him, she hurried down the stairs.

Timothy hurried into the parlor, and finding his sister standing by the door, he said, "She was in a fury!"

Alicia nodded. "Yes, I know."

"You should not have seen her without me present."

"On the contrary, my dear, it was much more to the point that I did. As you know, I have been much exercised as to what I would say this afternoon—and she has helped frame my answer."

"I hope that you will consent to an annulment, my dear."

"No," Alicia said firmly.

"But, my love, in the circumstances—" he began gravely.

"No," she interrupted. "It is my duty to remain Lucian's wife."

"But he has shown—"

"Timothy," Alicia said in a tone that brooked no argument, "I will not, cannot condemn the man I love to the maw of a tigress."

Lucian had been up all night, pacing back and forth in his library, cudgeling his brain for memories that remained elusive. In his mind's eye, he could envision all too clearly the unsettling events of the previous evening—above all, the face of the young woman who had, so shockingly, called herself

Lady Morley and who had the ring he had never taken from his finger since his father had given it to him on the occasion of his eighteenth birthday.

Late last night, facing an agonized and angry Barbara, he had heard her reiterate her theory that his "wife" had scoured the fields looking for what she could find. The allegation still shocked him as it had shocked the girl when Barbara had voiced it. He had not admired Barbara's attitude toward the "interloper," as she had called her when he had come to see her, but at the same time he could not blame her. She was grieving as he was grieving over his unaccountable lapse from virtue and honor.

"How could I have married her?" he muttered out loud, and saw the pale face of the woman who called herself Lady Morley and ostensibly had every right to use that name. She was so small, a poor little dab of a creature. She barely reached Barbara's shoulder. Her features were good but she never would have appealed to him—not in his right mind! His preference had always been for tall, stately women—or, rather, for one tall, stately woman, for Barbara, whom he had loved all his life. And unaccountably, he had turned from her, betrayed that love. Why? What had driven him to commit so shocking a deed? Barbara had said something about the Duke of Pryde. She had mentioned his jealousy. He had taken exception to the duke and gone off to Brussels without a word. He could imagine that, but the rest—to ignore the letters Barbara had written to him and to turn to this girl and to give her his signet ring, which, in addition to being a gift from his father, was a cherished family heirloom worn by every son of the house since . . . he could not remember when. He swallowed convulsively as he thought of his father's horror over that—over the entire terrible situation, his poor father who was dead, dead before he could even bid him a last farewell, another sorrow that had come upon him when he lay wounded. Yet, this latest tragedy, the loss of Barbara even eclipsed that! How could he have betrayed her, how?

Again he shut his eyes, willing that those two years come back to him, but to no avail. The darkness remained!

There was a tap on the library door.

"Yes?" he called.

Church appeared in the doorway. "Miss Barrington wishes to see you, my Lord. She be in the 'all."

"Oh, God," Lucian groaned, and hurried into the hall, to find Barbara pacing up and down, her face a mask of despair.

"Lucian, oh, Lucian." Unmindful of the butler, she sped to him and threw her arms around him. "We are lost, utterly, utterly lost, my darling."

"My love," he cried, "what can you mean? But come." He led her into the drawing room, indicating a sofa.

"No, I cannot sit down. Oh, my love, I have been to see her and I prostrated myself. Imagine, I fell on my knees before her and begged her to agree to an annulment, but I fear she will not! Oh, Lucian, I pray you, let us run away, far, far, far away. I do not care if you are wed. I wish only to be with you, my dearest, my love."

"Barbara," he said brokenly, "you are talking foolishly, madly. I cannot do that. If she will not agree to the annulment, I have no choice but to accept her decision."

"She will have to agree to it if we are together!"

"My shining angel," he said gently. "I cannot accept such a sacrifice. We must think of your reputation and more than that, of your mother, your uncle, everyone. You would be disgraced. No, what you propose is out of the question."

"Then we are lost," she moaned, "for she, I fear, will never give you up."

"Will she not?"

Barbara shook her head. "I think I read her very well. She sees this mischance as her chance for advancement. Oh, if you could have heard how she spoke to me this morning."

"You ought not to have gone there."

"I felt I had no choice." Barbara clutched his arm. "I was fighting for you, for us, for our love, and for my life, Lucian, but I lost. Underneath that meek exterior, there's an iron will. I offered her money and you can imagine what she said. She said she would have more, married to you!''

"She did not!'' he exclaimed.

"She did and talked of her own coach and going to Paris now that the war is at an end—and even to Rome. And, of course, she was delighted about having a house in town. 'Can you see me giving up all that?' she asked me, and smiled. I longed to wipe that smile off her face,'' Barbara sobbed.

"Oh, my darling,'' he groaned. "She must be the very soul of duplicity, for last night she did not seem so grasping.''

"She was talking to me not to you, Lucian.''

"Sure, she must have known that you would tell me.''

"I am sure she did, but she has her marriage lines and she is also sure that you do not want to divorce her. I would you did. Why will you not?''

"I have no grounds,'' he said miserably.

"Is not what I have just told you grounds enough? I will swear to it.''

"I have not heard it from her own lips, Barbara.''

Barbara's eyes flashed. "Are you suggesting that I am not telling you the truth?''

"Never, my love, but she can always deny anything you have said, and given her character or, rather, the lack of it, she will. And besides, I have no wish to involve you in this imbroglio.''

"But you cannot want to remain married to her,'' Barbara cried. "She entrapped you, Lucian, I know not how—but there could have been no other reason for you to wed her. She's not even pretty. Oh, God, if you could only remember!''

"I cannot,'' he groaned. "I have tried all this night but nothing came to me, nothing.''

"Oh, my poor love.'' Barbara expelled a caught breath, expertly turning it into a long sigh. "And so you will suffer in these unbreakable bonds?''

"Unless she relents.''

"I tell you she will not relent," Barbara said fiercely. She looked about her and saw a small marble image of Psyche. Pointing to it, she cried, "That statue will crumble to dust before she changes her mind. She is an adventuress and totally without scruples. If you could have heard her . . . But"—Barbara's eyes gleamed—"I think . . . Oh, my dear love, I think I have happened upon a solution."

"A solution?" he said despairingly. "What manner of solution? I will not involve you in anything that would detract from your fair name, my dearest, so long as I shall live."

"And you are mine," Barbara said in a tone as solemn as his had been. "But, Lucian, hear me. There is the abbey."

"The abbey?" he said blankly.

"Yes, yes, yes," she cried triumphantly. "Take her to the abbey or merely mention your intention of doing so. That might cause her to change her mind, and without further ado—but if she decides to hold out, think on the fact that it has not been occupied for a dozen years, not since your poor father decided to live in Sussex with your Aunt Margaret. He left because of the cold and the damp. Remember how he used to say that the climate chilled his very bones?"

"I remember," Lucian sighed.

"Oh, my dear, I do not want to fill your head with unhappy memories, but heed me. She has been living in Brussels, which, while it is not warm, contains houses that are well-insulated against the cold. And in winter . . . But I need not remind you what the abbey is like in winter with the winds howling down from the moors and she quite likely to be snowbound. I know you have a fondness for the old place and so do I, since 'twas there that we met when we were children. However, she will have no sentimental attachments and I am sure that she will hate it. She's been living in a large city. How will she respond to the loneliness of the abbey and its distance from London? How will she enjoy looking out of the windows at those shattered ruins? I used to find them beautiful. I loved to sketch them. Do you remember?"

"I do," he said. "I do remember that time, Barbara."

"I know, dear, and it is tragic that you cannot remember meeting her, but if our plan is successful, you'll be rid of her very soon. And do not forget the legends attached to the abbey, the ghostly monks who walk through the broken corridors when the wind is high and, on occasion, chant—"

"Ah, that is arrant superstition," he exclaimed.

"Yes, we know that, but will she? Living there, she is bound to hear about it from one or another person. And from my observation, she is rather a simple little women." Her eyes widened. "Lucian, what if we were to hire someone to chant?"

"No," he protested quickly. "That is going too far."

"Perhaps so, but I am sure that the loneliness of the place will be enough—that and the fact that she is living with a man who knows her for an unscrupulous schemer and treats her accordingly. Sure that will bring out her true nature and you will have grounds for an annulment or a divorce. She will get what she deserves and we will finally be together, with no importunate stranger to separate us ever, ever again."

"Oh, my dearest Barbara," Lucian groaned, "how can you want to be with a man who has so cruelly betrayed you?"

"Lucian," she said softly, "knowing you, I feel there must have been some extenuating circumstances. I feel that, rather than you having betrayed me, you were the one betrayed by that creature who has gained possession of your name—by what means we cannot yet know."

"She looks so innocent," he mused.

"To your eyes, perhaps, my dearest. It takes another woman to tell the difference between the real and the assumed. That she does seem innocent to you makes her all the more dangerous. If she insists upon your honoring this bond she secured through God knows what means, I beg you will be on your guard."

He took a turn around the room, his limp more in evidence

than it had been in the last weeks. "Can you imagine that I will not?" he burst out. "Can you imagine that I will not be thinking of you and missing you every hour of every day, every minute, indeed! Yet, Barbara, perhaps she will relent. I will certainly make it worth her while. Oh, God, how came I to this coil?"

"My love, I cannot bear to see you suffer," Barbara moaned. "But again I assert that it cannot have been your doing. That woman and possibly her brother, more than possibly." Her eyes flashed and she smote her hands together. "Of course it was her brother. He might have caught you with her—"

"Barbara,"—Lucian moved to her and seized her hands—"I could not have been with her, being in love with you!"

"Perhaps she came to your room, trapped you, and he, waiting outside the door, found you together. This, of course, is mere supposition. I have no proof. Unless you were to regain your memory, we have no way of telling how she managed to inveigle you into marriage."

He pushed his hands against his forehead. "No, we have no way. It all remains a blank. It would be more comfortable to believe I was trapped."

"What other explanation could there be?" she asked reasonably. "Unless, of course, you *were* in love with her."

"No!" He threw his arms around Barbara and held her against him. "I could not have been, never!"

She remained in the circle of his arms for a moment and then gently but firmly extricated herself. "My love, we must not allow ourselves this luxury. You are not free."

"True," he groaned. "I offer you my apologies."

Barbara sighed. "And I accept them and wish . . . But there is no use in wishing. If this creature does not relent, Lucian, promise that you will take her to the abbey."

"You have my word on it, my angel," he cried. "Once she has made her stand, I will make mine or, rather, ours.

And then we will leave for the abbey as soon as possible. I will not even make arrangements to have it opened."

"Ah." Barbara smiled. "That is good. She will see it shuttered, empty, and cold—but you, my love, ought not to be exposed to that dreadful chill."

"There are parts that can be warmed quickly. I beg you'll not concern yourself about me, Barbara." A grim look darkened his eyes. " 'Tis the least I can do, and I assure you she will not be happy in this situation. Indeed, she will feel most uncomfortable."

"Ah," Barbara said, "I could hope for no more."

"You should have been able to hope for so much more, my love, and I as well," he said sadly.

"If you follow my advice, that hope must soon be realized. Oh, Lucian." Barbara managed a tiny sob. "I know 'tis wrong, since you are not free, but I *want* you to hold me close now. It might be the last time."

He enfolded her in his arms again. "I promise you, Barbara"—he stared into her eyes—"indeed I swear to you that there will be many, many more times, a lifetime, in fact." He kissed her.

The hour had struck, and Alicia, her brother, Lord Barrington, Barbara, and Lucian were assembled in the library at Barrington House. Having nothing else to wear, Alicia was still in her black garments. These, she reasoned dolefully, were suited to the occasion, for on looking at Lucian's face as he entered and meeting his stony eyes, she had been struck by the notion that, after all, the man she had called husband was dead. Indeed, for a brief moment she had actually entertained the idea of consenting to the annulment. Then she happened to look in Barbara's direction and caught a gleam of triumph in her eyes. It occurred to her that Barbara's early-morning visits had not ceased with herself. Undoubtedly, she had gone to Lucian as well, and who knows what poison she had poured into ears that were, alas, only too receptive?

Certainly Lucian's attitude was changed from the previous night. Then he had been miserable and confused. Now he was actively antagonistic. More coals had been heaped on that particular fire, certainly, and she did not doubt that it was Barbara's hand that held the scuttle. Consequently, she braced herself and kept her eyes on Lord Barrington's face.

His demeanor was calm, and when he began to speak, his words matched it. "Well, now, last night we were all shocked and confounded by the revelation that Lucian had contracted a marriage while in Brussels. Upon due reflection, however, I, for one, am exceptionally glad that this intelligence was given us before rather than after the event of my niece's marriage.

"I wish, however, that more light could be shed on the circumstances that led to the contracting of a marriage while Lucian was still betrothed to my niece." His cold glance shifted to Alicia's face, and she, meeting his eyes, read condemnation in them. She took and momentarily held a deep breath, the while she clamped her teeth together lest she tell him that she did not believe that Lucian had still been betrothed to Barbara at that time. Such an argument was futile in the circumstances. Lucian, with his clouded understanding, could not have refuted the supposition and, she realized with an actual pain in her heart, would not have wanted to refute it. Clearly he was in Barbara's corner—kept there by guilt and, she had no doubt, by Barbara's lies. The big guns in this engagement were all on Barbara's side and she had only the ring and her marriage lines to bolster her position.

"I wish so, too, sir," Lucian spoke. "No light, however, has pierced the darkness here." He touched his head.

"Such memories cannot be forced." Lord Barrington's eyes were on Alicia again. "I have made inquiries of my physicians and it is very possible that Lucian will remain in this condition for the rest of his life. Perhaps you are not aware of that, Lady Morley."

"I am aware of it, my Lord," she said steadily.

"I am glad to hear it. You seem a sensible young woman and I am sure that you will not want to remain in a situation that can hardly be to your best interests. Since I have no way of knowing why Lucian contracted this unfortunate marriage—"

Alicia raised her hand. "At the time, my Lord, I can assure you that he did not believe it unfortunate."

"Liar!" Barbara flashed.

"My dear," Lord Barrington said quellingly, "let us have no more outbursts akin to those of last night. They serve only as interruptions and it is to everyone's interest that this matter be brought to a close." He turned to Lucian. "You, my boy, wish, I think, to dissolve this alliance. Is that not so?"

Lucian, his eyes on Barbara, nodded. "Yes, if Miss—Lady Morley will agree to it. I have spoken to my man of business and am prepared to offer a settlement that, I hope, will be satisfactory." He stared at Alicia. "I am offering ten thousand pounds."

"Lucian!" Barbara exclaimed with a gasp.

Out of the corner of her eye, Alicia saw Timothy frown. She put her hand on his arm and, meeting his eyes, gave an almost imperceptible shake of her head. To Lucian, she said, "That is a great deal of money, sir."

"A very great deal, indeed. A fortune," Lord Barrington said in a shaken voice. "Are you sure, my boy, that—"

Lucian's eyes were fixed on Barbara's face. "I am quite sure," he said steadily, turning toward Lord Barrington then.

"Well, Lady Morley"—Lord Barrington was still out of contenance—"will you accept this most munificent offer? If so, we can bring this matter to a conclusion now."

Alicia said softly, "I do not accept it, my Lord."

Lord Barrington's eyes opened wide. His face paled. "You do not?" He glared at her. "Am I—I mean, I hope I am mistaken in assuming that you are demanding more?"

She rose to her feet. "I am asking considerably more, Lord Barrington. In the name of the rings I have on my finger and the lines inscribed in the registry of the Church of St. Stephen in Brussels and in the name of the words that Mr. de Jong pronounced on the morning of June eleventh, I demand that my husband remain with me."

"Harpy!" Barbara actually leapt from her seat and lunged at Alicia. She was immediately confronted by an angry Timothy.

"I charge you, stay back," he rasped.

"Barbara"—Lucian, also rising, took her arm and escorted her back to her chair—"I beg you'll stay here." He confronted Alicia, adding heavily, "Does it mean nothing to you that I cannot love or—or even like or respect you?"

"You'd not speak to my sister in such a way were you in your right mind," Timothy growled.

"I beg to differ with that," Barbara cried.

Alicia spoke only to Lucian. "If you were cognizant of the events attendant upon our marriage, Lucian, you would understand my position. I can only say that I live in the hope of your memory returning."

"You have picked yourself a hard row to hoe, young woman," Lord Barrington said sharply. "His physicians are in accord in telling me that there is very little chance of that."

"Yet, such things have been known to occur," Alicia replied. "And I will be faithful to the vows I made my husband. I can only tell you that if he should awaken from this stupor, as it were, he would not thank me for refuting them—especially for money."

"On the contrary," Lucian cried, "I would go down on my knees to you."

Alicia's mouth trembled, but she said steadily enough, "I beg to differ with you, Lucian." Her eyes rested briefly on Barbara's flushed face. "I think you will live to thank me for a most happy release."

Barbara gasped and Lord Barrington glared at Alicia. "I will not say what I think of your manner, Lady Morley."

"That is just as well, my Lord, for it would avail you nothing," Alicia responded.

"She is without shame," Barbara accused.

"True," Lucian agreed. He was very pale. Facing Alicia, he said, "I find your attitude insufferable, but since I did wed you, I must, it seems, abide by that bond. Consequently, I suggest, my dear wife, that you ready yourself for a long journey."

"A journey?" Timothy moved to Alicia's side. "What would you be meaning by that, sir?"

"He means," Barbara said coldly, "that she will not be able to queen it over society here in town, Mr. Delacre. He means—"

"Barbara," Lucian interrupted. "I think, my dear, that I must furnish the explanation. I mean, sir, that your sister and I will be leaving for Yorkshire on the morrow. We will travel to Morley Abbey, which is our family estate. It is not far from Richmond and we will remain there for the rest of the winter."

"Yorkshire in the winter," Timothy exclaimed. "No, I will not have it!"

"I fear, sir, that you have nothing to say about where I choose to live with my . . . wife," Lucian reminded him coldly. "The house, I might add, has not been open in quite some time and I feel I owe it to my tenants to put in an appearance there. I wish my . . . wife to accompany me, unless, of course, she chooses to change her mind regarding my offer."

Alicia said, "I will abide by your original offer, Lucian."

His eyes gleamed. "You mean you will take the money?"

"I mean that I will be your wife. I will love, honor, and obey you till death do us part. And I will be ready at such time as you wish me to be."

"We will be leaving at five in the morning, then," he said icily. "I advise you to take some warm clothing with you. The weather there is uncertain at this time of year."

"I thank you for your advice. I will see what I may purchase before the shops close," she returned equably. She looked up at her brother. "With that in mind, Timothy, I think we had best bid Lord Barrington, Miss Barrington, and my husband a good afternoon."

The clock chimed four, and Alicia looked down compassionately at Effie, who had been ready betimes but who had dropped off to sleep again, her head on a leather bandbox. In a low voice, she said to her brother, who had just appeared at the door to her bedroom, "Let us go into the salon. There's no sense rousing her until he arrives."

"Very well," Timothy also spoke in a hushed tone. He moved back and was followed by his sister, who shut the door behind her quietly. "I wish," he began, and staring at her determined countenance, he shrugged and said no more.

"What do you wish?"

"I am sure you know without my telling you, since we've talked of nothing else.

"We have argued, you mean," she emphasized. "And no, my dear, the scant sleep that I have had has not minded me to change my plans."

He frowned. "I cannot help but think that you are stepping into folly. Yorkshire in the winter is very cold, and you will be doubly cold. He is not the man you married and might never have been."

She said firmly, "I could not have been so mistaken in Lucian."

"It happened too quickly—your marriage." His frown deepened. "I told you that at the time, if you will only remember."

"And reminded me of it not four hours since, as if I needed to be reminded. Timothy," —Alicia gazed at him earnestly—"you know what he was like in Brussels. Do you see much of the man we knew?"

"No. He has changed, but he seems most attached to that young woman. I hate to point this out—"

"You have also pointed that out before," she interrupted. "And I tell you, my dear, that were I his mother rather than his wife, I would not want to see him joined in matrimony to Miss Barrington. She breathes insincerity. Undoubtedly, Lucian sees none of this and I am sure that he was once very much in love with her—or thought himself to be. No, I will allow that he was, but I am certain that the Lucian who married me was not displaying any of the symptoms of a past disappointment. Cast your mind back, Timothy. Sure you must agree with me."

"I suppose that I do," he said reluctantly. "But that Lucian has been, in effect, blotted out of existence. And as you have been told, you have no guarantee that he will ever return, and in these circumstancs, I say again, Licia, that I hate to see you deliberately bring more misery down upon your head. You have suffered too much already."

"I suffered because I thought he was dead. I could not bear that, but"—she gave him a long resolute look—" all else I can bear. I feel in my bones that the man I love will come back to me, and I am willing to wait."

She received a dour look. "And I feel in mine—"

"Hush, do not say it." She put her little hand over his mouth.

He caught her hand and held it warmly. "Licia, I beg you will promise me that if you are ever in trouble, you will send for me."

"If I am, of course, I shall, but I do not think I will need to," she assured him with more confidence than she actually felt. Close upon her statement, she was startled by the chiming of the clock as it struck the three-quarter hour. Inadvertently, she glanced at it and instead saw her face in the mirror. She sighed, wishing she had not. It was always a shock to find her pale visage staring back at her. Grief had wrought heavily upon her and she knew that a good part of Barbara's insistence on her duplicity was based on her diminished beauty. She did not expect that a hectic journey to the north would improve her appearance. Happiness might help but, for the nonce, she could not expect that either. She swallowed a groan. She had never been vain, but she had become used to being thought beautiful and she mourned the loss of the brightness and color that might have helped to assure Lucian that he had not been trapped into their marriage. A wave of unhappiness washed over her, and mixed with it was fear. Had she been too stubborn in clinging to Lucian despite his rejection of her? And would the Lucian she had known so briefly ever emerge again? If he did not, her life would be miserable indeed and, she thought dolefully, she would get more than a taste of that when he arrived.

"You could change your mind even now, Licia," Timothy said with the perspicacity he had shown on so many occasions.

She turned to him and then stiffened at a knock on the door. Glancing at the clock again, she saw that its little gold hands, indicated a minute before the hour. Timothy opened the door, and as Lucian, cloaked and booted, strode in, the clock chimed five.

His gaze fell somewhere between the brother and sister. "Good morning," he said curtly. Without waiting for a response, he continued, "The coach is below. 'Tis well-sprung and you will have plenty of room. Your abigail may ride with you and my man Jacob will also accompany you. I myself will be on horseback. My housekkeeper, butler, and a few other servants will be traveling behind us in another coach."

"Should you be on horseback all the way?" Alicia asked worriedly. "Your leg—"

He cut her off sharply, "I beg you will not concern yourself over that. As I am sure you must be aware, I am a soldier. I have been in many campaigns where I have sustained even greater injuries. My leg is nearly healed. But we waste time talking. Are you packed?"

"I am, Lucian," she said. "I will awaken Effie."

"Awaken her?" he repeated with a frown. "She is yet abed?"

"On the contrary. She is ready and has been ready for the last hour, but fell asleep waiting," Alicia said crisply. "We are both ready and eager to be on our way."

She received a hard look. "Very well, I shall be in the hall." Lucian's chill glance fell on Timothy, who regarded him with equal coldness. "You, sir, are remaining here, I trust?"

"No, I am leaving for Dover as soon as I have settled the bill," Timothy replied.

"I will do that," Lucian said curtly.

"No," Timothy responded. "We do not expect that. We are not your pensioners, sir, but we are your in-laws." Evidently not trusting himself to say more, he moved to his sister and embraced her. "I will be below to see you off, my dear."

"As you choose, my love." She moved quickly into the inner room and, to her relief, found Effie awake and ready.

The girl had a concerned look for her. "Oh, milady, 'e do sound ever so angry an' so different."

"No matter, Effie," Alicia responded in a low voice. "I am sure you understand."

"I do, milady." She still appeared concerned. "I 'ope—"

"We must hurry, Effie," Alicia said.

The abigail looked as if she had much more she would have liked to say, but she nodded and, picking up the bandboxes, followed Alicia out of the room.

As Effie bobbed a curtsy at Lucian, Alicia was struck anew by the strangeness of his disorder. Once he had laughed and teased Effie; now he regarded her indifferently and nodded her out of the room. He offered his arm to Alicia, who, after a second's hesitation, took it, feeling, as she did, his inadvertent tensing.

Though the sun was still only a band of red across the eastern horizon, London was already awake. The street in front of the hotel was filled with drays. There were also post-chaises carrying weary merrymakers home from an evening on the town. There were a few drunken fops on the pavement and there were responsible citizens hurrying to various offices. Waiting at the curb was a large coach drawn by eight horses. It was painted a dark green and on the paneling was a coat of arms that she knew well, since it was duplicated on her ring. Inadvertently, she removed her hand from Lucian's arm to touch the ring and in the next moment was whirled into her brother's warm embrace.

"Godspeed, Licia," he said with a catch to his voice. "I wish—"

"For my happiness, of course, Timothy," she said in a half-whisper.

"Of course, my dearest."

"And you must tell Papa very little of what has happened. You promised, remember?"

"I do remember," he assured her. "And I shall abide by my promise."

The brother and sister broke apart, and seeing that Lucian stood beside the door of the coach, waiting for her, Alicia produced a fleeting smile for Timothy and joined her husband. He indicated the three steps that would bring her inside and silently proffered his arm. She grasped it briefly as she negotiated the steps and a moment later she settled down on a comfortably padded seat inside. Effie was there waiting for her; beside her was Jacob, Lucian's valet, who had not been with him in Brussels and consequently stared at her with a quotient of his master's disapproval. She greeted him coolly and looked beyond him to the windows.

A footman slammed the door and in another few minutes they were under way, with Lucian, glimpsed fleetingly as he rode swiftly past the window, his expression moody and his posture stiff. Her heart was pounding in her throat, and though Alicia tried to close her mind against the memory, she seemed to hear Lucian, her Lucian, saying, "I would have you remember, my love, that I am known to possess a charmed life, and when this is over, I will come back to you.'' He had been right and wrong, she thought unhappily—but while there was life, there was hope.

As the milestones multiplied and the sun, passing its zenith, began to descend, the small hope with which Alicia had begun her journey flicked like the tiny spark in a candle end. Beyond the dust kicked up by his horse's hooves, beyond a flash of the dark brown coat and the buckskin breeches Lucian had donned for the journey, she saw very little of the man she had once so joyfully accepted as her husband. Though she could blame this on his infirmity and on the dark insinuations of his fiancée, it did not make her situation any the easier.

She quite dreaded their arrival at the next posting inn where, rather than another silent meal in the common room, they must be prepared to spend the night. She flushed, again not wanting to think of the brief nights of their marriage and of his ardent but gentle lovemaking, which had brought a whole new dimension of feeling to the inexperienced young woman she had been. And now he seemed reluctant to so much as touch her hand. A quavering sigh escaped her and her determination wavered. If she were ever to call him husband in the true sense of the word, she would have to overcome mammoth obstacles.

Barbara, of course, was the greatest of these, but almost as great was his sense of having betrayed the woman he loved by contracting this marriage to a stranger. At present, he must be undergoing a deep crisis of conscience. Her heart went out to him—how he must be suffering as he attempted to lift the veil of darkness that had obscured two years of his life. Had she done the right thing in insisting he honor his vows? Yes, because, in a sense, she was saving him from a folly he must once have regretted deeply. She could not believe he had entertained any lingering passion for Barbara Barrington when he approached her. His mein had not been that of a brooding and disappointed lover; he had been charming, gay and light-hearted. By then, Barbara must have been discarded, or perhaps she had done the discarding.

Alicia would have given much for a half-hour alone with the prideful Duke of Pryde, who seemed to have done his share of discarding. An image of Barbara's beautiful proud face arose in her mind. She must have been badly shaken by her experience with the duke and then, fortuitously, Lucian had been invalided home.

Alicia gazed out the window at the countryside. She saw a small boy leading a herd of cows home from the pasture. It was a peaceful scene. They had passed many peaceful scenes, or so they appeared on the surface. Who knew what went on in the minds of those who stood and watched the coach with its footmen, its postboys and coachman, its eight horses and its outriders, with another coach behind? It was possible that many people envied the occupants their progress in a well-sprung vehicle that might have cost more than they spent in an entire lifetime.

Alicia sighed and, shifting her gaze, met Effie's commiserating glance and the valet's cold stare of silent disapproval, one he had worn for several hours. Undoubtedly he had been a party to his master's late agonies and believed her an adventuress. That was certainly a strain mantle for her to don! She wished . . . But wishes were futile unless she were a character in a fairy tale! And again she remembered the one wish that had been granted, the one forlorn hope fulfilled. She must keep that in mind and through actions, not words, show Lucian that he had not been trapped into this marriage he had tried so hard to escape.

6

"Red sky at mornin', sailor's warnin'," Effie said, glancing out of the window in their bedchamber at the inn.

Alicia, fully dressed save for her hair, which Effie was just about to pin up, cast a weary glance at the vivid sky. The red glow was already fading and dark-gray clouds were rolling in.

" 'Twas all that was needed," she remarked, and saw Effie nod. She never had to explain her thoughts to the abigail, and as she often had during the past three days, she felt a rush of gratitude for the lucky chance that had brought Effie to her while they still lived in England all those years ago.

Effie had been the daughter of a housekeeper who had caught a quinsy and died. At that same time, Alicia's former abigail, who had also served her late mother, had been on point of retiring. She had found little Effie, aged ten, already deft with her needle and particularly clever about fixing hair. She had given her further instructions in the care of her young mistress, and for the last nine years Effie had been a friend to Alicia and often her confidante. She did not say much, but what she did say was always pithy and to the point. In the last month, her sympathy and understanding had proved greatly comforting.

"Per'aps, 'twon't be so bad," the girl said. But as if to

contradict her words, a low rumble was heard overhead. Effie rolled her eyes and added, " 'Accordin' to 'is 'Ighness" —her nickname for Lucian's superior valet—"we ain't too far from the abbey."

Alicia said, "I should think we are no more than a half-day's journey, but it might take longer if it rains." She did not quite manage to conceal the strain of anxiety in her tone.

"It might that." Effie spoke apologetically as if, indeed, she were holding herself accountable for the pending uproar in the heavens. But Alicia guessed that she was only wishing she had not mentioned the possibility of a delay. She knew that the girl was as distressed as herself at Lucian's continuing refusal to address Alicia—except at such times as it was absolutely necessary. Generally, he was totally silent at mealtimes. On the past three mornings, she had had her breakfast served in her room, but that left dinner and supper to be consumed in a silence broken only by his brief directions, generally addressed to the servants. And would he always be so silent? Alicia stifled a sigh and said to Effie, "Have you finished your tea, then?"

"Oh, yes, milady." She cast a glance at Alicia. "I'll do up your 'air, then."

"Yes, for we must soon be on our way, and let us hope that all sailors remain in the sunshine."

"Eh?" Effie looked blank and then she giggled. "Oh, yes, milady, let's 'ope so."

Some two hours later, after more rumbling, accompanied by alternate brightening and darkening of the sky and eventually by jagged flashes of lightning, the storm broke with pelting rain to the accompaniment of high-screaming winds that must certainly have caused the sailors to batten down the hatches and furl the sails. The rain descended in sheets, the horses neighed, the coachman shouted, the outriders and the footmen also yelled, and Lucian stubbornly remained on horseback.

Leaning out the window, Alicia stared after him. He had

urged his horse to a gallop and he was far ahead of the coach. She could see only his cloak, which usually flew out behind him but which now drooped in sodden folds about his shoulders. She longed to call out to him, but she doubted her voice could be heard above the clamor of the storm and the clatter of the coach wheels. And if he did hear her, it would have made no difference. He had refused to heed her one timid suggestion that he rest his leg from time to time and ride inside.

He had said accusingly, "Barbara would be able to tell you that I have always preferred to ride outside." That reply, she knew, carried a twofold message: he was bemoaning his lost love and, at the same time, he was suggesting that she ought to have known his preference and would have known them had she been a real wife.

At this moment he would never have believed that there had been no occasion for coach travel in Brussels, or if there had been, the Lucian she had known would have wanted to spend as much time as possible with the girl he had professed to love more than life itself.

"Milady," Effie said worriedly, "you'll be gettin' wet stickin' your 'ead out like that."

"I wish Lucian would ride inside." Alicia frowned. "It cannot be good for him—out there in all that rain."

"The master don't like to ride inside," Jacob spoke almost as pointedly as Lucian himself.

"The more fool 'e," Effie snapped, and then added nervously, "beggin' yer pardon, milady."

Alicia, who had continued to stare into the stormy distances, cried out. Lucian's horse had suddenly shied, tossing his master from his back.

"Wot's 'appened?" Effie demanded.

"Lucian has been thrown . . . Oh, dear, we must stop the coach," Alicia cried.

"Wot?" The valet leaned toward her. " 'Is 'e 'urt, can you see?"

She continued to stare out the window and at first she saw nothing, but in another second Lucian came into view. He was brushing mud off his face and garments. The horse, she noted, was nowhere to be seen. In that same moment, there were shouts ahead and the coach came to a sudden jolting stop some little distance beyond the place where the mishap had occurred.

The valet thrust open the door and jumped out with Alicia, immediately behind him, following him as he and two of the footmen ran back through the driving rain, only to be met by Lucian. He was limping and his clothes were muddied, but to Alicia's relief, he did not seem much the worse for his accident. He was immediately surrounded by the three men, all talking at once.

"No, no," his voice rose above their concerned queries, "I was not hurt and . . ." He paused, evidently seeing Alicia for the first time. He stared at her in surprise. "Why are you out of the coach?" he demanded.

"I saw you fall. I hope you did not hurt your leg," she said concernedly.

"No," he responded coolly. "I have had worse falls, I assure you. The ground has been much softened by the rain."

"And your leg?" she pursued.

" 'Tis nothing," he answered curtly, and stepping forward, he thrust her toward the edge of the road. As she regarded him in hurt surprise, she heard the sound of hooves and, glancing in that direction, saw the other coach dashing toward them. Two of its outriders immediately dismounted and hurried over to Lucian while the vehicle itself pulled to a stop farther down the road.

A few moments after the outriders, the butler and a footman had assured themselves that their master was unhurt.

Alicia, moving toward him, said, "You are very wet. Had you better not send the other servants ahead to open the house and set fires in some of the rooms?"

He stared at her a second before replying and then said in a rather self-conscious tone of voice, "I expect you are right. That would be the thing to do."

She wondered why the other coach had not gone before them all the way, and judging from his manner, that it had not was possibly deliberate on his part or . . . Barbara Barrington suddenly walked through her head and out. However, now was not the time to dwell on such suspicions. She said, "I think that you must ride inside, Lucian."

"Oh, milord, surely you must," Jacob urged.

"I expect I had better," he said reluctantly. "My horse . . . 'tis gone." Moving forward, he suddenly stumbled.

Alicia sprang to his side. "You must lean on me," she said quickly. "You did hurt your leg, after all."

" 'Tis nothing," he said insistently.

She glared at him. "Oh, I beg you'll not be so stubborn! Do not be forever dwelling on how much you resent me but rather think what you are doing to your poor innocent limb, which has no quarrel with anyone."

The valet let out a sound that much resembled laughter, but he said soberly enough, " 'Er Ladyship be right, my Lord. Pray lean on me."

"I expect I had better," Lucian allowed reluctantly. He took his valet's arm, and turning to Alicia, he added, "You'd best hurry to the coach; you'll catch your death standing here in all this rain."

"I am coming," she said.

Some forty minutes later, they were on their way again, and in that period the storm had spent its strength. By the time they had covered another league, the descending sun was in view again and the sky so clear that it was hard to imagine the lightning and the thunder.

Lucian, sitting near the window, was very quiet. Effie, now beside Jacob on the facing seat, darted shy glances at him from time to time, but only Jacob, who had insisted on his master placing his leg on his lap, occasionally broke the silence by asking if he were in pain, receiving only a shake of the head. Alicia guessed that had she not been present, he might have said more. She had the uncomfortable feeling that he had promised Barbara that he would speak to her as little as possible, and he certainly had fulfilled that particular pledge throughout the journey. Would he be equally taciturn when they arrived?

Hard upon that thought, Lucian startled her by saying, "We ought to be nearing the abbey very soon."

"I am glad of that," she said softly. "You must divest yourself of those wet garments."

"I beg you'll not trouble your head about me," he said coldly. "As I think I have mentioned more than once, I am used to campaigning, and not all our marches have taken place in clement weather."

"I am sure they have not, but you've not been on duty of late and the body can adjust itself to comfort as well as to hardships."

"No doubt, but I am very strong . . . Still, be that as it may, I do not think I have told you much about the abbey, or have I?" There was a touch of uncertainty in his tone.

She guessed that he was referring to his infirmity. "No, you have not. You told me only that you came from Yorkshire."

"But I did not discuss the abbey?"

"No."

"That seems strange," he said accusingly. " 'Tis my home."

"You spoke mainly of your house in London." She stifled a sigh, remembering the other Lucian's oft-repeated remarks about introducing her to his friends and taking her to Carlton House, where the Regent would fall in love with her. "I will need to hang a sign upon you, my own, saying that you belong to me exclusively," he had teased. Alicia winced and banished that memory to the place where she stored the words and images that had an unfortunate habit of reappearing in her dreams.

"Well," he continued, " 'tis time I did tell you a little about the place."

"Time and past," she agreed calmly.

"It's known to be haunted."

"Haunted!" Alicia echoed. "You'll never tell me that!"

"H-haunted?" Effie breathed.

"That be true." The valet nodded.

"Are you afraid of ghosts?" Lucian asked Alicia.

"I?" She regarded him with considerable surprise. "No more than I fear elves or fairies or fire-breathing dragons or man-devouring ogres."

"Indeed? Then I trust you'd not be disturbed were you to hear the chanting of those monks who were turned out of the abbey during the Dissolution. 'Twas in the middle of a high wind such as battered us this afternoon. And 'tis said that when the wind blows from the north, you can sometimes hear them. And since their services began at midnight with the ringing of the matins bell, you can also hear that bell on certain stormy nights."

"Really?" Alicia smiled. "And the clapper so rusted by now?"

There was a touch of asperity to his tone as he responded, "Nothing of the bell remains . . . only the sound."

"Ooooh, milady," Effie murmured.

Alicia had a comforting smile for her. "I beg you'll not take fright, my dear," she said calmly. "The Dissolution of the Monasteries took place at the command of Henry the Eighth in the fifteen-thirties. Is that not right, Lucian?" She bent an inquiring glance on him.

"Fifteen-thirty-six," he amplified. "You seem to be well acquainted with history."

"I have always enjoyed reading about the past. The Tudor period is particularly fascinating. Just think someone among our ancestors might have met and even walked with Shakespeare, but I must tell you, sir, that I am very skeptical regarding the phantom monks that appear at one or another ruined monastery throughout the length and breadth of England. I am sure that the poor souls sleep soundly while they await the trumpets of Judgment Day, but I should like to hear more about the abbey itself. When was it built and by which order?''

"The ruins date back to the twelfth century."

"Would they be Cistercian, then?" she asked interestedly. "That was the period of a great religious revival—unless I am mistaken."

"You are not," he sounded almost sulky. "And the order was Cistercian."

"Ah, then the abbey must once have been very beautiful. The Fountains Abbey and Tintern and, I believe, Kirstall were all Cistercian." Her eyes brightened. "I shall want to sketch those ruins."

"Oh, milady, you must," Effie exclaimed, and then blushed, "beggin' yer pardon, milady."

"There's no need to beg my pardon, my dear." Alicia smiled at Effie.

"You are an artist, ma'am?" Lucian asked.

"Not an artist," she demurred. "I sketch. All young ladies are taught to sketch, you know."

He nodded, "Yes. Barbara's governess often brought her to the ruins for that purpose."

"Does she enjoy sketching?" Alicia inquired politely, privately bestowing a small curse upon that particular pedagogue.

"She has little talent for it," he admitted. "But," he added fondly, "she does have a most beautiful singing voice."

Alicia bit down a sigh. She had steered the conversation into the wrong channels. She should have refrained from making inquiries about Barbara. She said merely, "That is a gift. I do hope, by the way, that some little part of the abbey ruins remain intact."

"Some of the cloister, a bit of the church tower, and . . . But you will soon see it for yourself," he said dismissively.

Alicia was not to be so easily discouraged. "I expect that some of its stones were used in the building of the house?"

"Some were, I believe," he said shortly.

"And the house itself, is it Tudor?"

"Tudor and with some additions over the centuries."

"Would these be Palladian?"

"In part."

"And are there secret passages? But if your family bene-fited from the destruction of the monasteries, I doubt that they would be priest-lovers . . . or did they change their faith to suit the times?"

The horses were slowing down and Lucian said thankfully, "There are books in the library and records in the muniment room that will tell you far more than I could."

That marked rebuff did not discourage Alicia as much as it might have earlier, for, she reasoned, at least she had per-suaded him to speak to her about matters other than those attendant upon their journey. She would use similar ploys in the future, she decided, for while he had been speaking, she had caught a tiny glimpse of the man she had once known. His voice had softened and she guessed that he had a fond-ness for this place, which he had designated as her prison. This notion brought her up short. Had he?

Yes, she was sure that his purpose in taking her so many leagues out of London was to, as Barbara had put it, "de-prive you of a chance to queen it in town," something she would not have enjoyed half so much as seeing the old house where he had been born. And furthermore, here in Yorkshire he would not be beguiled by the attractions to be found in London: the court, the balls, the routs, the clubs, the theaters. Also, it was far better for him to be here in the country, where he could rest and give his leg a chance to heal.

And perhaps the sight of the old buildings would help to jog his moribund memory. As for herself, she would have plenty to occupy her, getting the house in order, and perhaps in her spare time she could sketch. She might even try her hand at oils. Old Pierre de la Rocque, her teacher, had often urged her to try them, but oils were dear and she had never wanted to strain the family budget by purchasing them. Now she could afford to buy them and perhaps find a room in the house where she could work—even one that might overlook the ruins. She adored old ruins, of which there were some of note in Brussels, but she did have a preference for her native land, which she had not seen since she was a child. And maybe . . . But she would not dwell on that particular "maybe." In that direction lay frustration, a frustration that could easily match that of her husband, for, if he were mourning a lost love, so was she! However, it was futile to think about that and she must continue to remind herself that Lucian was alive, not lying in some nameless grave.

It was dark when they finally reached the entrance to the abbey grounds. In the wake of the rain, there was a damp chill rising from the ground, and the wind blew cold. It was evident that Lucian was feeling the effects of his fall, for he was huddled in the corner of the coach and every so often he rubbed his leg. It was important that he get to bed as soon as possible. However, Alicia knew better than to make such a suggestion. Were she to mention that he must retire, he would remain on his feet as long as he could possibly endure the pain and general discomfort. She must use a different method. She could not like the light in which it would place her, but she must needs resort to it if he were to be made comfortable.

After negotiating a circular driveway, the coach stopped. Descending from the vehicle, Alicia felt as if her legs were about to give out. Facing her was a massive building that seemed uneven in outline. It had a pillared portico that she realized must be a later addition. She was glad to see lighted windows and a reflection of flames on a wall. There was a fire laid on inside and the warmth would be welcome. Even more welcome would be bed . . . But she could not think of that yet. She must see to her husband's comfort and in a way that he would not notice it. Approaching the door, they had no reason to lift the massive knocker that centered it; the portal was opened by Church, who welcomed them with a broad smile that seemed to embrace them both.

"Oh!" Alicia exclaimed, glad that she did not have to pretend her approval of a huge entrance hall; the fire she had seen from the windows blazed on an immense grate set in a huge stone fireplace. Exchanging polite greetings with the butler, she hurried to warm her hands and beckoned Effie, who had hung back shyly, evidently overawed by her surroundings. "Come, my dear, you must be warm, too." She longed to say the same to Lucian but did not, knowing instinctively that he would immediately deny any feelings of discomfort.

Gazing about her, Alicia was glad that there was no parade of servants to be greeted and to greet her, she having met them all at the various inns where they had stayed. Possibly, there ought to have been such a gathering; it must certainly have been there had Barbara come thither with Lucian, but the less combined disapproval, she garnered at this moment, the better it would be. That word had already seeped among them, had been evident in their attitudes. She dismissed that memory and looked about her with considerable pleasure. The hall had architectural beauties she had not anticipated.

The ceiling, though only one story high as dictated by Elizabethan builders, was decorated with plaster panels and strapwork. The staircase was also Elizabethan: its short flight of six or possibly seven steps ended in a broad landing, and then another flight of steps made an angular progression to the second floor. Flanking the stairs were a pair of armored figures. One held a mace and the other seemed to be leaning on a sword. It seemed to her that they were staring at her through their headpieces. She impatiently shrugged that fancy away, fixing her eyes on the staircase again and noting its width. It had been made, she knew, for the wide farthingales of the period, and no doubt, it had been joyfully utilized by those females of her grandmother's day with their hooped skirts. She decided that the stone fireplace was of an earlier vintage, and longed to study it more closely . . . but now, of course, was not the time.

As she had anticipated, the fact that she had asked only Effie to join her at that roaring fire moved Lucian in that direction, and now it was time for her next stratagem. "Oh," she gushed, " 'tis all so beautiful. I hardly know where to look. I do hope you will take me through some of the rooms tonight, Lucian. I am aching to see my new home."

She heard a gasp from the butler and she received a glare from Jacob as Lucian said stiffly, "I think you must wait until tomorrow. I find myself rather fatigued by the journey."

She made a little moue of disapointment. "Oh, I see. Well, I expect the fall has tired you, but you will show me through tomorrow, I hope."

"Tomorrow," he agreed wearily. "But now I must leave you. The housekeeper will conduct you to your chamber." With a brief bow, he added, "I must bid you good night, ma'am."

"Good night, Lucian," she said as brightly as if she herself were not drooping with fatigue. Waiting until he had gained the second landing, she turned to the butler, and pretending to be unaware of his disapproving stare, she said, "I will be pleased if you send the housekeeper to me now and I do hope there will be a place for Effie in my quarters."

"There'll be the servants rooms on the third floor, milady," he responded.

"No, that will never do," she protested. "Effie must be near me."

She received another disapproving glance. "Well, I expect there can be a trundle bed made up in the dressing room, milady," he responded.

"That will be satisfactory," Alicia still spoke brightly. "And now, I believe that I, too, will retire. It has been a long day."

"Yes, milady," the butler said pointedly.

Due to the antiquity of the house, the rooms on the second

floor led into one another, and Alicia, following Mrs. Gibbs, the housekeeper, through a series of them, caught glimpses of paintings and fine wallpapers briefly illuminated by the flickering flame of the candle the woman was carrying—the which made her ache to see them by daylight. The room she was given was large, and there was an equally large sitting room adjoining it. Alicia wondered if, beyond it, lay Lucian's suite of rooms. At the thought, she felt a lump in her throat and a hardness in her chest. She had no trouble divining his intentions. He would not crown what he must consider the ultimate folly of his life by resuming the duties attendant upon the marriage he had forgotten. They would live as strangers in this house and she must not let herself remember the six nights when they had been so joyfully together.

It might be that in time he would come to her—out of duty and in hopes of an heir—but it would be duty alone, untouched by love. She felt tears gathering in her eyes and blinked them away. If only . . . But she must not think of that either. There was a chance his memory would return, but there was an equal chance that it would not.

"Would your Ladyship care to retire for the night?" Effie inquired in a low voice that reflected her own weariness.

"I would that," Alicia said with alacrity. "And may we not need to take so long a coach journey soon again."

"Amen to that, milady," the girl agreed. " 'Tis a very big house," she added.

"It is indeed and we shall enjoy exploring it, I'm thinking."

"Oh, yes, milady!"

The bed to which Alicia eventually came was immense. It made her feel even smaller than she was, but it was soft and the linens were scented with lavender and there was a hot brick inside. She had expected to lie wakeful in the darkness, but when next she opened her eyes, there was a thin line of white light seeping through heavy damask draperies, which she had scarcely noticed the night before.

She felt better. Much of her weariness had gone and, with

it, a portion of the depression that she had tried to keep at bay during the journey. It had been difficult. Lucian's determined effort to remain as far from her as possible *had* hurt, even more than she had anticipated, as she contrasted his frozen manner with that of the young man she had known, alas, so briefly and loved so passionately. Yesterday, and on the preceding days, she had been weighed down by the situation in which she was placed . . . She hesitated in her thinking; she would have said "no fault of her own," but of course, she did share some of that fault. If she had not insisted on her husband honoring his forgotten vows, she would not be here. She would be at home or, at least, what she had been forced to describe as home for the last decade. And would she have been better off there? The answer to that question slipped between her lips in a defiant and audible "No." "No," she repeated. It was better to be with the man she loved than alone and pining for him while he, oblivious of her very existence, married Barbara Barrington and lived . . . happily?

No, that was part of her reasoning. He could not have been happy with her. She breathed duplicity—but to lie here brooding over those circumstances would avail her nothing. She was here in Yorkshire and she wanted to see all that fatigue had denied her the previous evening: the house, the abbey. Indeed she wanted to see the ruins even before she went through the rest of the house.

The sound of hooves broke into her cogitations. She sat up, listening in surprise. Who would be riding at this hour? Or was it as early as she imagined? Habit brought her eyes to the mantelpiece—but of course she was thinking of the one at home. She giggled at the sight of a mantelshelf in that same place and a clock, ormolu rather than the little wooden clock at home. The golden hands indicated a few minutes past six. The continued sound of the hooves worried her. Would it be Lucian out there in the cold? Given his troubled state of mind, she would not be surprised.

Slipping from bed, Alicia went to the window and pulled

aside the draperies, which, in addition to being heavy, were also dusty. She grimaced. That was a condition that must soon be amended. Yet, those few servants they had sent on ahead had work cut out for them. Judging from the size of the rooms, they would need a small army to care for them properly. She sucked in a breath as, looking out, she found the distances nearly obliterated by a heavy mist. Yet, still she could make out a motionless figure on horseback. The swirling mist blotted out features and dimmed its shape to the point where it appeared almost insubstantial. The horse seemed restless and tossed its head frequently, the result, she thought, of a strong hand on the reins. Whose hand? The figure appeared burly, which, of course, ruled out Lucian. It, or rather he, was wearing a wide-brimmed hat. As she looked, the horseman suddenly turned and rode away.

Alicia stared after him, feeling vaguely disquieted. Who was he? And why had he been there so early in the morning, staring so fixedly at the house? Was he someone who worked on the estate? She doubted that. She had seen the vague outline of saddlebags on the horse. A traveler? Travelers did not usually trespass on private grounds or, she smiled derisively, had he been one of Lucian's ghosts? However, though it was early in the morning, it was well past cockcrow, and all reputable spirits, in common with Hamlet's father, had fled to their uneasy habitations. She would have to mention him to Lucian. She sighed. The resolve came so naturally to her and yet she doubted that she would bring it to his attention. His attitude precluded confidences, at least from her. To Lucian, she was there on sufferance, and no doubt he, in his chambers, lay wakeful thinking of what might have been. Had Barbara occupied these apartments? But she would not have been here. They would have yet remained in London, awaiting the moment when they would be walking up the aisle of the St. James's Church to be married.

"If this were not wartime, I would have brought you to St. James's, my darling," Lucian had told her all those weeks ago. "I was baptized there . . ." And, she thought unhappily, he would have been married there but for Octavia's perusing of the *Morning Post*. She owed a great deal to Octavia, but to think of that was to make herself even more unhappy. Still, at the same time she was relieved, for what would have happened had they gone through with that marriage?

"I would have died," she murmured, and frowned. With Lucian alive, it was hard to remember the despair that had wasted her body and robbed her of the glowing beauty that had attracted him in the first place—but that had not been all, he had told her.

" 'Tis your kindness, your sweetness that shines forth; beauty is a magnet, but it is nothing without the rest." And yet . . . and yet, he had been willing to ally himself with Barbara, whom he had known all of his life, and there was no kindness in her, surely. Alicia suddenly felt cold. Had Lucian been lying to her? Had he been attracted by her appearance alone? It did no good to indulge in such reflections. She had made her stand. She had accomplished part of her purpose, and Lucian had, after all, agreed to honor those vows that had been chains, binding him to a stranger.

She would not continue to dwell on that. She must concentrate on her marriage and try to make Lucian comfortable, if not happy, and hope for the improbable to become possible. Meanwhile, the ruins beckoned her as well as the house, and she thought with a surge of unanticipated happiness, she *was* in England, which she had missed during her long Brussels exile. Furthermore, Yorkshire was a part of the country unknown to her and all the more fascinating for that.

She looked out the window again and found that the fog was lifting and through it she could see walls, tall and irregular. With a surge of excitement, she saw that her room did overlook the abbey, and as she tried to distinguished more of it, she realized that the horseman had been riding through the abbey itself! That was strange. If she were superstitious . . . But she was not, she reminded herself. Though he had

appeared vague and almost insubstantial in the swirling mists,
he was corporeal and a trespasser. She did not know why she
was so sure of that. No, she did know. There would have
been no reason for anyone who knew the house to linger there
in the cold and stare at it. And what was his reason? He must
have had a reason, but now the fog was floating away and the
rising sun illuminated the battered ruins of the abbey!

Gazing at them, Alicia felt a lump in her throat. They were
so beautiful and so sad. And the man on horseback had
ridden over what must have once been part of the cloister.
There were the pointed, broken arches. The artist in her
thrilled to the sight and to the shattered stairs that lay a few
feet distant. And farther away rose a tower that appeared to
be in a better state of preservation while directly below she
found that scraggly weeds had forced their way between the
paving stones. Eventually they and the stones would be covered with snow. How many winters had passed since the
monks had chanted their matins. She wished that ghosts did
exist so that she might hear them, but it was better they were
at rest rather than drifting through these sad ruins. Still,
shattered as they were, the sun rendered them beautiful! She
ached to visit them, but hesitated at the thought of leaving the
house so early. The servants would be expecting . . . What
did they expect from her? Instructions, of course, and the
house must be put in order. She would have the housekeeper
show her through. Fortunately, she knew a little about the
running of a great house, having lived in one before her
father's excesses had driven them abroad. Her governess had
also tried to give her some instructions. She had an ironic
little smile for that memory.

"You are so very beautiful, my child; sure you will marry
well and to a noble of high degree." Miss James had been
very romantic, an avid reader of novels from the circulating
libraries, some of which had made their way into Brussels
bookstores. She had told Alicia that she resembled a fairy
princess or a heroine out of one of those tomes. "Beauty such

as you possess, my dear, will win you a rich husband, even though you have no dowry.''

Alicia chuckled at that memory and then stiffened, realizing that, in a sense, Miss James' prophecy had come to pass, except that she was no longer beautiful and her husband, though rich and titled, did not love her.

"But I can be useful," she muttered. "I will be useful!" Purposefully, she turned away from the window. She would speak to the housekeeper this morning.

Her decision made, she looked at her own surroundings, really taking stock of them, approving the bed with its gold silk hangings. There was a writing desk in the center of the chamber and a dressing table near it that she remembered from the previous night. The two windows facing the abbey were wide and tall. An oval mirror hung between them and a similar mirror hung over the mantelpiece, both having gilt frames and, judging from the condition of the glass, both were old. To one side of the door that might or might not lead to Lucian's suite of rooms stood a large armoire that she also recalled from last night. With a little thrill of pleasure she found that the floor was covered by an Aubusson carpet; it was yellow with golden scrolls to match the draperies and the bed hangings. The ceiling was sculptured and in each corner was the bas-relief of a nymph draped in garlands of fruit and flowers. It was a lovely chamber but it wanted cleaning and airing. She guessed that the whole house required similar treatment and wondered how long it had been since anyone had lived there. The dust in the draperies suggested years. She wished that the Lucian she had known had been more informative about his home. However, beyond saying that he could scarcely wait to present her to his father, he had said little.

He had been fond of his father, she knew, and it must have been another cruel blow to learn that he was dead—when to his knowledge of two years back, he had not even been ailing. *Two* years, what could it be like to have them removed from your mind? In retrospect, two years did not seem very long, but the twenty-four months that had been erased from Lucian's consciousness had been particularly vital. She shook her head. She could not continue to dwell on this cruel loss that had made such a terrible difference in her life as well.

She went to the wardrobe. Effie, she remembered, had unpacked some of her garments last night, and she needed to don something serviceable, a gown adaptable for dusty passages. Miss James came to mind and she laughed, albeit a trifle ironically, as she recalled her governess saying, "And he will dress you in silks and velvets and drape pearls about your throat and put diamonds on your every finger."

Lucian had promised her a diamond, too, to replace the ring he valued so highly. She caressed that crested ring and then sighed. It was ridiculous to let the past arise to depress her. She chose a morning gown of brown chintz, remembering, as she did, Lucian's ecstatic references to eyes that one might have expected to be blue but that were a glowing brown. Reluctantly, she moved to a mirror, something which, of late, she had tried to avoid. She heaved a second sigh. In addition to the pallor that had replaced her once vivid coloring, the shadows under her eyes seemed even deeper and the bright white light flowing in from the windows was not kind to her complexion or her hair. She grimaced, wondering if she could ever regain what she had lost. It did not bear thinking on, save that it might have lent more credence to those claims Lucian could not understand. Again, she thought of the Incomparable Barbara and angrily dismissed her from her mind. In that direction lay self-pity. She had no time for that. There was a house to be put in order.

7

One of the first things Alicia learned, as she had followed Mrs. Gibbs, the housekeeper, from room to room was that Lucian's apartments were on the other side of the house and that he had given orders that she occupy those suites reserved for guests, at least during the tenure of the late viscount, whose family had been limited to Lucian.

"All the other children did not survive infancy. 'Er Ladyship nearly died givin' birth to 'is Lordship, as you probably know." That information had been given with a sharp glance based, Alicia knew, on the housekeeper's suspicions concerning her marriage. All the servants regarded her with much the same attitude. That had been apparent at breakfast. Lucian had not joined her then, nor had he come to the midday meal. He still remained secluded in those rooms to which the housekeeper had not been able to conduct her.

She had tried not to be depressed over that or over the fact that she had been placed as far away from him as possible, given the confines of the house. Yet, at first she had not been able to keep the image of the man she had married from striding, ghostlike, at her side. She had envisioned his tender smiling glances at every turn and heard his voice in her ear—a spirit she must needs exorcize if she were to have any peace of mind. However, she had been fascinated by the house. Though it showed definite signs of neglect—as it well might, having not had an occupant for the last twelve years—it was beautiful. She had been particularly fascinated by the long gallery with its portraits, so many of which had features similar to those of her husband.

There was his mother, a chestnut-haired girl, painted holding a favorite spaniel, and his father, to whom he bore a great resemblance. There was his fabled Spanish ancestress in her stiff farthingale, she who had given him his blue-black hair and his olive complexion. She had also seen the man who had married her—with his fair hair and his gray eyes—silvery rather, like those of Lucian. She remembered the tale of their meeting . . . How had that Spanish beauty faced the chill winters and cool summers of Yorkshire? The dates beneath her portrait had given her sixty-eight years of life—a long time in that era, longer than Lucian's mother, longer than her own. She banished thoughts that bordered on melancholy. She had, at any rate, made a more favorable impression on Mrs. Gibbs by saying that they must hire more servants, and soon, to relieve her of the heavy work attendant upon getting the house in order. She had also asked her to make a list of what most needed to be done. After the midday meal she had visited the kitchens to see if it was the cook or the stove that had delivered up a repast so indifferent that she was actually glad that Lucian had not deigned to join her.

The kitchens had proved to be huge, dirty, and with a stove that might have come to the house in the wake of Lucian's Spanish ancestress. An exaggeration of course, but when she had mentioned that it must be replaced, she had perceived tears in the eyes of Mrs. Bradley, the cook, and gratitude written large on the pale face of Milly, the girl who assisted her. To her further suggestion of more helpers, the woman had named three, including a lad to do the cleaning. She had added timorously, "If . . . if the master'll agree."

"I am sure he will," Alicia had assured them. She had read doubt in the cook's eyes, a reflection of that she had noted in the housekeeper's manner. It could be a reason for further depression, but again she was determined not to let the odd circumstances attendant upon her acceptance as mistress of the house rankle. That way lay indecision, and the house must come first! It had been neglected far too long. She could imagine the condition of the cellars but forbore to examine these as yet. However, she would have to find Lucian and . . . Where was he? She had half-expected to find him in the library, but that vast room—one that had pleased her with its floor-to-ceiling bookcases, its huge mahogany desk, its sculptured fireplace, and its numerous chairs for comfortable reading—had not yielded Lucian. She had reluctantly questioned the butler, but beyond being informed that at some time in the morning the master had gone out, she had learned nothing. She found his continued absence frustrating as well as depressing. Since he had agreed to honor his vows, at least to some extent, he should not have left her without any word as to where he had gone. Would he always ignore her? Was that part of his plan?

Plan?

Did Lucian have a plan, or rather, did he and Barbara have a plan to let her flounder in this house alone? She recalled her earlier suspicions and decided that, probably, they did. Certainly that had been his reason for insisting that they journey to Yorkshire. He might have had more than one reason for that—the other being that he did not want to embarrass Barbara by remaining in London with his so-called wife while she dealt with the conjectures of the *ton*. The thought that Lucian might have wanted to spare her, Alicia, such speculation arose in her mind and vanished in that same moment. This man did not care what she thought, and again she wondered what manner of mischief Barbara had brewed.

That she was malicious went without saying and that she could manipulate a conscience-stricken Lucian was also possible. No, not possible, probable! At the very least she would have made him feel guilty, and for a man as honorable as Lucian that would be a very heavy burden to shoulder—

especially now, when he was so confused and not entirely recovered from his wound. Alicia loosed a quavering breath. In a sense it would be better were he to be free of both of them, but if she were to leave, Barbara would come, and in her estimation, that was not the lesser of two evils!

Alicia sighed. In spite of her resolutions, the depression she had endeavored to hold at bay swept over her. It was hard to be living among those who regarded one with distrust and, in Lucian's case, dislike. If her father or her brother were with her, it would have been easier to face this situation. As it was, she was half-inclined to go to bed and sleep away the hours that must intervene before evening, but the sun was bright, and judging from all she had heard about the northern climate, there would not be many more days of fine weather—rather there would be the winds and rains of yesterday. Furthermore, she did want to stroll through the abbey ruins and she had denied herself that pleasure long enough.

With that in mind, she went up to fetch her cloak, congratulating herself on finding her chamber without any assistance from the servants. As she entered, she discovered Effie sewing on some of her garments. She had not seen the girl since they had gone through the upstairs rooms in the wake of Mrs. Gibbs earlier that morning.

"I am going outside, my dear. Should you like to accompany me to the ruins?"

Effie had looked pleased until Alicia mentioned her destination, then her face clouded, "Oh, no, milady. I wouldn't go in 'em if I was you."

"And why not?"

"Nobody does from the 'ouse. 'Is Lordship'n Mr. Church, too. They says as they be 'aunted."

"I cannot believe his Lordship was serious," Alicia said. "As for Church, has he seen any of those ghosts?"

" 'E says as 'ow 'e's 'eard things'n Jacob 'as, too." For some reason, Effie blushed as she mentioned Jacob's name. They had become a little more friendly toward the end of the journey, Alicia remembered.

"And what have Jacob and Church heard?" she asked.

"Noises in—in empty rooms." Effie shuddered. "An' Jacob told me that he knows folk who've 'eard the monks chantin' just like 'is Lordship says. It 'appens when the wind be 'igh. Papists they was, wicked Papists, 'n when they was turned out o' the abbey, they laid a curse on all who done it'n all 'oo'd come after 'em an' look wot's 'appened to the poor master."

"The poor master was wounded in battle. Such things occur in wars, Effie. As for the poor monks being wicked, they were gentle folk for the most part."

"Gentle," Effie exclaimed. "Beggin' yer pardon, milady, but they was Papist, like I said, 'n known to conjure up the devil."

"Effie! I beg you'll not heed whoever has been filling your ears with this childish nonsense. That they were Papists—or rather, Roman Catholic, to give them their proper designation—goes without saying. That they worshiped the same God that the Protestants do is also the truth. And that they were cruelly treated by those that coveted their riches and their lands is another truth. I would guess that the only ghosts Jacob and Mr. Church have heard are those that dwell in gin glasses. I beg you'll not give credence to these tales. There is enough wickedness abroad in the world without needing to borrow more from the ether."

Regrettably, Effie still appeared unconvinced, and Alicia, not wishing to press her, took her cloak from the armoire and went on down the stairs. If the truth were to be told, she was just as pleased to be alone. Yet, at the same time, she was annoyed at the prevalence of the ghost rumors. It might be hard to hire servants, especially if Jacob and Mr. Church were already fomenting trouble among the staff. She would have to speak to them, or better yet, have Lucian undertake that duty.

The unhappiness that was never far away rolled back and over her. Lucian should have made some effort to be with

her, she thought bitterly, and again her common sense inter-
vened to advise her that the present circumstances precluded
that. But how long would he continue to avoid her? She made
another effort to bury these conjectures. They lived in the
same house, and though it was large, he could not remain
closeted away from her forever. He needed time to adjust to
his new circumstances and meanwhile, she thought philo-
sophically, she would have to make the best of it.

She laughed mirthlessly. In the ten years since she, her
brother, and her father had fled England, pursued by the
baronet's creditors, she had become well-versed in "making
the best of it." Even before that, at the tender age of seven,
she was confronting the heavyset, ill-natured men who came
to the door of the mortgaged London house. With big round
eyes, radiating innocence, she would say that Papa, currently
cowering in an upstairs bedroom, was from home and she did
not know when he would return. Huge brown eyes coupled
with golden curls had always had a profound effect on these
gentlemen. Some had even given her a penny or, on two rare
occasions, a shilling. The rest of them had patted her head
and gone on their way. She did not know why that particular
memory had come back to her, or did she? Lucian, encour-
aged by Barbara, probably believed her an out-and-out liar.
Consequently, she was glad he knew nothing of that background. It would have served only to strengthen his suspicions. Still, in a sense, that early training was standing her in
good stead. Faced with his doubts, she could pretend she did
not notice them. She shook her head as if to clear her brain of
these unhappy reminiscences and went on out through the
main hall and onto the pillared portico.

Coming down the steps, she stared about her with a mixture of dismay and determination. Having arrived in the
darkness on the previous evening, she had not been vouchsafed a view of the grounds. Now she found that the grass
was badly in need of mowing and much overgrown with
weeds. The drive needed regraveling and the trees wanted

pruning. They must hire gardeners and . . . The sound of an approaching horse interrupted her speculation. Looking up, she saw a rider at the curve in the driveway. Lucian? No, disappointment brought a lump to her throat as she saw that the rider was in skirts, her hair flying in the wind. A moment later, she realized that the hair was red—indeed, it was the precise shade of Barbara Barrington's locks.

Alicia stiffened. Had Barbara come to Yorkshire? That assumption was quickly dismissed as the rider came nearer. Though she shared Barbara's coloring, she was older, and though attractive, she did not possess Barbara's startling beauty. Her features were too irregular for that. Alicia was further startled as the woman hastily dismounted, almost throwing herself from her horse. She wound the reins around one hand and came forward, leading her horse and staring at her with frank curiosity.

"Are you, Lady Morley, then?" she demanded in a deep and pleasant voice.

"I am." Alicia returned her stare, perplexedly.

"I pray you will forgive my trespassing. You really ought to hire a new gatekeeper. Old Matthews is as deaf as a post. But of course you have only just arrived, have you not? I, by the way, am Matilda Barrington-Hewes. Do you not loathe the name Matilda? Though I think it belonged to some queen or empress or such—something to do with Salic law—but I insist my friends address me as Tilda and I have finally convinced Hewes that he must do the same, poor lamb. He would much prefer it were I more dignified and stodgy like the rest of his family. However, I do exempt him, else he could never have married me nor I him. And *you* are the lady who singed Barbara's beard? She does not have a beard—an Incomparable never would—but you do know what I mean. Amd I am delighted. I hope that you will not let the fact that la Barrington and I are first cousins put you off. I wish I could disclaim the relationship myself, for I truly loathe her and I was absolutely delighted when I heard via the grapevine this morning she had gotten what she deserved for the cruel set-down she gave to poor Lucian and just before he was off to Brussels.''

"Set-down?" Alicia said weakly, feeling nonplussed and even a little battered by her visitor's frank and rapid speech.

"Indeed, yes. Imagine, she thought she could circumvent the Duchess of Pryde, a most unpleasant old witch, and snare the duke. She succeeded in the latter but failed in the first, and as usual, the duchess emerged the victor. She has picked out a bride for the duke and eventually he will marry her even though she is even plainer than the duchess herself, but far richer than Barbara and considerably easier to manipulate. With Barbara, she would have met her match when it comes to manipulation. My cousin is a formidable enemy and has absolutely no scruples. However, even she—according to my abigail, Nancy, who had it from Milly, who had it from Mrs. Gibbs, who was informed by Church, your butler—could not contend against your marriage lines. 'Tis a pity about Lucian's loss of memory. One prays that it will return. What a coil it is, is not? Still, I am delighted to know you. You will need a friend here, for if the news has reached me, you can wager that it is circulating through all the district and every-one will have formed an opinion. Mine is that anyone who can outface Barbara must win my support. So, will you accept my friendship?"

Alicia could not keep from laughing. "I am delighted to meet you, er, Mrs.—"

"Lady Hewes, but we need not be formal, since I have made up my mind to love you—if only because you have put my cousin's beautiful nose so far out of joint. I do not think that noses have joints, do you?"

"I do not think so either."

"Well, 'tis a good expression and I pray you'll not mind that I came unannounced and so quickly. I wanted to meet you and warn you that Barbara is utterly determined to make your life miserable and see you ostracized by those of us who are mad enough to remain here in Yorkshire during the winter. I received that news between the lines of a letter from my mother that arrived this morning. Naturally, I was itching to see you and I am delighted to find that you are so beautiful."

"Beautiful," Alicia echoed. "I—I might have been thought to be, once, but of late—"

"Nonsense, I expect you have been unhappy. You need not tell me why. I have figured out what must have happened. All I really needed was Barbara's furious outpouring to my parents, concerning the 'bride' who so unexpectedly turned up just when she was about to announce her engagement to poor, unsuspecting Lucian. Undoubtedly, you believed he was dead and were pining away from him. Am I not correct?"

"You are," Alicia acknowledged. "But—"

"And naturally, you were much in love with him, else you never would have insisted upon coming into this wilderness with Lucian, unless you are, as Barbara described it, a 'fortune hunter' or huntress determined on clinging limpetlike to his side, despite his all-too-apparent hatred of you. That description, faithfully detailed to me by Mama, comes under the heading of 'opening gun' in the battle she means to wage against you here, but I have an arsenal myself, and that is why I am here: to see if you are worth my using it. I made up my mind directly I saw you. And I am even more determined now that we have spoken. Never mind that I have not given you much opportunity to answer me. I see you for what you are. It is written all over your face, and that my parents could not see it I put to the fact that Barbara is a consummate liar. I cannot imagine you saying any of the things attributed to you during your interview with her. However, my parents are not so discerning nor, I fear, is Lucian. However, I can see that you are honest. I like you. I will give a dinner and I will invite my friends and you will be my guest of honor—you and Lucian, of course."

Alicia smiled and sighed almost simultaneously. "You are kind, but I cannot think that Lucian will accept."

"He'll not dare refuse," Lady Hewes exclaimed. "My husband is a power in this place. Justice of the peace and . . . But I will not enumerate the reasons why Lucian will not refuse his invitation. Another one, of course, is that he likes Hewes. Everyone does. And furthermore, we have the best cook in the county—French, of course—and everyone's trying to snare him from our kitchen. The bribes, my dear! But they will not succeed. Etienne is tremendously loyal. Imagine, he was a soldier under Soult, Napoleon's man. Hewes found him wounded in Madrid, or was it Lisbon? I do not know the whole of the tale, something about him making ragout for Hewes in gratitude once he recovered because he had seen the man was well cared for. Anyhow, Etienne believes the sun rises and sets on Hewes and would not leave him for the Prince Regent, as has already been proved. I must go—but first, a word to the wise: see that Lucian takes you to church next Sunday. He might demur, but you must insist and I will be there to see that you are properly introduced and welcomed. Will you insist on it? It might be difficult. They—I am talking about the local gentry—will stare at you very rudely because everyone has been apprised by their servants . . . and, I would like to bet, by Barbara, who will also have written letters. No one has said anything to *me*, of course, but you can be assured that her pen was not idle. However, I will come to your rescue, see if I do not."

"You are kind," Alicia said a trifle breathlessly. It was difficult for her to assimilate all that Lady Hewes was telling her.

"I am kind and I am also determined that my cousin gets beaten at her own game, so you see that I am not entirely altruistic. But I feel much more so—now that I have met you. You are exactly as I hoped you would be and I am determined that we must be bosom friends. I hope you agree."

"I—I do," Alicia said hesitantly.

"Good." Lady Hewes clasped her hand strongly and warmly. Releasing it, she moved back, adding, "I must go, but first let me add that I am very glad that Lucian has decided to open the abbey again—whatever his reasons. This house has been empty too long and caretakers are not always efficient. Rats gather when there is no cat to chase them. The same goes for prowlers and vagrants and the like. I would not wander around these grounds alone, until I had hired myself several keepers.''

"You are saying . . ." Alicia began.

"I am saying that any house that stands too long empty needs to be thoroughly searched, if only as a precaution," Lady Hewes said firmly. "And the abbey has not been visited much since Lucian attained his majority. His father rarely came here . . . the weather, poor man. He was a prey to rheumatism, but I am sure you know that. Mind you, I cannot point to anything specific. I am only speaking from past experience with a lodge that Hewes' family once owned." She moved to her horse. "I will say farewell for the nonce and hope that I see you on Sunday next." In another second she had, with amazing ease, vaulted into her saddle, and waving at Alicia, she urged her horse into a canter and was soon lost to sight.

Alicia stared after her outspoken visitor in amazement. Her nonstop conversation had been both amusing and shocking, first with its hints of Barbara's intentions . . . But those had been more than mere hints. They had been warnings, and she could not be surprised by them. Barbara's enmity had been early established, and naturally she would try and do her utmost to see that she, Alicia, would continue uncomfortable in her determination to remain Lucian's wife. Lady Hewes had not really told her anything she had not guessed already, but her allegations, uncomfortable as they had been, did carry some comfort with them.

Barbara's cousin had evidently received a favorable impression from her and would be her friend. As for herself, she did like her, but could she trust her? Trusting did not come easily to her, Alicia realized. Excepting her father and her brother, there had been only one other person in whom she had put all her faith, and that had been Lucian. Yet, she could not count herself actually deceived by one who knew her not, and as far as Lady Hewes was concerned, time would tell. Alicia would give her the benefit of the doubt by insisting that Lucian take her to church on Sunday.

Meanwhile, she would still visit the ruins. She frowned, thinking on what Lady Hewes had said about vagrants and prowlers and remembering, of a sudden, the horseman in the fog, who had ridden through those same ruins. Did she mean that the house had been occupied? But that could not be. In her tour through the rooms, she had noticed many objects that could easily have been stolen, had the caretakers been less efficient. As for the vagrants and the prowlers, she doubted that any of them would show themselves in broad daylight, and besides, she was aching to view the ruins. Purposefully she went down the path, from where she expected to determine their exact location. She was rewarded by a glimpse of them through the trees—tall elms, their leaves splashed with the reds and golds of autumn. With the determination that was an integral part of her nature, she happily made her way in that direction.

Seen close up, the broken walls were taller than they had appeared from her window. As she approached them, Alicia noted that behind them were squares and oblongs marked with thin shards of stone that, some three centuries ago, must have been rooms, their walls knocked to the ground by anvil-wielding soldiers. The stones, she guessed, had indeed gone into the building of the house, which, in effect, gave the owners the right to call it Morley Abbey.

She skirted those sad, ravished squares carefully. There were many loose stones about, some small and jagged that could and had already bitten into the thin soles of her shoes. In a few more minutes, she had arrived at a standing wall. It was oddly painful to see how carefully the stones had been set in place, carefully and lovingly by parishioners who were

working for the glory of God. It was their faith that had
helped to raise the edifice. She imagined that the main buildings, with their ornamental arches and their once-vaulted
ceilings, must have been erected by stonemasons, that mysterious brotherhood responsible for the building of most churches.

The sun was shining through the pointed arches that she
had seen from her window. Long ago, those rays would have
sent a pattern of reds and blues, greens, yellows, and browns
upon the pavement from the stained glass that had been set in
them. A few feet away from the archway, she saw an oblong
slab of stone marked with dates and a cross, and she knew it
to be the tomb of some holy abbot whose good works had
earned him the right to be buried here. At that moment, she
was doubly glad that she did not believe in the existence of
ghosts, for sad it must have been had his spirit been forced to
return to this shattered abbey. And . . . Her thoughts were
summarily scattered. She had heard a sound: footsteps, crunch-
ing over pebbles a few feet away. Reluctantly, remembering
Lady Hewes' mention of prowlers, she cast a glance behind
her, regretfully eyeing the rock-strewn ground and wondering
if she had best not make a dash for it, but in that same
moment a man came into view. Alicia caught at the stone in
front of her. It was Lucian, at last. He was walking with his
head down and what she could see of his face was so unhappy that her heart went out to him. However, she stifled
the greeting that had risen to her lips; it were better that he
did not see her. Yet, how could he help it, framed as she was
in the onetime window? She moved hastily aside, but stones
crunched under her feet and, startled, he looked up, frowning
as he sighted her.

"What are you doing here?" he demanded so coldly that
her feelings of pity fled. He was regarding her as he might
regard some trespassing stranger or even one of Lady Hewes'
prowlers.

"I wanted to see the abbey ruins," she explained with a
comparable chill in her voice.

"Indeed? You are"—he hesitated, as if weighing his words—"very brave."

"Brave?" she repeated. "What may you mean by that?"

A small derisive smile played about his lips and was quickly smoothed away. "Did I not tell you they were haunted?"

Alicia produced a smiliar smile. "You did, Lucian, but as I told you then, I will tell you now. I am inclined to believe that such rumors must needs come under the heading of old wives' tales."

Again there was a slight hesitation before he spoke and a touch of anger in his gaze. "Not . . . entirely."

Her eyes widened. "Will you still attempt to frighten me with stories of phantom chanting and ghostly chimes? I cannot believe that you credit such fancies."

"These ruins are old," he persisted.

"Obviously, they are. I'll not deny that, or that they might harbor owls or bats, but ghosts? Not to the enlightened mind, sir."

A look of surprise flickered in his eyes, but it was swiftly replaced by one of derision "And do you possess an enlightened mind, ma'am?"

Nettled, she said bitterly, "Were you in full command of your senses, you'd not need to ask me that."

He flushed. "I cannot believe that I could ever have been in command of those senses you mention to have done what I have done or was pressed to do through means I cannot fathom." He moved to her and stared into her eyes. In anguished words that seemed wrenched from the very depths of his soul, he continued, "How did it happen? I try and try to think, but no explanation offers itself. I, like you, find it very difficult to believe in ghosts, but under the circumstances, I will not rule out witchcraft."

Alicia winced. "I waved no magic wands over you nor did I drop some mysterious potion into your drink."

"How did you exact my promise to wed you, then?" he

demanded in a pain that was edged with anger. "I am not generally in my cups, but have on occasion drunk too deep. Did I become foxed and fall into your bed and did your vigilant brother force—"

Alicia drew herself up. "You insult me and yourself as well, not to mention Timothy, who was not entirely in favor of the match, saying it was contracted too hastily, But you— you," her voice quavered. "You'd not have it any other way and I wanted to—to oblige you." She swallowed a lump in her throat and blinked desperately against threatening tears.

"You wanted to oblige me?" he repeated sarcastically. "And you—you knew nothing of Barbara or that we were plighted, had been plighted close on three years?"

"I swear I never heard her name until my friend Lady Octavia sent me the clipping from the *Morning Post*!"

"Oh, God." Lucian brought his hands up to his head. "Am I to believe you, then?" He glared at her. "No, I cannot, I cannot. And you, you must know that Barbara has told me all that passed between you when she came to beg you to accept my offer and proceed with the annulment."

Lady Hewes' assertion was back in her mind. She had said she did not believe all the things that Barbara had insisted Alicia had said during their interview. That artless comment had confirmed her suspicions and now Lucian was providing further confirmation.

"And what did she say I said?" she demanded.

He regarded her contemptuously. "I hardly think I need repeat it," he said stiffly. "I am sure you are quite aware of that already."

"I am no seer, Lucian, but I think I can guess the manner of lie she must have concocted," Alicia said shortly.

"Lie, ma'am, you dare to speak of *her* lies, who must be the very soul of deceit! How you acquired my name, my ring, and my signature on the marriage register I cannot begin to understand, but I will tell you that you'll not be the happier for whatever strategems you have practiced!" He strode away from her, and then, with a startled cry, he fell heavily, lying at full length on the stones.

"Lucian!" Alicia clambered through the window, jumped down, and rushed to his side. "Are you much hurt?"

"My leg," he said gratingly through clenched teeth. "It does not yet respond well." He made an attempt to rise and a half-suppressed groan broke from him.

"But you must not try to get up," she cried. "I beg you will remain where you are until I have brought help." Without waiting for a response, she ran back the way she had come, reaching the house in minutes. Fortunately, she had left the front door on the latch, and on the latch it still remained. She hurried inside and, seeing a passing footman, sent him for the butler and at the same time requested him to find another man and bear Lucian to his chamber. A few minutes later, confronting Church, she ordered him to send for the doctor.

He regarded her dubiously. "I cannot think that his Lordship will be wanting the doctor to come, milady. He does not hold much with doctors."

"His wants need not concern us at this time. Have the goodness to do as I bid you. I will take responsibility for his presence."

Thus adjured, the butler regarded her with considerably more respect than he had shown heretofore. "Yes, milady," he said. "I'll send the lad for him."

As he went out of the room, Alicia sank down on a chair. She felt shaken, and the memory of her confrontation with Lucian still filled her with pain. She looked wistfully at the stairs. She would have liked to retire to her own room and weep, but she could not do that. For better or for worse she was yet the mistress of the abbey.

∼ 8 ∼

Alicia, sitting in the great hall, heard footsteps on the stairs. She rose swiftly and moved toward them, looking anxiously upward. The doctor must be returning. She had not gone with him to Lucian's rooms, guessing that, since she had not been vouchsafed as much as a look at them, she would not be welcome there.

In a minute she saw Jacob descending and behind him Dr. Hepworth, who was talking in a low voice, obviously giving him instructions as to the care of his master. The doctor was, as she had noticed earlier, a younger man than she had expected, but she thought, he did inspire confidence. Almost as fair as herself, he had a frank, open, and handsome countenance, lighted by deep-blue compassionate eyes. For the rest, he was tall and broad-shouldered. He dressed plainly but wore his garments with a decided air. That he was gently bred was obvious, both in his manner and in his speech. As they reached the first floor, Jacob turned and hurried up the stairs again. The doctor moved to Alicia, and in answer to her anxious query, he said, "He is resting easier, milady. I gave him a little laudanum to alleviate the pain."

"Is he in much pain?" she asked.

"Some. Fortunately, he did not jar the leg as badly as I feared. Whoever set it did a fine job. However, he should not do any strenuous walking, nor should he wander through the

114

ruins where a misstep can easily result in . . . well, what has just taken place."

"I know. 'Twas unwise of him," she said regretfully. "He is much troubled in his mind and not careful where he steps. You do know of his condition, I am sure."

"I do that, milady," he said commiseratingly. "A most unfortunate turn of events."

Though she had already received answers aplenty, Alicia could not keep from demanding, "Do you believe that he will ever regain his memory?"

"I think it likely, milady, though, of course, I cannot ascertain when this awakening will take place."

She felt a surge of hope. "You've treated similar conditions, then?"

He nodded. "One or two. There was one I did not treat, but 'twas a most extraordinary case. Should you like to hear about it? It might take some time in the telling."

"Oh, I should," she assured him hastily. Pointing to a settee that was nearest the fire blazing on the hearth, she said, "But pray sit down."

"I thank you, milady." He sat in a corner of the settee.

Alicia, also sitting down in the opposite corner, added, "Should you care for a glass of wine?"

He shook his head. "I thank you, milady, but I never partake of spirits whilst I am on call."

"You are to be commended, sir," she said warmly. "I can think of physicians who are not so circumspect. But, please, I beg you will tell me of this extraordinary case."

"Of course." His eyes lingered on her face for a second. "I know you must be anxious, but the condition can be cured or, rather, changed at any time. The man to whom I refer, I met in Glasgow, in the hospital where I took my medical training. He worked as an orderly, scrubbing the floors, emptying out, er, the most menial tasks. He had been there several years. He had been brought in as a patient, much bruised and battered, clad only in a shirt and trousers—boots and jacket gone and not a penny in his pockets. The theory was that he had been set upon by thieves in some Glasgow close, struck on the head, and left for dead. When he regained consciousness, it was discovered that he had lost his memory. However, his condition was considerably worse, say, than that of your husband, for he had not lost two years only—he had lost an entire lifetime.''

"Oh, dear." Alicia clasped her hands. "How tragic for him . . . for his loved ones."

"Tragic indeed, and probably even more tragic for them, who did not know what could have happened to him." Again the doctor's eyes were on her face. After a moment he continued, "Since this unknown man could not produce an identity and, indeed, seemed afraid, even after he had regained his strength, of leaving the hospital, the doctors, finding him willing and dependable, retained him in the capacity I have mentioned. His speech, however, was good. It bespoke an education and we were sure he had been a man of substance once."

As he paused, Alicia asked, "Were no inquiries put about, no descriptions circulated?"

"There had been when he first came, but there was no response. 'Twas the general assumption that he had come from out of town, which might have accounted for his wandering into some part of the city dangerous to travelers. There are many such enclaves in Glasgow and 'twould also account for his terror of venturing out of the hospital—some memory of violence must have been lodged in his brain.

"All this speculation was corroborated later, when in scrubbing the stairs one morning, he slipped and, falling, struck his head. Knowing that he and I had a certain bond, the other orderlies brought him to me.

"At first I was much alarmed, for his head was covered with blood, but though it was bleeding profusely, 'twas not a bad cut. As I was bandaging it, he suddenly opened his eyes and demanded to know where he was. Before I could answer him, he had recognized me and talked wildly, I thought, of a castle in East Lothian and of one Jeanie, his wife. But 'twas not wild talk merely. He was a member of the MacKenzie clan, an earl, with a young wife and two children whom he could scarce bear to be parted from. He had come to Glasgow on business, and being unfamiliar with the city, he had lost his way. As 'twas ascertained, he had been set upon by thieves, robbed, and beaten senseless.''

"Oh, dear." Alicia clasped her hands. "His wife, had she waited?"

"She had that, and summoned, she arrived still in the very deepest mourning with a girl of fourteen and a boy of twelve." He swallowed. "Their reunion was most affecting and at the same time sad, for the children had been but seven and five at the time of his inexplicable disappearance."

She liked him for the emotion that still colored his speech. "His wife must have been very happy," she said wistfully.

"She was . . . and they still are. At their urgent request, I have managed to visit them from time to time."

Alicia said gratefully, "I do thank you for telling me. As you said, Lucian is certainly better off, for he has but forgotten two years and—and the events therein."

"You must have faith, milady," he said compassionately. "One day, when you least expect it, there will be recognition in his eyes."

"Oh, I pray that you are right," she breathed.

"Think of the Highlands chief," he said. "And at least you do know where he is and are not in ignorance as to whether he is alive or dead."

There was an excess of bitterness in his tone that surprised her, and glancing up, she found that his eyes had grown somber and his expression gloomy. She had a feeling that he too must have suffered some loss—but meeting her eyes, he said merely, "I must go, milady. See that his lordship rests for the next two days. I have told him he must, but he might not heed me. Active people often lack patience."

Alicia rose. "I . . ." she began and, pausing, flushed,

"But what is amiss, milady?" he asked, smiling at her now.

Warmed by his sympathetic manner, Alicia said, "He does not remember me, nor that we were married in Brussels. 'Twas just before Waterloo."

"Ah." His gaze grew intent. "That would account for— for an attitude I found inexplicable, if you will pardon me for mentioning it, milady."

"I am pleased that you did. He is sadly confused. I did want you to understand. And I have told you because 'tis best you communicate whatever orders you have for him, to him directly or to his manservant. 'Tis possible that if I were to issue them, he would do quite the opposite. I tell you this is the very deepest confidence, sir."

"You may be sure that I will respect that confidence, milady."

The understanding and the sympathy in his eyes made Alicia want to cry, but she was able to maintain her poise as she responded, "I thank you, sir. Will he be well by Sunday, do you imagine?"

"Sunday is five days off, milady. He should be quite recovered by then. If he is not, do send for me."

"I will, of course." She managed a smile. "I will have your horse brought around."

"No need, milady. My cottage is but a mile or two distant. I walked here. I am a fast walker, lest you imagine I took your husband's accident lightly."

"I am sure you did not," she said. "And I do thank you for all you have told me. 'Tis very comforting to hear."

"May you have greater comfort than I can bring, and soon," he said gently.

At the kindness in his tone, tears once more came into her eyes. She blinked them back hastily, hoping that he had not noticed them. "I do thank you," she repeated gratefully. "I will pray for it."

"And I," he said gravely.

After he had gone, Alicia went to her chamber. She felt unexpectedly weary. The events of the afternoon had drained her. Yet, despite her unsettling confrontation with her husband, the day had not been entirely miserable. She had acquired a friend—two friends, if she could believe all that Lady Hewes had told her. And upon mature reflection, she did not see why she should not. To be sure, she was a chatterbox, but her chattering had been to the point. As for the physician, she could never, never doubt his sincerity.

She found herself wondering about him. Clearly he was a gentleman. Why, then, had he chosen to practice in this small village? Did he have a history similar to her own? Had his father spent too lavishly and left his children impoverished? She thought of poor Timothy, heir to a baronetcy that was only an empty title, and of herself, who had no dowry, something that had not mattered to the Lucian she had married, but that must be very puzzling to the man he was now, the man she did not know and was not even sure she liked.

That startling thought gave her pause. Had she fallen out of love with him in one fell swoop? She moved restlessly around the room and, coming to the window, stared out at the ruins, thinking of their unpleasant confrontation among those stones. He had looked at her so coldly and . . . Had he been serious when he had accused her of witchcraft? His other accusation had been equally hurtful, the suggestion that she had trapped him into marriage when he was foxed. The Lucian she had known could never have said such cruel things to her, but had she really known him?

A tap at the door brought her out of these most uncomfortable speculations. "Yes," she called. "Come in."

"Milady." It was the housekeeper who appeared on the threshold. " 'Is Lordship be askin' for you. Would you come please?"

"Oh, yes, at once. I thought he must be asleep," Alicia

said to cover the fact that she had not gone to him for fear he would not welcome the intrusion.

" 'E did sleep a bit, milady, but 'e's that restless. An' 'e do want to see you."

Lucian had finally asked for her, but as Alicia followed the housekeeper across the front hall and toward the wing where his chambers lay, the events of the afternoon were still large in her mind, and marching beside them was uncertainty. She could not be sure of her reception and she did not rule out another unpleasant altercation. And if that were in his mind, she would not stay to listen, she thought determinedly. Indeed, if she were subjected to another scene such as that she had experienced in the graveyard, she would go back to Brussels.

As she had been walking after the housekeeper, she had been so occupied with her own thoughts that she had scarcely noticed the rooms through which they had been passing, but having made her decision, she did look about her. It seemed to her that these, unlike those on her side of the house, showed signs of a continued occupancy. One chamber must have served as a sort of nursery, for there were shelves of toys and books set about. The next had a definite feminine atmosphere—possibly this one had belonged to his long-dead mother. She was sure that once they had passed through a dressing room hung with delicate Watteau engravings and having among its furnishings a dressing table with triple mirrors and, on it, a silver-backed hand mirror with matching brush, comb, and jars. In other circumstances she, as mistress of the house, must have occupied these quarters, she knew.

The housekeeper was knocking at a paneled door that must lead to Lucian's rooms, but Alicia had half a mind to turn and leave. However, in that moment, she heard him say faintly, "Come," and found that she was not impervious to the weakness in his tones.

The housekeeper opened the door. "Please go in, milady," she said, and dropped a respectful curtsy.

"Thank you, Mrs. Gibbs." As Alicia moved inside, she heard the door softly closing behind her. She had come into a large room, and facing her was a huge canopied bed with green velvet hangings. Sweeping velvet draperies of that same hue covered the windows, and another Aubusson carpet picked up some of the green in its patterns. All this caught her eye as she entered and was as swiftly dismissed as she saw Lucian, lying back against his pillows and looking almost as pale as their linen covers.

Some of her resentment melted away. He must have been more shaken by that fall than the doctor had admitted.

He said, "Ah, I am glad you've come. I'd not have blamed you had you refused. I beg you will pardon my imputations, though I fear you will believe them as unpardonable as I do myself, in retrospect." A flush mounted his cheeks. "One does not, you understand, like to see himself in the light that I am bathed at present. The situation between myself and Barbara Barrington has been of such long duration that—that when I found myself wed to you, 'twas difficult for me to understand. I looked about for some excuse in which to clothe my perfidy. And Barbara thought . . . ." He flushed. "But never mind that. She is prone to exaggeration and she, too, was much hurt and disappointed. Our engagement was about to be announced and our wedding to follow fast upon it, but all this you know. And considering the hurtful and unjust manner in which I spoke to you in the ruins, I'd not have blamed you had you left me there to get back to the house as best I might, but you did not, for which I thank you."

"You are welcome, sir. I do not believe you were aware of how much you had hurt yourself."

"I was not, but the doctor has told me 'twas well you flouted my orders and sent for him. And I agree. He is new here and seems most capable." His flush deepened, "I have been rude again, I see, keeping you standing so long. There's a chair near you." He pointed to a padded Queen Anne chair not far from the bed. "Will you not sit down?"

Alicia remained standing. "Should we not converse when you are more rested?"

"No, please," he actually begged. " 'Tis time and past that we spoke. I pray you will sit down."

"Very well." Alicia took the proffered chair.

He gave her a long look, and she, being closer now, read shame in his eyes. "I wish you to know that I do respect you. Given the circumstances attendant upon our situation, you have been very brave to have come this far. It bespeaks an affection . . . Oh, God!" He pressed both hands against his head. "I do wish I could remember, but"—a long sigh escaped him—"I cannot."

"I know it must be very confusing, very difficult to bear," she said softly.

"It is terrible," he burst out. "Not to *know* and to learn that some you loved are dead—my father and my best friend, Dick Seeley."

She nodded. "I can imagine that it must be very, very hard."

"Yes . . ." He was silent a long moment before saying, "I have been thinking that I ought to take you back to London—sure the winters there are easier—but since I have come to the abbey, I realize that I have been most neglectful of my old home. When I was a lad, I was very happy here, very proud to be here, too. 'Tis odd that I should have forgotten it, for unlike those of more recent vintage, these memories remain intact and I can conjure up visions of my mother, my father, and others who are gone. I find it much to my liking and would like to see it refurbished as it should have been before now. If you feel you can bear the coming winter and"—he flushed—"myself, I should prefer to remain. Mrs. Gibbs has told me that you asked to be taken through the rooms. Having seen them, what is your decision? Would you prefer to live in London? 'Tis your choice."

She had been, she realized, anticipating another sort of

proposition—one involving her return to Brussels. Despite her earlier resolutions, she had discovered that she did not want to go. Indeed, as Lucian had been speaking, she had found that her anger had evaporated. She had, in fact, seen something of the Lucian she had known . . . how long ago? It seemed years rather than a few months. He was regarding her anxiously, she thought, and again she was reminded of that other Lucian who had looked not unlike that when he had proposed to her. And in a sense this, too, was a proposal, though she could not deceive herself as to the spirit in which it was proffered. She said, "It is a beautiful house."

"Beautiful?" he questioned. "I cannot quite concur with you on that. It could be, I expect, but much needs to be done. In recent years my father never came here. I, of course, was with Wellington's forces, and my mother died young."

"I know," she said gently.

He reddened. "Of course, you would," he said quickly. "You must pardon me if I tax you with much that you must have heard me mention before."

"You did not mention this house," she responded.

"Did I not? It was not often in my mind, I expect. I imagine that I did speak of the London house."

She nodded, regretting the memories that sprang once more to the surface of her mind.

" 'Tis closed now, but it can be opened easily enough," he said tentatively.

"I have seen London, but Yorkshire's new to me and life here will not be so demanding."

He gave her a grateful look. "That is true. And as I was saying, I should like to see the abbey put in order. After all, 'tis our family seat. The room before mine, for instance, belonged to my mother; my grandmother once resided there and before her my great-grandmother, but my father closed it after my mother died. He avoided this entire wing."

"I can understand that," she said gently. "He must have been very much in love with her."

"That is true, but"—his face darkened—"he did not mourn her overlong. There was a Madame Violetta from the opera, but be that as it may, I have put you in one of the guest chambers and I think that is not right. You ought to be occupying the adjoining rooms."

"No," Alicia said quickly. "I would prefer to remain where I am for the nonce. I am willing to stay and help you get this house in order, but as for the rest, I am entirely aware of your difficulties." She paused. Hovering near the tip of her tongue were the words that would grant him the freedom he might still greatly desire. It was even possible that he regarded her in the same light that his father had regarded the mistress he had taken after the death of his wife: as some manner of inferior substitute for the woman he had really loved. But Barbara Barrington was not dead, and were she, Alicia, to be so magnanimous, there was the possibility that in the long run Lucian might suffer as much as herself even though he would not be aware of it now. "I think," she continued determinedly, "that before we resume our marriage, as it were, we must be friends rather than mere acquaintances. I am sure you must agree."

The long breath he expelled before answering her told her that he had been holding it. "I can only commend you on your wisdom." He sounded actually eager as he added, "But you will stay and will try to forget all that passed between us this afternoon—prior to my fall, I mean?"

"I have already forgotten." She rose. "And now I think you must sleep."

"I will be able to sleep now," he told her. "I do thank you, Alicia."

It was the first time since they had met again that he had called her by her name, she realized. Tears threatened yet again, but as before, she determinedly willed them away. "Good afternoon, Lucian," she said as brightly and as calmly as though she had never lain clasped in his arms, her lips ready for his ardent kisses. "Sleep well, my dear." Without waiting for his response, she hurried out of the room.

Reaching her chamber, Alicia found the curtains billowing out and a shutter banging. A wind had risen, and as she hurried to close the window, she saw gray clouds scudding across the darkening sky. Probably it would rain very shortly. She went into the dressing room, hoping to find Effie there, but she was not. She was sorry for that. She did not want to be alone with her thoughts. These were too inclined to lead her backward into a glowing past, a sorry contrast, indeed, with the present and, she feared, the future. Uppermost in her mind was the feeling that in spite of the fact that she had gained a small victory, she might have made a grave mistake in insisting that her husband honor those forgotten vows. Though he had just made a definite concession in her favor, his pain and confusion were still present, and in coming here, she had taken on a burden that she could compare to that of Sisyphus, forever pushing the stone up the hill with Barbara at the summit ready to kick it back down again. True, Lucian was making a valiant effort to abide by his promises, but such efforts could not make for a happy union. She smiled mirthlessly. It would be a union of three rather than two, for there was no dismissing the Honorable Barbara. She might be residing in a spot some two hundred miles distant, but to all intents and purposes she was here, a potent force in their lives.

"And what did you expect?" she murmured. "Did you imagine that he would forget her the moment the coach rounded a bend in the road?"

That self to whom she had addressed the question made answer, "You are too impatient, Alicia. 'Tis but four and twenty hours since you arrived."

She frowned. Had so much happened in so brief a time? Their arrival, her going through the house, her meeting with Barbara's talkative cousin, her visit to the ruins, her encounter with Lucian, his anger and fall, her subsequent conversation with the young doctor. It seemed almost too much for one day, never mind a very few hours. An ominous rumble brought her back to the window. The clouds were coalescing. Presently there would be rain and more rain and more rain. The roads would be muddied and eventually snow-laden, and through all this winter would Lucian be the resentful young man she had met earlier in the ruins or the polite husband who was doing his honorable best to accustom himself to this stranger he had so unaccountably married?

"Oh, God, it is hard," she whispered. "I ought not to have come, but supposing . . . supposing he does remember me? He'd not understand why I deserted him."

It was a very fragile thread on which to build a hope or to hang a marriage, but at the same time it was strong enough to bind her to this man. "I will stay," she whispered defiantly, and winced as hard on that resolution came an ominous roll of thunder.

"Miss—oh, milady . . ."

There was a hand on her shoulder gently shaking her. Alicia, coming out of a deep sleep, filled with fragmented dreams of Lucian, opened her eyes to rainbow colors that, she realized a second later, were candle flames caught in the prisms of her sleep-wet eyes. She blinked the effect away and stared up into Effie's pale, frightened countenance. "What is it?" she demanded.

"Oh, m-milady, can you not 'ear?"

A crash of thunder resounded through the room and the wind shrieked around the corner of the house. "The rain . . . the wind," Alicia mumbled.

"Listen, milady, oh, do l-listen," Effie's voice trembled. " 'Tis *them*. out t-there in the r-r-ruins."

Alicia was silent, straining to hear whatever it was Effie was talking about. Then she tensed. There was a sound that was not of the storm, a droning; more than a droning, it rose and fell, like *chanting*.

"Do you 'ear it now, milady?" Effie whispered.

Alicia sat up. She nodded, and slipping from her bed, she ran to the window, staring down into a darkness intermittently relieved by vivid flashes of jagged lightning. The eerie sound still filled her ears, and behind her Effie broke into tears.

"Hush, my dear," Alicia whispered.

"Oh, milady." Effie clutched her arm. "Supposin' that they come in 'ere?"

"Shhh." Alicia frowned.

"They was turned out from there when—when the wind were 'igh . . . all them Papist monks. J-Jacob s-says they was wicked."

Alicia hardly heeded her. She was thinking of that motionless figure she had seen that morning. It had been equally eerie. However, as Effie continued to sob, she said calmly, "I beg you'll not be alarmed. 'Tis highly unlikely that what we are hearing comes from any supernatural source. I cannot fathom the reason why anyone, let alone a group of people, would care to serenade us at this hour and during so furious a storm, but I am rather sure we'll take no harm from them. Now I beg you'll go back to your bed and try to sleep. I shall do the same."

"You do not b-believe that—"

"That the dead return?" In dreams, perhaps, but since you and I are both awake, Effie, I think that sounds we are hearing are issuing from human throats."

"But why?"

"I do not know why," Alicia responded, hoping that she sounded reassuring enough. "Now please go back to bed, Effie."

"Yes, milady." Effie sounded a trifle calmer as she went toward the dressing room.

Left alone in her chamber, Alicia stared into the darkness. The chanting had ceased, but the storm had not. It still raged about the house, and listening to it, Alicia wondered how many hours must pass before she could confront Lucian with a description of what she and Effie had heard. In her mind, she went over their conversation of the afternoon and heard him say hesitantly, "I have put you in one of the guest chambers."

And she had been in haste to assure him that she was quite willing to remain there. Had he anticipated her response? Had he deliberately placed her in this chamber that overlooked the ruins because he planned to frighten her into leaving? It was well within the realm of possibility. Yet, thinking of the Lucian she had known, such a device seemed foreign to his frank and open nature. He could not have changed so drastically! Yet, he had mentioned the haunting of the ruins yesterday in the coach and again this afternoon. Had he been trying to prepare her for that unholy chorus? Unexpectedly she yawned. She was growing sleepy again. She must needs ponder these questions in the morning.

Mrs. Gibbs was angry. Alicia had heard her voice from the top of the stairs, and now, as she reached the lower hall, she saw the housekeeper, arms akimbo, as she faced Mary, the parlor maid, and another girl whom Alicia did not recognize. Both were wearing their cloaks and carrying bundles of what appeared to be clothing and both looked defiant.

"An' so yer goin' an' because o' wot ye 'eard last night . . . as if you was goin' to be 'armed by them."

" 'Twas terrible." Mary shuddered. "They come up outa 'ell!"

"An' do you say your prayers at night?" Mrs. Gibbs glared at her. "Do you?"

"Y-yes, but—"

"But they don't 'old with nobody but the wicked," the housekeeper said sharply. "An' the godless," she added.

"I'm not stayin' where there's ghosts," Mary said.

"Me neither." The other girl's voice quavered.

"Then he'd best leave off bein' a servant . . . 'round 'ere at least. 'Alf the places 'ereabouts 'ave their ghosts'n I never did 'ear of anybody bein' 'armed by 'em."

Alicia concealed a smile. Joining them, she said brightly, "Good morning, Mrs. Gibbs." She had a smile for Mary and the other girl. "Do I understand that you are leaving us?"

Mary gave her a glance that was half-timid, half-determined. "Me'n Bessie 'ere, we 'eard *them* last night . . . the monks."

"An' so did the others'n you don't see 'em turnin' tail'n runnin' off," snapped the housekeeper.

"There've been other things," Mary said stubbornly. "Noises in the cellar—"

"An' don't most old'houses 'ave the same?" demanded Mrs. Gibbs. "Still, if yer that set on goin', I'll not 'old ye 'ere. But ye'll not be gettin' yer wages an' the 'iring fair's already been 'eld." She bent a stern glance on Mary. "Yer ma'll not like ye comin' back now, Mary Middleton. An' nor will yours, Bessie Smith."

"Us d-don't mind," Bessie said.

"Then go, an' good riddance," sighed the housekeeper, rolling her eyes in Alicia's direction. "I've said all I'm a-goin' to."

"If they are uncomfortable here, they ought not to stay," Alicia added. "Though in my estimation there's more to be feared from the living than from the dead."

"My thoughts exactly. "Mrs. Gibbs directed a sharp glance of approval at her.

"What is all this talk of the dead?" came a voice from the stairs.

Alicia turned swiftly and saw Lucian standing on the first landing. "Oh, should you be from your bed?" she cried.

"I am well enough. Holding on to the balustrade, he came down. The two servant girls, instinctively backed away and then, belatedly, dropped curtsies. He smiled at them. "I understand that there was a disturbance in the night. My valet also tells me that there have been other sounds that have given you cause for alarm. What manner of sounds, may I ask, Mary?"

Finding his eyes on her, the girl reddened, but she said, "There've been noises in the cellar, my Lord."

"And not attributable to rats?" Lucian inquired.

"Charlie, oo 'eard them said 'as 'ow they sounded like—like footsteps," Mary said.

"But you, I take it, did not hear them?"

Mary flushed and shook her head. "No, my Lord."

"An' in my estimation neither did Charlie," the housekeeper put in.

"But the worst were *outside*," Bessie whispered. "Them voices wot were in the ruins. The monks . . . *singin'*."

"Stuff!" snapped Mrs. Gibbs.

"You was asleep, ma'am," Mary said.

"As you should've been." Mrs. Gibbs glared at her.

"For what it is worth," Lucian said, "I lived here as a child and there were also tales of phantom monks, but none in this house ever heard or experienced anything out of the way. If last night there was such a chorus, I can only think 'twas of the earth—earthly and some prankster thinking to play a trick on us. You may, of course, believe as you choose, but that, I am sure, is the explanation." He looked at Alicia. "I am pleased that my wife, who must also have heard it, has chosen to dismiss it." His eyes rested on Alicia's face and it seemed to her that he looked oddly ashamed. "You," he continued, his gaze on the two girls, "may of course go or stay. I would rather you stayed; still, if you feel you cannot remain, I will see that you are given such wages as you have earned."

The girls regarded him somewhat uncertainly and Mary looked a trifle sheepish. "Well, I . . . I expect I will stay, your Lordship."

"That's more like it," Mrs. Gibbs exclaimed. She turned her sharp eyes on Bessie. "And you?" she demanded.

The girl still appeared nervous, but she said, "Guess as I'll stay if Mary do."

"Very good, then, get to your tasks," Mrs. Gibbs ordered, "but first 'ave a cup o' tea in the 'all."

As the two girls curtsied and hurried from the hall, Mrs. Gibbs turned to Lucian. "I do thank you, your Lordship." She shook her head and said with considerable annoyance, "I'd like to know oo it were was out there last night. 'Tis 'ard enough as 'tis to keep servants without some fool scarin' them outa their silly minds. 'Twas well you come when you did, my Lord."

"I am glad I was able to reassure them. And"—he smiled at the housekeeper—"I am pleased by your good sense, Mrs. Gibbs."

The housekeeper reddened with pleasure. She said gruffly, "We've enough trouble wi' the livin' without me exercisin' my mind about a passel o' dead monks. Do I 'ave your leave to go, my Lord?"

"You have, Mrs. Gibbs."

"Thank you, my Lord. There be breakfast laid on in the second dinin' room." She bustled out of the room.

Lucian turned to Alicia. "I am sorry you were troubled in the night."

" 'Twas none of your doing," she said. "I am only glad that you came to soothe those girls. I know from what you've told me that those tales of phantom monks are not new, but if these rumors were to circulate again, we should have trouble getting other servants to come and we have a slender staff as it is."

"I know. We will need to hire more," he agreed.

A question was hovering on her tongue, and almost without volition she voiced it. "Would you have any notion who it was might wish to frighten us away from the house?"

It was a moment before he responded. "I have no idea who would do it," he said finally. "But in common with you, I am sure that the sounds were of a human origin."

"How could they not be?" she said reasonably. "I am sure

the dead sleep well and soundly. But enough . . . I hope you are feeling better this morning, Lucian?''

''I am. My sleep, at least, remained undisturbed.'' He paused. ''Shall we go to breakfast?''

Despite suspicions that she had yet to wholly abandon, Alicia could not help experiencing a surge of something that, while not pure happiness, could be considered pleasurable. ''Yes, please,'' she assented. She was even more pleased when he held out his arm. Taking it, she had an odd sensation, one she might be forced to relinquish later, but at this precise moment she did feel as if she actually belonged here.

❦ 9 ❦

The attics of Morley Abbey were immense. There were rooms filled with old furniture and others stocked with trunks of household goods, draperies, and garments. Indeed, there was a family legend to the effect that somewhere in three centuries' worth of bundles and bales lay a fig leaf plucked from a tree in the Garden of Paradise and brought back from the Holy Land by a crusader ancestor.

"I doubt," Lucian said upon regaling Alicia with this piece of apocrypha, "that you will find it, since the Sieur de Morley who embarked upon that mission was dust and ashes some four centuries before this estate was deeded to his descendant. But 'tis an interesting tale, the usual souvenir from the Holy Land being a piece of the True Cross."

Remembering that anecdote as she and Effie stood in one of the several low-ceilinged rooms said to contain some of the materials left over from the last time the house had been redecorated, some thirty years earlier, Alicia smiled. In the four days that had passed since they had arrived at the abbey or, rather, she amended mentally, since that moment when Lucian had persuaded Mary and Bessie to remain, he had been much less antagonistic. That there was still considerable constraint in his manner went without saying, but he did not avoid her as much as she had feared he might—even given their conversation late in the afternoon of the day she had encountered him in the ruins. She had an odd feeling, however, that that had less to do with his change in attitude than the advent of that ghostly choir.

It seemed to her that Lucian, in fact, had been embarrassed by it, even though he had dismissed it as a prank. Did he know more about it than he had admitted? Had he, in effect, been trying to frighten her away and had he later repented that childish attempt? She wished that she did not still harbor these suspicions but they did seem an eminently reasonable explanation for the so-called unexplainable.

"Milady."

Alicia started. She had been so deep in thought that she had actually forgotten Effie's presence. The girl had come with her to search through the old trunks in the hopes of finding a bolt of the green brocade that had been used to cover the chairs in the drawing room. The fabric on two of these was sadly worn, but it was beautiful and, in addition to matching the sofa, it blended with walls of a mellow gold, a combination chosen by Lucian's mother shortly after her marriage.

Had every bride redecorated? Alicia wondered. She had not discussed the subject with Lucian. She had limited herself to a tentative suggestion concerning the two chairs and he had mentioned the attic. He had spoken disinterestedly, strengthening her suspicions that he cared little about surroundings not shared by the woman he had longed to call wife. With a sigh, she turned to Effie. "We will start with this one." She pointed to a huge, steel-banded, nail-studded trunk in the corner. Producing a ring of trunk keys given her by the housekeeper, she slipped off several, adding, "You try these here, and I'll try that trunk over there."

"Yes, milady," Effie spoke with the suppressed excitement of an explorer on the edge of a new continent. "They are ever so big," she breathed, and sneezed. "It be dusty up 'ere. Jacob says as 'ow no one's been 'ere for ever so long."

Alicia concealed a smile. Effie had been quoting Jacob quite often these days. She said, "And does he also say 'tis haunted?"

"No, milady . . . not 'ere, but 'e's sure that the cellars are."

"I hope that they will be setting traps for those 'ghosts.' " Alicia laughed.

"Traps, milady?"

"With cheese," Alicia amplified. She had been trying various keys in the lock of the trunk, and finding one that fitted, she turned it and found to her surprise that the lid would not budge. She must have locked it. Turning the key again, she pushed at the lid and it opened easily. In that same moment, Effie said, "I declare to goodness, milady, this 'ere trunk is open."

"And mine also." Alicia shook her head. "Gracious, I wonder who was so careless."

"It must've been the last 'ousekeeper," Effie said staunchly.

Alicia smiled. "You like Mrs. Gibbs, Well, so do I. We'll not mention the oversight. But I wonder what we'll find?"

They found gowns carelessly packed or, rather, piled haphazardly in the trunks along with shoes and even bonnets, a few badly crushed. Alicia, shaking her head over the lack of order, suddenly remembered Lucian's disparaging reference to his father's involvement with Madame Violetta. He had had room in his heart for two loves, or had it been only one: the opera dancer he had not been able to marry? And did his son have something in common with him? He was presently tied to a woman he had married and in love with a woman he could not marry. She tried to shrug that most unwelcome comparison away, but if anything were to happen to her, would her garments be unceremoniously tossed into an attic trunk? No, that was most unlikely. Barbara would probably burn them!

"Oooh, milady, look 'ere," Effie cried.

Alicia turned and found Effie holding up a gown with wide

skirts with matching paniers. It was fashioned from pale-pink silk and embroidered with tiny roses. Fine lace adorned sleeves that must have ended at the elbow. More lace edged the paniers and the skirt. The neck was square-cut and also edged with a narrow border of lace. "Oh, that is beautiful," Alicia exclaimed. "And it must be at least thirty-seven or -eight years old."

"Aye, 'tis. I've seen pictures o' ladies dressed like this," Effie said. "An' they 'ad their 'air dressed 'igh'n tricked out wi' 'orse'air an' they slept on wooden blocks wi' grooves in 'em for their necks'n never took down their 'eaddresses till the rats nested in 'em."

Alicia laughed. "I think that is a bit of an exaggeration, Effie."

"No, 'tis the God's truth." Effie looked toward the ceiling. "My ma told me about it. She were a ladies' maid, too."

"It seems to me that my father once said that his mother wore such a headdress and topped it with a ship in full sail." Alicia moved to Effie's side. "Are there any more such garments in there?"

Effie bent down and rummaged through the trunk. "Oooh, 'ere's one." She pulled out a gown of shimmering gold brocade. Similar in cut to the pink one, its neck and the edge of the skirt were trimmed with gold lace.

"Ah, this is exquisite," Alicia said, taking it from her and holding it up. "It does not look as if it has been worn very often either."

"It don't, an' 'tis your color, milady."

Alicia laughed. "But 'tis not precisely my style."

"There's a lot of material in that skirt . . . enough for two gowns," Effie persisted.

"We are not here to dress me; we're to garb the chairs, remember? And do you see anything that looks like a bolt or even a length of green brocade in there. I have found only odds and ends in mine."

"I will look again, milady." Effie bent over the trunk, thrusting both hands inside. "Oooooh," she exclaimed again, and held up two necklaces. One was gold set with stones that resembled diamonds and a pink jewel Alicia had never seen before. The other was a gold filigree with delicate sapphire and ruby drops framed in diamonds. "Ain't they beautiful, milady?" She handed them to Alicia.

"They are indeed!" Alicia looked at them in surprise. "They look almost real, but of course they could not be, else they'd not be tossed in here. They are paste, but they are certainly cleverly done. 'Twould be hard to tell them from the genuine, they must be of French design." Moving closer to the windows, she held them up. "Yes, I am sure they are French. They have a genius for fashioning ornaments of paste." Alicia added musingly, "I think I might take these . . . I've not many jewels."

"You must, milady," Effie urged. She added with a frown, " 'Tis a great pity 'is Lordship 'asn't all 'is senses. 'E ought to be loadin' you wi' jewels'n would if he knew where 'e was at."

"Effie, dear," Alicia protested, "we must not discuss that."

"Yer pardon, milady," Effie said, but added mutinously, "but it be a great shame 'n it's lucky for 'im, 'e ain't wed to 'er . . . not from wot I've 'eard about 'er."

Alicia regarded her in some surprise. "What you have heard about whom?" she could not keep herself from demanding.

"Er, wot was goin' to marry 'is Lordship. Er, girl Jane wot I met when she come to yer 'otel told me on the sly as 'ow 'er mistress 'ad dismissed 'is Lordship outa 'and the minute Pryde cast an eye in 'er direction. 'Is Lordship were that angry'n called 'er a female Judas 'e did'n said as 'ow she'd betrayed 'im'n sold 'erself to the 'ighest bidder'n that 'e never wanted to look on 'er face again!"

"Oh, God!" Alicia gasped."Is this the truth, then, Effie?"

"As I be standin' 'ere, it is, milady. Jane 'eard 'em an' said as 'ow 'er mistress started snivilin' an' said 'e were cruel'n 'eartless'n 'e slammed out wi'out another word. 'Twasn't nobody more surprised'n Jane when 'e sent for 'er mistress after 'e come back from the wars—but o' course 'e were all wrong in 'is 'ead an' she gave Jane two crowns so's she wouldn't tell nobody nothin'."

"Effie," Alicia exclaimed, "why did you not let me know this before?"

"I—I gave my promise to Jane that I wouldn't breathe a word o' it, cross my 'eart'n point to 'eaven, an' 'sides 'e stayed wi' you, but that were the way o' it'n I'm not sorry I told, so there!" Effie spoke defiantly and inadvertently glanced upward, almost as if she were anticipating heavenly punishment.

"Oh, Effie," Alicia cried joyfully, "he did want to marry me—I mean in Brussels!"

"You couldn't be a-doubtin' that, milady."

" 'Tis difficult not to have doubts now," Alicia sighed.

"Once 'e remembers—" Effie began.

"There's no saying that he ever will."

"An' there's no sayin' that 'e won't," Effie returned stubbornly. "An' now that I let the cat outa the bag, as 'twere, maybe I could tell 'is Lordship a thing or two?"

"No," Alicia said quickly. "He'd not believe you. Oh, God, I wish . . ." Into her mind drifted an old nursery rhyme. "If wishes were horses, beggars would ride." She sank down amid the welter of garments on the floor, feeling frustrated and defeated. Even armed with Effie's surprising confidence, she could do nothing with it. Lucian would not believe her nor Effie even if the girl were to swear to it on a stack of bibles. This Lucian would believe only what he wanted to believe, and he would be positive that Effie had invented the whole of it to aid her mistress. He might even suspect that she, Alicia, had put her up to it. She sighed and shrugged. "Effie, we are here for a reason. We must try to see if we can find that material." She dropped the jewelry into the trunk.

"You'll not be keepin' 'em, milady?"

Alicia shook her head. "They are paste, Effie, paste ornaments for an imitation bride."

The girl stared at her openmouthed in amazement. "But," she said finally, "I've just told ye wot Jane said."

"Lucian does not know the truth, Effie, and until he does, I would just as soon wear nothing at all when it comes to jewelry . . . at least these ornate pieces. If he sees me decked out in imitation baubles, he will believe that I am, in essence, asking that he provide me with others that are real. I would prefer not to create such a false impression. Now, come, let us continue with what we are doing while still we have the sunshine."

Effie returned to the trunk and held up a third necklace. " 'Ere be another one an' it be all diamonds. My, 'ow they do catch the light."

"Put it back," Alicia said firmly. It occurred to her that it might have been better if Effie had not broken her promise to Jane. The confidence had thrilled her for the moment but it had also served to increase her frustration. Would he ever know the truth? Dr. Hepworth's story came back to her and now it did not seem quite as comforting as it had before. After all, it had been seven years before the highland chief had regained his memory. Could she endure seven more years of Lucian's doubt and distrust? She was not at all sure of that!

"But you are here! I was delighted to see you and Lucian come in!" Lady Hewes, looking very smart in a long golden-brown coat trimmed with a dark-brown fur and a turban to match, confronted Alicia, whom she had waylaid as the sermon ended and even before she and Lucian had come out of the family pew. Without waiting for a response, she cocked an eye at Lucian. "And how are you, dear?" she inquired. "You look a bit peaked, but I am delighted that the horrid war did not spoil your appearance." Her glance slipped back to Alicia. "And talking about appearance, yours has definitely improved, but though I much prefer gray to the black you are wearing the first time we met, I do feel you should wear blues or browns or greens. After all, you are not a widow, praise be. Yes"—she surveyed Alicia from head to toe—"you are looking much more the thing. I think it must be the country air. You, Lucian, were quite right to bring your beautiful bride here, the rigors of the town, you know. Have you seen Hewes? No? He is, no doubt, outside speaking with the vicar. Do join him! He is avidly interested in mangel-wurzels for cattle and is sure you must know something about it. Go and relieve his mind, I pray you."

Lucian, looking a bit battered by Lady Hewes' rapidly fired phrases, managed a smile. "I cannot believe that Christopher, unless he is greatly changed from when we last met, could be interested in cattle fodder."

"Would that what you have just said 'twere true. None would be happier than I, the partner of his bosom. But, alas, Lucian, you are wrong and I am right. Mangel-wurzels fill his mind and dominate his conversation. I have them for dinner and supper as well. I lay abed too long to breakfast with him, else I should hear about them over chocolate and rolls. Go and listen. I know you will agree with me, and besides, I want to be private with your bride." She gave him a little push, and Lucian, looking rather discomfited, went on out.

"There," Lady Hewes said triumphantly. "He has at last taken the hint. I must say Lucian is looking much better than I expected. And 'tis a pleasure to see him in civilian dress at last. Such a leg as he has, and shows it to perfection in those narrow black pantaloons. His coat is nearly a match for his eyes, too. I expect that Jacob is responsible for his cravat.

Hewes will not let Horace, his man, do anything half so complicated. He says it scratches his chin and gives him a stiff neck besides. Fashion means nothing to him, but never mind that. By the way I was perfectly serious about your gray gown. You *must* wear colors. And I've not had a chance to ask you what you think of our church. Is it not unusual with shops built into its sides and trade carried on in the aisles?''

"I did find it rather disconcerting," Alicia confessed.

"I find it delightful myself." Lady Hewes grinned. "It gives me something to watch during the vicar's interminable sermons. He is dull. But why did you not come last Sunday?" She did not wait for an answer but motioned to a pew. "Do sit down here. None will disturb us. They are all outside busily discussing you. I assume you were aware of the attention you were receiving even though you had your eyes glued to your hymnal?"

"I," Alicia began, "did not—"

"But," her irrepressible companion spoke over her tentative response, "you must not mind them. Some, of course, will have been primed by my cousin and believe you an adventuress and they will have helped her spread the word to the others, but I have words to counteract their words and I must say that your deportment is perfect and . . ." She lowered her voice. "Did I see you nodding at Dr. Hepworth? Do you know him?"

"He came to tend Lucian last week," Alicia said. "He—"

"He is a very good doctor, is he not? Such a sad story, and yet romantic. Imagine it has blighted his whole life, not that it did not benefit those about here who need a skilled physician, but he was due to go to London. He had been offered a position at the palace, no less! He is well-connected, the younger son of Sir William Hepworth, who has . . . or rather his elder son, Frederic, has an estate some distance from here. Dr. Hepworth has a nice house himself—small, of course—and his father was going to buy him another in

London when it happened. Sir William is dead now, but Frederic would be equally obliging. James, however—that is, Dr. Hepworth—prefers to remain here. I wonder if he ever will recover from the shock? 'Twas a great tragedy. I shall tell you about it quickly and then we must join the others. I am giving a ball, by the way, and you will be invited. I want everyone to meet you! Lucian is walking more easily. Will he be able to dance? No, matter, *you* will not want for partners. You really are looking so very much better. I expect you are more rested and less anxious. At least Lucian is not dead and he does not seem as disturbed as I anticipated, though, of course, none of the Morleys wear their hearts on their sleeves, but they are known to have tempers. The Spanish blood, you understand, way back but there. It has made Lucian quite divinely handsome and so delightfully un-English-appearing. I could never understand Barbara casting out lures for Pryde, especially when she ought to have guessed that she did not stand a chance with his mama . . . Oh, yes, I was talking about Dr. Hepworth, was I not? He was just out of medical school and she . . . Her name was Juliet, Juliet Cotterel. I do not expect Lucian has told you anything about this—or has he?—but I do not expect he knows. It happened some two years back. Has he said anything?''

"No, nothing," Alicia returned, trying to conceal a combination of curiosity and sympathy. She well recalled the aura of melancholy that had permeated the doctor's manner.

"No, I am sure he would know nothing about it. He was away when it happened. I expect Barbara would have heard, but she'd not believe it interesting enough to repeat. Nothing that does not concern my dear cousin is interesting to her, I can assure you. She is entirely self-centered, and certainly she would never have liked poor Juliet, if she knew her at all. I had only the most cursory acquaintance with the girl. She was, by the way, much on your coloring, but her hair was even lighter—a strange shade, almost silvery. She wore it in braids, very unfashionable, but one heard that when it was unbound she could sit on it. For the rest, she was very lovely, slender, sylphlike, and small, like you, poor child. She was just eighteen when it happened.''

''What happened?'' Alicia shot the question at Lady Hewes and then flushed, aware that her impatience must be very evident.

''Well, to make a long story short, Juliet and James Hepworth were very much in love. They had met at an assembly in Richmond. I was in London at the time, but I understand that it was love at first sight. Their families were in favor of the match. He is the younger son of Sir William Hepworth—but I told you that, did I not? She is a cousin of the de Courcys, and being engaged to young James, he obtained permission to take her to an assembly in Richmond again. She should have had a chaperone, but her Aunt Mildred, Lady Rande, who usually accompanied her, was ill with a quinsy and so they went alone, which was just as well, for dear Mildred at least. Juliet lived with her aunt—some distance from town, a fine old house, to be sure, but a bit out of the way, a long stretch of lonely road before the turnoff to the main highway.

''As I understand it, they were a little more than a mile from the house when it occurred. They are so bold, these rogues, which is why some roads are very little traveled at night unless one has outriders and postilions with guns. Unfortunately, young James had been away studying medicine in Glasgow and was unaware of the highwaymen, or perhaps they had been lying low. They do, you know, for months and of a sudden they emerge again to terrorize us. They are certainly elusive, they seem to disappear without a trace. The rest of us would certainly breathe easier were they caught and hanged, do you not agree?''

''I do.'' Alicia nodded. ''Was the poor doctor set upon by highwaymen?''

''Yes . . . and he tried to defend Juliet, who unfortunately was wearing her late mother's pearl and opal necklace, a lovely thing, I understand, an heirloom. They wrenched it from her neck and the doctor struck at them and was pulled from the curricle. He was beaten senseless. When he regained consciousness, the curricle and his horses, the most beautiful matched grays, I understand—Sir William had wonderful taste in horses—were gone, and Juliet with them.''

"Oh, God," Alicia breathed. "What happened to her?"

"Well, though the doctor was dazed and bleeding profusely, he managed to get to an inn some miles down the road and spread the alarm. The landlord sent out men to scour the district, but to no avail. Juliet was not found. In fact, my dear, she was never found. 'Tis believed that she was murdered and buried in an unknown grave—probably out on the moors. The doctor himself was ill with grief, and though the families, both of them, tried to persuade him to go to London, he refused. 'Tis said that he does not believe Juliet is dead and stays here in the hope that she might return. However, in my opinion 'tis a vain hope, for she has been missing two years and if she is alive . . . Well, one might wish that she were not."

"Oh, dear." Alicia shuddered and remembered his compassion and understanding on the day she had first met him. In a sense, she realized, his situation was comparable to her own, but in common with Lady Hewes, she found herself hoping that the girl was, indeed, dead.

"I do wish someone could get those men." Lady Hewes frowned. "They are the bane of the district. They have robbed innumerable coaches and held up solitary walkers as well. That is why I am always concerned when houses are left too long empty, but the abbey, I take it, has not been invaded?"

"Not to our knowledge." Alicia was suddenly reminded of that motionless figure in the fog but decided not to mention it. It would undoubtedly set her companion off on another lengthy discourse and, very possibly, that horseman might have a connection with the "phantom" monks. Besides, it was time and past that she joined Lucian.

Quite as if she had read her mind, Lady Hewes startled Alicia by saying, "I fear I have detained you far too long, my dear. Hewes will scold. He must have exhausted the subject of mangel-wurzels by now, I am sure, and your husband too. I pray I have not exhausted you?"

"No, not in the least," Alicia assured her.

"You are a love, and of course, I do not believe you. However, I am more than ever determined that we must be friends. And you will come to my ball and in return you must invite us to the abbey. If Lucian protests, insist. He must not be allowed to brood in sullen silence over his peculiar situation or over my most unworthy cousin Barbara. I have a strong feeling that the less he is left to his own devices, the better it will be for both of you. And, my dear, I will allow last Sunday, but I beg that in the future you will not be too considerate of him."

"Too . . . considerate?" Alicia repeated.

"Well, I intend to issue many invitations to both of you, and if he sometimes turns gloomy and refuses to accompany you, I beg you will come without him. And certainly you must never act apologetic when you make demands on his time. Remember that, Barbara or no Barbara, you are his wife. Indeed, it occurs to me that there are many points of interest you ought to view: ruined castles; the Aysgarth Force, which is a series of beautiful waterfalls; and there's Bolton Castle and Easby Abbey. None of these are far from here and you might also enjoy market day in Richmond. Do not hesitate to enlist Lucian as your escort and, my love, if he balks, I beg you'll find some other gallant to go in his stead. That, of course, might be difficult at first, since you do not know anyone, but I will remedy that and perhaps we will make a foursome. Hewes has a passion for farming that often takes him from my side and I have visited various places with one or another gentleman. But enough; we'll discuss these matters at another time. The ball comes first.'' Lady Hewes put a compelling hand on Alicia's arm.

Coming out of the church and into the town square, Alicia found Lucian surrounded by a group of people. He seemed a trifle ill at ease and she guessed that he was being questioned and at the same time scrutinized by those who were curious about his infirmity and, judging from Lady Hewes' remarks, equally curious about his marriage.

Before she could speculate further, Dr. Hepworth, who had been standing near the church door, came to her side. ''Good morning, Lady Morley,'' he said with a pleasant smile. ''And Lady Hewes.''

''Good morning, Dr. Hepworth,'' Lady Hewes said before Alicia could do more than nod. '' 'Tis a fine morning for mid-September, is it not? Though I expect the cold weather will soon be upon us and you kept close to the grindstone with cases of quinsy. Did I tell you I was giving a ball? If I did not, I have now and will send you an invitation soon. I do hope you will come. 'Twill be in honor of Lord and Lady Morley and—''

''I shall be delighted,'' he said quickly as she paused to catch her breath. He added, ''How is your husband faring, Lady Morley? I had not opportunity to ask, and as you can see, he is surrounded, at present.''

''He seems much better.'' She smiled. ''We are fortunate indeed that you were here to tend him.'' Into her mind swam Lady Hewes' confidence concerning the lost Juliet and she imagined she could see a trace of melancholy in his manner, for which she felt very sorry.

''I am pleased that I could be of help.'' He bowed slightly, his eyes lingering on her face. ''I will bid you good morning, then.''

''Good morning, sir,'' she murmured.

''Good morning, Lady Hewes,'' he added punctiliously.

''Good morning, Dr. Hepworth, and remember, I will be expecting you.''

"I shall look forward to it, Lady Hewes." He bowed again and walked away.

"Well, my dear," Lady Hewes muttered, "you have achieved a small triumph, though I am sure you are not in the least aware of it."

"I?" Alicia looked at her in surprise. "In what way?"

"I have the distinct feeling that our stricken doctor was waiting for you to emerge from the church."

"Oh, come, you jest," Alicia chided. "I cannot believe that!"

"I know I am right," Lady Hewes insisted. "Generally he leaves the church, immediately the service is at an end. And you are, as I told you, I think, much the same height as Juliet and with her coloring, save that your eyes are brown when hers were blue and her hair a paler gold."

"Nonsense," Alicia exclaimed. "He was only interested in Lucian's health. After all, he tended him last week."

"And has tended many of us in many weeks and 'tis the first time that I have seen him stop to exchange pleasantries with any of his erstwhile patients—not to mention their connections. Nor did I see him stray to Lucian's side. Do not discourage him, my love. I had not thought of him before, but James Hepworth is well acquainted with this district and eminently suited to be your guide."

Alicia visited an exasperated look upon her companion's countenance. "I will do nothing of the kind, Lady Hewes," she said firmly.

"You would be well-advised to heed me," Lady Hewes returned sagely. " 'Tis time that the sad memory of Juliet was effaced and a new interest put in its place. You need not encourage him, but . . . Well, we'll discuss the matter later. Come, you must join your husband."

Propelled toward the group surrounding Lucian by her determined sponsor, Alicia was showered by introductions that went in and out of her head. As she smiled and nodded, she was both surprised and pleased by her husband, who, taking her arm, said firmly if mendaciously, "My wife has yet to see the town and I have promised that I will also show her the castle."

"The very thing, my dearest Lucian." Lady Hewes, standing close to Alicia, nudged her with a sharp elbow. She continued, "Coming from the sophisticated city of Brussels, you must let her see that Richmond has its attractions as well. And do not forget, I will expect you both at my ball."

He smiled. "I will keep it in mind, Tilda. And now I will bid you all a good morning." As they moved away, he added, "What ball? Am I being forgetful again?"

"No, you are not," Alicia assured him quickly. "She has not sent out any announcements as yet."

"Ah." He appeared visibly relieved and cocked an amused eye at her. "Tilda, you must know, can be rather overwhelming. Her tongue hangs on well-greased hinges and is rarely still."

"I have found that to be true, but still, she is very pleasant," Alicia responded.

"Oh, she is," he agreed.

"And was Lord Hewes interested in mangel-wurzels?"

He shook his head. "He was far more concerned with the fact that a traveler was attacked on the road last week." He frowned. " 'Tis late in the year for highwaymen with the nights so cold."

" 'Tis a pity they cannot be apprehended."

"Oh, they are, but more appear. They are a plague upon those lonely roads, but come, let us go to the castle. You can see it well from this walk." As they had been talking, they had also been making their way along the street and now she saw a steep and narrow lane leading upward. "This will bring us to a walk that will take us around the cliffs near the castle," Lucian explained. "Do you know much about it?"

"No, save that it must be very old," Alicia responded, caught between pleasure and surprise. She had thought that his mention of the castle had been a ploy to remove them from Lady Hewes' chattering presence, but she realized now that he had been quite serious in his determination to show it to her.

"It is old," he said, "and 'tis a sight well-worth seeing. Careful that you do not trip. There are many loose stones on this path." His hand tightened on her arm.

"I am being careful," Alicia assured him. "You, too, must be careful. Your leg . . ."

" 'Tis much improved. I am grateful to Hepworth. He suggested that I have Jacob put hot poultices on it and they have helped me. He's a good man. I meant to say something to him this morning. I saw him conversing with you and Tilda, but he was gone before I could call to him."

"I expect he is busy even of a Sunday . . . Oh, listen," she exclaimed.

"What?" Lucian looked startled.

"The river . . . there must be a waterfall below."

"There are ledges, rather. The Swale falls into deep pools. Once we reach that bridge"—he indicated a massive stone span—"you will get a glimpse of it. The channel is nearly hidden in the shade of the woods." He pointed to a tree-covered slope on the other side of the bridge. "The river, too, is sinuous. I wish it were later in the day, for now that the trees are beginning to turn, you should see them in the sunset. The sky will be incredibly beautiful, all purple and gold and reflected in the river."

There was a note of excitement in his voice that Alicia had not heard for a very long time. She guessed that he had a love for this district, which, in common with his old home, he had been forced to put aside and which he might even have forgotten during the hectic war-filled years he had been away. That he wanted to share some of those beauties with her was immensely heartening as well as surprising. However, he had been in a better humor during the last few days, and that, she thought, might be due to the fact that she was helping to put the house in order.

Though he had not been particularly responsive when she had showed him the materials she and Effie had finally discovered in the attics, she suspected that she had surprised him. Had he anticipated that she would be at him with demands for money to buy new silks to upholster the chairs or, more to the point, to upholster herself, as it were, via visits to the local mantua maker? She could guess what Barbara must have told him, but she did not want to think about Barbara, not at this time when Lucian bore so close a resemblance to the man she had known and loved at first sight.

They had reached the path that led around the ivy-covered cliffs below the castle. "Oh," Alicia murmured, "the walls are so massive."

"And somewhere behind them, in the very depths of the castle," Lucian said in a sepulchral tone of voice, "the Once and Future King Arthur of England sleeps."

"King Arthur," she exclaimed. "There?" She pointed at the castle.

"Have you not heard the legend?"

In that moment, it occurred to her that she had, but seeing him primed to tell her, she shook her head. "No, I have not."

"Well . . ." He paused and leaned against the wall. "It seems that a certain potter by the name of Thompson had a scold of a wife who would run after him calling him a lazy good-for-nothing and proclaiming his misdeeds to anyone who would listen. So one day, hoping for a bit of peace and quiet, he climbed up to the castle and found a cave in a rock. He went inside and what should he see but huge figures lying about, like the spokes of a wheel? And in their center was a high raised dais on which an immense man with a long curling golden beard lay. He was clad in golden armor and wore a jeweled crown on his head. And a few feet away there was a huge round table and in its center were placed a horn and a sword. He tried to pick up the sword, but all the sleepers stirred and he heard a voice cry, 'Who dares to break the sleep of Arthur the King!' He dropped the sword and took to his heels. He was so frightened that when he got home he actually told his wife about the cave; she of course insisted that he lead her to it, but he could never find it again.''

"And his wife would give him no peace after that!'' Alicia laughed.

"I can imagine that she did not.'' Lucian also laughed. "I cannot tell you how many times I went searching for that cave myself.''

"I should have, too, had I been fortunate enough to live here,'' Alicia said.

"Fortunate?'' he repeated. "Do we not seem sadly rural after Brussels?''

"No . . . I was never very fond of Brussels. It was so very confining.'' She shuddered slightly, remembering that she had hated the city—after Waterloo.

"Where did you live before going there?'' he asked curiously.

She gave him a startled glance. For the moment she had almost forgotten that lapse of memory that had banished everything she had told him all those months ago. "We lived in London on Brook Street, but we went to Brussels when I was ten. The house was put up for sale. Papa had many creditors.''

"Did he gamble, then?''

Her eyes widened. "Do you remember my telling you that?'' she asked hopefully.

He stared at her blankly and then shook his head. "No. Generally, when there are creditors, there is also a gaming table in the background.''

Alicia sighed. " 'Tis only too true.'' Defensively she added, "My father did gamble a great deal, but even before he had reached his majority, my grandfather had had a similar run of bad luck. He sold his estates in Wiltshire to pay his gambling debts.''

"Really, that is a pity." Lucian was gazing at her intently. "I know that gambling often runs in families. Did your father continue his, er, way of life in Brussels as well?"

"He did," she admitted.

"I hope that Brussels offers less scope than London."

She gave him a rueful little smile. "No. There are numerous ways to gamble in Brussels, and Papa found them all."

"That must have made it very difficult for you and your brother."

"Occasionally, but Papa had runs of good luck as well as bad."

"Yet you never could have been very secure."

Into her mind flashed the memory of Lucian as she had first seen him, indignant because she was carrying such heavy bundles into the house. She had been marketing in another part of the town where the merchants did not know her and could demand that she employ the little sum that Papa had managed to give her to pay part of their outstanding bills. She usually took Effie with her on such excursions, but Effie had had the headache that morning. And then Lucian had come forward and insisted upon shouldering her burdens, and from that moment on she had ceased to bewail her father's proclivities. If it had not been for his gambling, she would not have met Lucian. It was that that prompted her to say, "No, we were not secure but . . ." She looked up at him with a smile that faded immediately when she saw the hard look in his gray eyes. He was staring at her so coldly and, she thought with a sinking heart, suspiciously as well.

"But what?" he prompted in a tone as hard as his stare.

With a touch of defiance, she replied, "We were very happy, the three of us. You saw . . . but you'd not remember."

"No," he spoke bitterly now and accusingly. "I remember nothing of Brussels—nothing at all!"

She stifled a sigh. " 'Tis a great pity. I wish that you could."

"And so do I." He bit the words off as he actually glared

at her. He added, " 'Tis very steep this path. Would you mind if we were to return to the town. I feel myself rather weary. I should like to leave for home.''

"Of course," she said hastily. "You must not tire your leg, certainly.''

"Come, then.'' He offered his arm.

Alicia stepped back. "I think I will walk behind you. I fear that my extra weight must put an undue strain upon your leg.''

"As you choose,'' he returned shortly. Wheeling about, he started down the hill.

Behind him, Alicia shivered. It seemed to her that the bright landscape had suddenly darkened, but that, of course, was only her imagination. The sun was just as golden and the sky was just as blue. In the distance, there was a scattering of little clouds. However, she would not have been surprised had they suddenly swelled into thunderheads. Certainly Lucian's mood had changed that swiftly—and what had been the impetus? As she followed him, she went back over their conversation. They had been discussing her father's gambling. Was it that he did not approve of gambling? No, in Brussels, she recalled, he himself had gambled and won. Furthermore, he had seemed fond of her father, even though he agreed with Timothy that it was a shame that he had, in effect, gambled his son's birthright away. Yet, when a shame-faced Timothy had told him that they were unable to provide her with a dowry, Lucian had guessed the reason and laughed it away, saying tenderly that to claim her as his bride would be riches aplenty. Alicia swallowed a lump in her throat only to have it replaced by another. If he could only . . . But remembering her favorite analogy, she doubted that one met many beggars on horseback.

Lucian could remember nothing about Brussels, did not want to remember anything about it, and undoubtedly felt himself saddled with a wife who had married him for his money.

And who had put that suspicion into his mind? Barbara, of course!

Alicia swallowed a bitter little laugh. Lucian had suggested that there was a ghost at the abbey—and he had been right. Barbara, having applied for that position, was filling it with considerable success. And she did not confine her haunting to its precincts alone.

∽ 10 ∽

"I do keep forgetting that you have these storied stones for your very own. You are indeed fortunate, and 'tis my opinion that when the weather allows it, you *must* give a garden party and let us all wander through these ruins at will. In the spring, I should say . . . May, perhaps. The gardens will be lovely in May."

Lady Hewes and Alicia were walking through the shattered cloister. Due to a north wind, both ladies were wrapped in cashmere shawls over a gown of green kerseymere in Lady Hewes' case and one of brown merino cloth that Alicia had fashioned from an older garment discovered in the attic, her own supply of gowns being inadequate for the cooler weather. Autumn-brightened leaves blown there by a recent windstorm were crunched under their feet, and overhead a lemon-colored sun was intermittently covered by gray-tinged clouds.

Gazing up at them, Alicia said musingly, "I wonder where I will be in the spring?"

Lady Hewes gave her an exasperated look. "I, my dear, am no prognosticator, but I am reasonably convinced that you will be here or there." She turned around and pointed to the house. Turning back, she said, "Where else would you be?"

"I fear—" Alicia began.

"Let me have no more of your absurd cavils, my dearest Lady Morley, but I am *not* going to call you Lady Morley

155

anymore. You are Alicia and I am Tilda, do you not agree? Well?"

"I should like that," Alicia said rather shyly.

"Then, 'tis done, Alicia. And as I was saying, you live to borrow trouble. Lucian may not acknowledge it, and I know 'twas unfortunate what happened on your castle walk two Sundays ago, but I would lay a monkey and not be the loser if I told you that he is not as miserable as you prefer to imagine."

Alicia came to an abrupt stop and favored her companion with an indignant brown glance. "I do not *prefer* to imagine that he is miserable," she emphasized. "I have told you—"

"You have told me that he spends a great deal of time closeted in the library or riding about the estate or walking, now that his leg is so much improved, and I tell you that if he stays away from you during the day, he does take his evening meals with you, is that not a fact?"

"Yes, but—"

"*But* that he does not act the loving husband must be blamed as much on his infirmity as on my miserable cousin Barbara. There is much that I would like to forget, goodness knows, but to have it wiped out of my mind would be most confusing, particularly were I to find myself in an entirely different situation than what I had expected and wed to a stranger! Be understanding, my dearest Alicia, as you have been, and I beg you'll not reach for the moon—just wish upon it."

Alicia sighed. "Oh, Lady—Tilda, you do make me feel ashamed. I know I ought not to be so impatient."

"If you were not, you'd not be human, and there's a great deal about you that is not in the least human but must, rather, border on the angelic. In spite of all my lecturing, you must know that I would go utterly mad were I in your place, but you must not. I know I do sound scatterbrained, but enough! Will you promise to do as I have suggested at my ball on Friday?" She visited a compelling stare on Alicia's face.

"Friday? Is your ball only two days off, then?" Alicia asked amazedly.

"It seems far too soon for me. The household's in a pother. 'Twas to escape my harried housekeeper and my tearful maids that I fled to you, and of course, because I wanted to see you. Oh, look!" Tilda suddenly pointed. "I keep forgetting that you have that lovely tower with most of the roof intact? Have you ever gone up to the top?"

"Yes, I have. One can see a great deal of the countryside. Would you like to come?"

"No, I think not. I am not enamored of heights, and are not the stairs rickety?"

"No, they are of stone."

"Oh, of course, they would be, with a brother climbing them two or three times a day. Think how grand it must have been when the bells still hung there."

"I often do," Alicia said, following her glance. "I do not wonder that some people believe that these ruins and others similar to them are haunted. Think of the anguish of those monks, driven out of here while anvils knocked down the walls and mallets shattered the stained-glass windows. They must have thought 'twas the work of devils and the people who perpetrated it must have feared they were committing a mortal sin—such memories live on even if there are no ghosts."

"True, and how like you to sympathize with them." Tilda suddenly put her arms around Alicia. "My dear, do you know that I am well on the way to loving you, and believe me, I do want the best for you."

"Oh, you are kind," Alicia said shyly. "I—I am so very grateful for your friendship."

Tilda blushed. "I have a confession to make. In the beginning I cultivated you because of Barbara. I have always disliked her greatly and I wanted to champion you merely, I blush to admit it, because I wanted to get even with her. I could not bear to see her annex poor Lucian after the horrid way in which she had treated him, but then I came to know and like you for yourself alone. You are such a dear and I can certainly understand why Lucian fell in love with you. I cannot see, however, why he does not recognize your true worth now. You have already done wonders with the house—it is more than a collection of ill-assorted pieces of beautiful furniture. Through some mysterious legerdemain, you have made it livable, and that Lucian cannot or will not see it I put it to his guilty conscience over his so-called betrayal of my undeserving cousin. I would tell him so, but he'd not believe me, knowing as he does that Barbara and I are enemies. Two things I do beg: do not lose patience with him—he must come to his senses one day—and please forgive me for my original and underhanded motives." Tilda looked both hopeful and ashamed.

"But I guessed you had something of the sort in mind." Alicia smiled.

"Did you? You always manage to surprise me, my dear, and quite frankly I do not understand—Barbara or no Barbara—why, in spite of what I have just told you, Lucian cannot see you for what you are. Still, I do not think him as unhappy as you seem to imagine. I just have a notion that he is not yet aware of the prize he has in his possession."

"That is a most cryptic observation," Alicia teased.

"I mean it to be comforting, and see if I am not right.I must go now. Oh, I can hardly wait until Friday night. I wish I had planned my ball for this evening. I do expect great things of it, you know."

"What things?"

Tilda's glance was enigmatic. "Well, 'twill serve as a further introduction to such members of the *ton* as I have been able to capture for the night . . . But I will let you see for yourself, my dearest."

Alicia was thinking of Tilda's words as she sat at her dressing table on the night in question, with Effie arranging her hair. She had half-expected that Lucian would, at the last moment, refuse to accompany her, but he had not. Could that be significant? She exhaled a short little breath. She could not be sure and was tired of searching for meaning in everything he did or did not do. Furthermore, she was tired of always feeling as if she must make herself as scarce as possible for fear of treading on his foot or, rather, his mood. In the beginning, she had hoped . . . But she did not want to dwell upon her past hopes either. She would concentrate, instead, on the ball. She did love to dance and . . . She exhaled another breath, an inadvertent sigh, as she remembered the Duchess of Richmond's ball, when she had danced every set with Lucian, looking so brave and so handsome in his scarlet uniform. She remembered the careful way he had held her, remembered the ecstatic look in his eyes . . . but, she recalled reluctantly, there had been another ball after that, and another Lucian, staring at her as if she were a stranger. And he still regarded her that way! And this evening . . . Inadvertently she fingered the heavy gold brocade of her gown and then had an anxious look at Effie.

"Do you think that he will guess—" she began.

"Oh, milady," the girl interrupted, "I am sure he'll not guess 'twas cut down from that old gown we found in the trunk. The color's most becomin' to you. But 'tis a pity you'd not take one o' them necklaces we found. I could still run up an' 'unt for it."

"No," Alicia said firmly. She touched the delicate gold necklace with three cameos that Effie had just clasped about her neck. "This belonged to my mother, as you know, and it, at least, is not paste." She rose and glanced in the mirror that hung over the fireplace. Stepping backward, she could see her full-length reflection, and not for the first time she sent thoughts of gratitude winging to Brussels and the little French maid who had taught her to sew.

The girl, Eugénie, had been employed in the hotel where she, her father, and her brother had stayed before moving to the house Sir Anthony had purchased after a fortunate night at the tables. She had come to clean the room one morning and found ten-year-old Alicia struggling to mend a tear in her gown. Gently she had taken it from the child's plump little fingers.

"You do . . . so." She had spoken in a mere whisper, her habitual way of speaking. She had walked softly too, and she had a habit of suddenly looking over her shoulder as if she feared someone was walking behind her. One morning she had turned swiftly, a scream welling up in her throat because Papa had entered hastily, slamming the door behind him. Eugénie had dropped the sewing basket, and the spools had spread their bright threads on the dingy carpet.

In her mind's eye, Alicia could still see them, could still hear Papa questioning Eugénie gently, see his arm encircling her thin shoulders, and a few minutes later, she had learned that the hotel maid who in her spare time served as her unofficial sewing instructor was the Comtesse Eugénie de Montfort, who had escaped the Terror in Paris by hiding in a farm cart full of produce piled on top of her, the only one of a family composed of two sisters, a brother, and her parents who had not gone to the guillotine. However, the suffering she had endured and the privations she had experienced had undermined her delicate constitution to the point that she was already ill with consumption when they met her. Papa had insisted that she come with them when they moved to their house, and consequently she had been able to die in relative comfort some two years later. In that time, Eugénie had passed on to Alicia her expertise with a needle, taught to her in the convent where she had been sent to finish her schooling. Consequently, it was to Eugénie that she really owed this golden gown with its puffed sleeves and round neck cut just above the swell of her bosom, the whole of it fashioned from the skirt of the gown in the attic. Eugenie would have approved, Alicia thought.

"There is much virtue in scraps," she had told Alicia.

"And you, *ma fille*, are the little artiste *avec ses doigts*." She had patted Alicia's fingers. "But one day you will marry a man *très riche* and will not need those so-clever fingers save to paint your lovely pictures."

With a little shock, Alicia realized that Eugénie's prophecy had, in common with that of Miss James, her governess, been half-realized. She *had* married a rich man, but after all, she needed her "clever fingers," and she thought with a touch of pride, they had served her well. She need not be anxious, not in the least, and if Lucian did not choose to dance with her, no doubt there would be other gentlemen present who would!

Alicia's defiance had, however, vanished by the time she descended the stairs to the great hall and found Lucian waiting at the bottom, looking breathtakingly handsome in his well-cut evening clothes, which, in accordance with the dicta of Beau Brummell, were black. Despite the fact that she had not asked him to provide her with garments for this occasion or for any other occasion, inadvertently she did owe this gown to him! And, for the first time, she wondered uncomfortably who its original possessor had been. Could it possibly be a treasured heirloom? She would soon know. Drawing herself up and regretting as always the lack of inches that made her a delicate rather than an impressive figure, she said with a touch of defiance in her tone, "Good evening, Lucian."

"Good evening, Alicia," he said punctiliously. He added, "That is a lovely gown. Its color is most flattering. It is a recent purchase?"

Alicia swallowed nervously and said, "I made it, Lucian." She paused and then added, "I found an old gown in one of the trunks when I was looking for material to refinish the chairs. It had a wide skirt and—"

His brows drew together. "Surely you need not have done that! Why did you not go to a mantua maker?"

"There was no necessity," she said evenly. "I enjoy sewing. And my mother's necklace goes well with it." She handed him her cloak. "Should we not be on our way?"

"Yes, but . . ." He drew a deep breath and continued, "I never suggested that you go about in made-over garments."

"Even when they are of a color you have called flattering?" she questioned. "I thought so myself when I saw the gown. I feared only that you might not want me to cut it up, but it had lain there in the trunk for many years."

"I pray you'll not give it another thought, please," he said coldly. "When your wardrobe needs replenishing, I beg you will come to me. There are many experienced mantua makers in Richmond."

To her surprise, she found that he was actually angry and, she guessed, also embarrassed. It was an attitude that heartened her, since it suggested that he held himself to blame for her reluctance to approach him on the matter of her wardrobe. It might also be a straw to show which way the wind was blowing . . . or, again, it might not. It had been easy enough to read the mind of the Lucian she had married, mainly because he had never seen the need to conceal his thoughts from her. This Lucian, however, was a different matter, and when would she ever be able to stop thinking that she had married two men?

"Come," Lucian said, scattering her thoughts, "we must go." He draped her cloak about her and in another few minutes they were in their post-chaise and on the way to the ball.

In his corner of the vehicle, Lucian kept his eyes on the night sky as seen at intervals through the interlocking branches of the tall trees edging the road. Usually the sight of the sky had a soothing effect on him. He could remember when, resting in his tent in Spain or Portugal, he would look through the flap up into the dark canopy overhead trying to trace the constellations. He could see Orion from here, but the sight failed to soothe him.

The stars that formed the constellation glittered like diamonds, the diamonds that should have been adorning his wife's throat on this, the occasion of her introduction to

Richmond society. His mother's jewelry lay in a vault in
London. It had been intended as a bridal present for Barbara.
And must he needs get it out for the likes of Alicia? He
expelled a hissing breath. The gold necklace with the three
cameos that she was wearing did compliment her gown, but
compared to the gems that would be worn by other females at
the ball, it would seen no more than a bit of trumpery. And
her gown . . . he had to admit that it was becoming. She had,
in fact, looked very pretty this evening. Her hair was no
longer the dull "color of faded straw" that had been one of
Barbara's contemptuous descriptions. He remembered it had
been apt at the time. However, tonight her locks had been
beautifully arranged and they had looked extremely lustrous.
There was a glow about her skin as well. Indeed, if one
admired brown-eyed blondes, she was very well-looking and,
in her way, beautiful. Still, she could not compete with
Barbara, and she was so small! He had never admired small
women. There was a pain in his heart as he thought of
Barbara's tall, slim figure and her crown of red-gold hair.
Her eyebrows and eyelashes were darker than her hair. Nature had been very kind to Barbara . . . But why was he
torturing himself by thinking about her? It was useless.

No doubt she had found another to love by now. He wondered if Tilda had written to her telling her how happy his
so-called bride appeared to be. Tilda, of course, had no
notion of Barbara's plan. He grimaced. He, too, had been
positive that Alicia must hate Yorkshire. He had never expected her to settle into the abbey so easily, and though he
was loath to admit it, she *had* made some improvements in
the house. There had been the new cushions for the chairs,
and she had arranged the furniture differently so that the
rooms did not appear so cluttered. Unlike Barbara, she actually seemed to like the abbey and the ruins, but he doubted
that she really did. Her supposed interest in the house was
merely a ploy to win him to her side, and her home-made
gown was also a ploy. Undoubtedly she was clever, but in

this instance she had been a little too clever. "The very soul of duplicity." That was how Barbara had described her, and by heaven, she had been right!

The gown was, as he had earlier noted, quite becoming, but why had she not patronized Madame de la Tour, who was an excellent seamstress? Surely Tilda would have mentioned, her and he himself would have suggested the mantua maker had Alicia come to him. That she had not was further proof of that "duplicity" Barbara had mentioned. Clearly Alicia had wanted to prove that she had not married him for his money and his title, and so she had made her own gown out of fabric that must be near forty years old.

He could see the workings of her mind. In time, he had no doubt, she would approach him and ask for monies to send to her indigent parent and her brother. And eventually . . .

"Lucian . . ."

He started. "Well?" he demanded harshly, his response coated with his churning anger.

"We have arrived."

"Oh, have we?" he responded unnecessarily since the post-chaise was drawing to a stop and from his window he could see the crush of other vehicles and the brightly lighted facade of the Hewes mansion. One of the footmen had placed the stairs in front of the carriage door, and Lucian, coming down them, turned to escort the woman he must perforce call wife to her first ball and into a world in which she had no right to be moving. It occurred to him that he would far rather have set her on the stage to London, but something told him that would take a much more detailed plan than either he or Barbara had originally ascertained.

Because, as Tilda had confided to Alicia, half the county would be present, the ball was held in the long gallery in front of what the hostess called a "singularly unprepossessing gaggle of ancestors." "If Hewes would allow it, I would drape the lot of them in black velvet," she had said frankly.

That she had exaggerated was evident, Alicia thought as

she scanned them. Though the Hewes generations had a definite family resemblance, none of them was ill-looking. However, before she had had an opportunity to view more than the seventeenth-century Hewes—one Lord Geoffrey, brave in falling curls and petticoat trousers—she was seized by her hostess and introduced to various people who banished any nervousness she might have been experiencing by being extremely cordial. She lost sight of Lucian, who had been in one of his silent moods—silent and, she had no doubt, disapproving. Obviously he was lamenting the fact that he was not being accompanied by the lovely Barbara Barrington. She belonged here and would have known every person present. More than merely acknowledging introductions—but, of course, she would not have needed those either—she would have been inquiring after their parents, their mutual friends, and so forth. She must not think about Barbara, she decided. That way led to depression and she wanted to and *would* enjoy herself tonight!

"Might I have the first waltz, Lady Morley?" A tall young man had come to confront her.

She had scarcely consented and inscribed his name on the spokes of her little ivory fan than another older man was asking for a country dance, and in a few minutes Alicia found to her surprise that she was surrounded by gentlemen. She smiled and was reminded of the assemblies at Brussels when she usually did not sit down during an entire evening. Dr. Hepworth also claimed a waltz, and a few minutes later there was Lucian also asking for a waltz—probably, she thought as she stared up into his unsmiling face, because he felt it was his duty to do so.

She consulted her fan. "I have one left," she was pleased to tell him, equally pleased because it would not be taking place until much later in the evening.

"I thank you," he said stiffly, and moved away.

She wondered a little at the anger she read in his eyes, but she forgot it as her first partner claimed her. She had always loved to dance and, she realized with surprise, she had not danced since the eve of Waterloo. She swallowed a lump in her throat, resolutely banishing the memories that had accompanied that thought, and let the music carry her along.

An hour later, coming off the floor from a country dance, Alicia remembered Tilda's mysterious comments concerning the ball and guessed that she had instructed the young men who thronged about her, to demand dances. She smiled. She could not help but be pleased that three of these gallants had asked wistfully if she had another dance to spare and had seemed mightily disappointed to find that all had been requested. They had praised her grace with flattering surprise. Her thoughts fled as Dr. Hepworth came to claim his waltz.

He, she knew instinctively, would have required no prompting from his hostess, and as he approached, she felt the warmth of a flush on her cheeks. She could not deny that she found him attractive, and he was looking particularly well this evening. In common with Lucian, he was wearing black. The hue emphasized his broad shoulders and his slim waist, and under the light from an immense chandelier his fair hair shone like spun gold. She was pleased that he did not seem as somber as usual and she found him an unusually graceful partner. Furthermore, even though he said very little, he did seem to be enjoying himself. As she thought of his history, Alicia's sympathy was mixed with empathy, and for a reason she did not care to examine too closely, she almost wished that Lucian had not asked her for a dance. He had done so out of duty, she was sure, and in a sense, it would almost be like dancing with a ghost. Another waltz with James Hepworth would be much more enjoyable.

The music came to an end and Dr. Hepworth bowed. He said a trifle breathlessly, "That was most pleasant, Lady Morley. Might one hope that you have another waltz to spare?"

She flushed, remembering that vagrant hope, and shook

her head. "Alas, I wish I could give you an affirmative answer, but they are all taken."

"And I wish they were not." His blue eyes lingered on her face for another second, and then, bowing, he moved away.

As Alicia stood waiting for her next partner, Tilda came to her side. "I vow, my love, you are a great success. Several of the gentlemen have been begging me to add more dances, mainly so they can once again claim you as a partner. If you will look about you, you will see a number of females who have turned pea green with envy. You are marvelously light on your feet, my love, a veritable nymph." She frowned. "But I do wonder what happened to the Duke of Pryde; he was supposed to be present tonight."

"The Duke of Pryde?" Alicia demanded in some surprise. "Do you know him?"

"Did I not tell you? 'Twas in my company that my cousin met him. We were both at the home of Lady Ponsoby, who did not know better than to invite us at the same time—it being in London. Pryde came and, seeing me, stopped to exchange a few words, whereupon dearest Barbara quite forgot that she and I were not speaking and *voilà*! I cannot think what has kept him away. I had thought to introduce you. I am sure that Lucian has heard some of the *on-dit* concerning the beauteous Barbara and his Grace. I thought it would do him good to meet his rival. Alas, the best-laid schemes o' men an' mice—or, I think, mice and men—gang aft agley, but no matter, I think I have achieved one purpose: you are approved, my dear, and are pronounced quite unexceptional, even by those ladies who envy your success tonight. I am entirely delighted myself, and if you do not mind a word of advice, you must plan a dinner. I will help you with the list of invitations."

"I will, of course," Alicia said warmly. "And . . ." She paused, remembering Lucian. "But my husband—"

"He will concur, never fear. He has his pride, my love. Years ago, when his mother was still alive, the dinners at the abbey were famous, and even more so in his grandfather's day. But enough! The music is starting and here comes Sir John to claim you for the quadrille.''

The quadrille was at an end and Alicia, fanning herself, found Dr. Hepworth at her side again. ''I am happy to tell you that Lady Hewes has consented to add another two waltzes to the program. I hope that I am the first with this news, and may claim you for one of them? Unless, of course, you are too weary. Were I your physician, I might advise against such exercise as you have had tonight.''

She laughed. ''I do not believe I have ever heard so quaintly worded a request, Dr. Hepworth.''

'' 'Tis a matter of conscience *versus* desire,'' he said with a slight bow.

''And which am I supposed to heed?'' she inquired.

''I hope that you will brush my professional scruples aside,'' he returned, his blue eyes intent.

Alicia hesitated, aware of an emotion beyond mere pleasure, one that was resulting in a dangerous quickening of her pulse. That Dr. Hepworth admired her was evident, and given her situation, such admiration was sweet. Furthermore, in common with herself, he too had suffered. She said softly, ''Of course, I will be delighted to dance with you. Which of the two waltzes will it be?''

He looked extremely gratified. ''I would say both, but I must not be so selfish. May I be awarded the first?''

''The first will be yours, sir.''

''I thank you, Lady Morley. I am honored. And I will be back to claim it directly it is announced.'' He bowed and left her.

Music was in her ears again. ''My dance, I believe,'' Lucian said.

When she looked up at him, all else faded from Alicia's mind. Silently she moved into his arms. In her ears were the opening bars of the waltz, not the one they had played that night, but she could not help harkening back to those moments in the Duchess of Richmond's vast ballroom. Even though this Lucian was not in his bright regimentals, the face above the beautifully tied cravat was the same. She had promised herself that she would not be visited by memories, but as they came onto the floor, these flooded over her. She blinked against moisture in her eyes, and then they were dancing. He did not speak and neither did she, nor did he smile. His face was grave, his eyes intent. He danced well, but not with the freedom of movement he had displayed on the night of that never-to-be-forgotten ball. Alicia wondered if his leg might pain him. She looked up at him and the question died on her lips. He had such a strange expression on his face: his head was cocked as if he were listening. Meeting her puzzled glance, he said haltingly, "Do you hear guns, Alicia?"

"Guns?" she whispered, her heart beginning to pound heavily in her throat.

"It seems to me that . . . I hear guns," he said, staring down at her dazed look in his eyes.

Across the floor, someone cried loudly, "Good God, what has happened, your Grace?"

Some of the dancers halted, Lucian among them, the dazed look beginning to fade, and Alicia, also glancing in that direction, saw that everyone was turned toward the door near the end of the gallery where a tall, heavyset man, his garments muddied and a streak of blood coursing down his face from a wound in his forehead, stood clutching the door frame.

Several of the men had stepped forward and now Lucian followed them. "What's amiss?" he called.

"Highwaymen!" the newcomer cried. "They attacked the coach. My coachman fired at one of them. The postboy thinks he's wounded, but meanwhile, Charles, our coachman, is dead, they have the horses and my mother's diamond necklace."

There was loud talking and two of the women seemed near

swooning. Alicia, following Lucian, moved forward almost automatically. She saw Dr. Hepworth striding in the direction of the heavyset man, heard him say, "Your Grace, let me tend your wounds. The bleeding must be stanched."

"No, Dr. Hepworth, see to my mother, if you will, please. I carried her to the hall; she has swooned. Her health's in a precarious state, as you know."

As Dr. Hepworth nodded and hurried out of the gallery, several other men ran out.

"We'd best go." Lucian turned toward Alicia.

"Do you not think you should stay here?" Tilda asked, her face pale and her hair disarranged where evidently she had been running her hands through it. "The highwaymen must still be at large."

"They will have done enough mischief for the nonce," Lucian told her. "They never attack twice in a night. You know that, Tilda." His face softened. " 'Tis a pity your ball had to end on this note. 'Twas a very pleasant evening."

"I—I had hoped it might be," she said distractedly, and moved away.

"Come." Lucian turned to Alicia again. "Unless you are afraid?"

"No," she said dully, "I am not afraid."

"Good." He grasped her arm. "We will fetch your cloak, then."

Going to bed that night, Alicia buried her face in her pillow and wept as she had not wept since Lucian's supposed demise. Tilda's plan to introduce the duke to Lucian had gone sadly awry. She remembered her husband's face as he had mentioned the guns—the guns heard, if he but knew it, some five months back, when they had been waltzing in the ballroom of the Duchess of Richmond's hired mansion in Brussels. His gaze had been far away. Had he been on the brink of remembering? She would never know, never, never, never! She sobbed, and then, most unwillingly, she recollected her slight exchange with Dr. Hepworth. For a moment or two she had felt oddly drawn to him and knew, instinctively, that he had experienced a similar sensation.

They did have a certain kinship in that they had suffered in much the same way. And he was dangerously attractive. Was she being punished for having experienced that attraction, however briefly? That, of course, was ridiculous! And in the moment that Lucian had asked her about the guns, the ghostly guns of Waterloo, Dr. Hepworth had been completely blotted from her mind. She could not even understand that momentary attraction. No, she was not being honest with herself. She could. In her unhappiness and her frustration over Lucian's continued coldness, combined with his determined efforts to avoid her, she had reached out for comfort. Comfort was what she craved—not love—and she guessed that Dr. Hepworth had perhaps experienced a very similar feeling.

She sat up in bed, staring into the darkness. "Oh, Lucian, Lucian . . ." she whispered. "Will you never come back to me?"

Her only answer was the mournful soughing of the wind around the corners of the old house. To her mind, it seemed to be moaning, "Nooooo, nooooo, noooo."

11

The sky was an unprepossessing gray and the winds were chill. They were systematically stripping the trees of their brilliant autumn plumage. In another fortnight they would be bare, Alicia thought as she stood at her window staring into the ruins, bleak under an appearing and disappearing sun, a shy sun that had only been up for a half-hour. She had a half-smile for the fancy. It vanished as the panes rattled under a gust of wind. She shivered slightly, drawing the shawl she had put over her nightshift tighter, and cast a glance over her shoulder at her tumbled bed. It would be warmer there, but she was not moved to go back. She had risen, drawn by the light, a north light that was kind to artists. She had yet to paint the ruins. She smiled wryly. She had purchased her paints, but she had not used them.

In the three weeks that had passed since the Hewes ball she had not had the time to think, much less spend a morning at her easel. There had been invitations to routs, to another ball given by Lord and Lady Cavanaugh, whom she had met at one of Tilda's routs. She had also been bidden to join an excursion to Easby Abbey in company with Tilda and Lady Shelbroke, or Charis, as she had been bidden to call her. She and Lucian had subsequently joined Lady Shelbroke and her lord at the Theatre Royal in Richmond for a revival of *Love in a Cottage*. She smiled at the recollection. She had been half-afraid that Lucian would refuse to accompany her, but contrary to these expectations, he had. He had also seemed to enjoy himself, even though the production could not meet London standards of excellence.

Alicia had also enjoyed it and had been able to assure the Shelbrokes that it was much above anything she had viewed in Brussels. Somewhat to her surprise, she had found that in the eyes of the Shelbrokes and other county families, her years abroad had given her an aura of sophistication that they both envied and admired. Indeed, Lady Shelbroke began many a sentence with "Of course we are not world travelers like yourself . . ."

Discussing this unearned reputation with Tilda, she had been advised not to protest it. "Let them defer to you, my love. It cannot harm you, and it will, I believe, impress dearest Lucian."

Though Alicia had laughed, albeit rather wryly, at what she had not hesitated to call a "flight of fancy," she had found to her surprise that Lucian was pleased, if not impressed, by her increasing popularity among the county families, to the point that when she tentatively suggested that they give a dinner to return the many invitations they had received, he had pronounced himself completely in accord.

The event had taken place last night—after a week of agonized preparation. Present had been Lord and Lady Cavanaugh, Lord and Lady Shelbroke, and Lord and Lady Hewes and their houseguests, Mr. and Mrs. Thomas Rowley. Also present had been Dr. Hepworth and his cousin Clara MacAuliffe from Inverness, who was currently visiting friends in the vicinity. It had been a very pleasant evening. The cook had outdone herself, and Lucian, a charming and unusually gregarious host, had complimented her on a very pleasant evening before taking himself off to bed.

A sigh escaped her. She wondered what her guests would have thought had they been aware that she and her husband still lived as strangers—she on one side of the house and he on the other. No, she corrected herself, they were not quite strangers. Of late, he was becoming a little more friendly, and there had been the matter of her wardrobe and the necklace.

On the morning after Tilda's ball, Lucian had actually insisted that she replenish her wardrobe, telling her that if she would not make an appointment with Madame de la Tour, he would make it for her.

"My wife," he had continued angrily, "must not dig her garments from a blasted rag barrel."

"But, Lucian," she remembered replying, "there was nothing ragged about the gown I wore to the ball. I imagine that the material would be much more costly today than—"

He had raised his hand. "Enough. That is not at issue. Will you speak to Madame de la Tour or must I?"

Taking him at his word, she had had several ensembles made at a cost that had easily equaled the London prices and that had filled her with trepidation. Lucian, however, had not complained. He had actually praised her taste and had seemed to have a special fondness for a golden-brown kerseymere that, he had said, was the exact shade of her eyes. And last night he had surprised her by coming to her chamber, something he had not done in the nearly three months they had been residing at the abbey. He had brought with him a flat, velvet-covered casket that had proved to contain a magnificent diamond necklace; he had explained that it had been in the family since his grandmother's day. He had insisted that she wear it. She had agreed to do so and had told him she was delighted. However, even though it had glittered like ice around her slim throat and had looked particularly lovely with the white satin gown she had just received from the mantua maker, she had not been delighted.

Despite a certain softening in his attitude toward her, Lucian was undoubtedly still suspicious and still on the alert for any crack in what he might yet believe to be the facade that concealed her true nature. Barbara had done her work well, and of course, coupled with that was Lucian's continued awareness of having betrayed his betrothed. Would nothing ever change his clouded mind?

James Hepworth had not been particularly encouraging when, on meeting him in town last week, she had told him of the episode at the ball before the Duke of Pryde had stumbled in.

James Hepworth . . . *James and Jacob*.

Alicia's cheeks grew warm as she unwillingly remembered the ramifications attendant upon that encounter.

As usual, when on going to the mantua maker's she took the gig, Effie accompanied her, and on this particular afternoon Jacob, of all people, drove them. Effie, who always enjoyed going to Richmond, had been unusually quiet and had darted shy glances at her on the way. When they arrived at Madame de la Tour's little shop, which was also her home, Effie had asked if Alicia would mind if she and Jacob went for a short drive. Knowing the attachment that had sprung up between the abigail and the valet, Alicia had given her permission, only asking that they return in an hour, at which time she expected to be finished with that final fitting. Effie had promised faithfully that they would be ready and waiting, but unsurprisingly, they were not.

Alicia had stood in front of Madame de la Tour's white wicket gate for the better part of a half-hour when the doctor passed her in his gig and, seeing her, stopped to exchange a few words with her. Learning why she was there, he had insisted on driving her back to the abbey. She had agreed and left a message for Effie with one of the mantua maker's assistants. "And," Alicia muttered to herself, "that is all there was to it."

Unfortunately, that was not true. Her disobedient mind, ignoring her pleas to desist, provided an accurate recreation of that troubling incident.

Once more she was standing just beyond the gate of Madame de la Tour's house, squinting against the sunlight and with increasing impatience looking in the direction she had expected Jacob and Effie must come. She had heard the jingle of a harness and the snuffle of a horse and, looking up, saw Dr. Hepworth with the sun glinting on his bright hair.

In that same moment he saw her, and immediately pulling his horse to a stop, he called, "Good afternoon, Lady Morley."

"Good afternoon, Dr. Hepworth."

After that exchange of greetings, why had she asked him if he had seen anything of the gig driven by Jacob? Naturally, he would want to know why, and of course, she had explained; even more naturally, he had offered to drive her back to the abbey. But, of course, none of it was natural! She should not have asked, should not have explained—it was a direct invitation to him, which he had accepted with alacrity, even though on the surface it had seemed as though she was the one who had accepted his kind offer.

And anyone could have seen her up there with the doctor, but unfortunately no one had. He had driven out of town rather rapidly, slowing down only later, when they had turned into a quiet country lane, a shortcut, he had explained, one that would lead them to the abbey in less time than it usually took.

His manner was so sympathetic, so understanding, and of course he had asked about Lucian.

She had said immediately, "I had been hoping I would meet you. I had wanted to tell you what happened at the ball."

"Tell me," he had urged. He had listened carefully, as if he were afraid to lose one syllable of what she was saying.

"And he believed he heard guns?"

"Yes, and it was just like that night when—when he left with the rest of them and did not return. And then, the Duke of Pryde came in." She had clasped her hands. "Did you ever notice anything similar in your patient the Highlands chief?"

He had frowned and said slowly, "Occasionally, there seemed to be a blank look in his eyes, as if he were staring beyond us into another place."

"Another time?" she had asked eagerly.

"I cannot really say."

"I see."

He had given her a long look and then said in a low voice, "Oh, Lady Morley, what does it matter if he cannot remember? He is not without you."

She had believed that he must be remembering his own sad circumstances and his lost Juliet, but she never, never should have answered so despairingly, "But he does not want me. He was betrothed to Barbara Barrington again—can you not understand?—and all he can think on is the fact that he is married to me, whom he does not, cannot love." Tears had sprung to her eyes and she had not been able to restrain her sobs.

Dr. Hepworth had stopped the gig, and putting his arms around her, he had held her against him. "He is a damned fool," he had said in a low furious voice. "Were I in his place, I would count myself the most fortunate man in the world. How can he be with you? How can he look at you without wanting you?" He had kissed her then, passionately, and she had responded. Had she responded passionately? She had! It had been such a long time and she had been so very starved for affection and . . . Was she really attracted to him?

"Oh, God," Alicia moaned, and then silently thanked her creator for not having allowed her to act even more foolishly. She had moved back. He had apologized profusely and said that he would make some excuse so as not to come to her dinner on the following Friday. And she had insisted that he must come, else it would seem strange. And he had come and everything had passed off easily enough—as easily as though she had never betrayed herself and her husband by her impassioned response to James Hepworth's embrace.

They had met again before dinner last night—at the Assembly Rooms in Richmond, whence she and Lucian had gone with Tilda and Lord Hewes. They had even danced together. And Lucian had danced with her, too. Twice. She had hoped that he might experience a sensation similar to that on the night of Tilda's ball, but he had not. She shook her head. She ought not to be dwelling at length upon this situation, for that way lay frustration, mingled now with guilt and also a corroding bitterness, intensified last week by Tilda's delighted confidence. After three years she was finally breeding again.

"My dearest Alicia," she had said, "I was beginning to give up hope that we would have a third. I do hope 'twill be a girl this time, not that I do not adore my two boys, but 'twould be pleasant to give them a little sister, do you not agree?"

Alicia sighed. She had always wanted children. She and Lucian had talked of a family all those months ago. He had spoken of having four and had mentioned the difficulties as well as the loneliness attendant upon being an only child. That conversation seemed to have taken place in another lifetime, but it had not. Today was but the second of November and her husband had left her side on the evening of the seventeenth of June—five months earlier, five short months that, at present, seemed twice their length. And could she continue living with him in this pretense of a marriage?

Doubts, gnatlike, stung her. She needed more than a marriage in name only; she needed Lucian's love to protect her. To protect her from what? From searching for it in different, dangerous places. The episode with Dr. Hepworth had frightened her. It had shown her a side of her nature she did not even want to contemplate. She craved affection, and there was no persuading herself that she had not wanted Dr. Hepworth's arms around her, had not welcomed his kisses. But had it been he or was she mentally putting Lucian in his place? However, if anyone had witnessed that episode, they would not have shared her doubts.

"Oh, God." She shuddered. "What am I to think? What will happen to me if . . ." She did not want to consider the questions inexorably seeping into her mind. She stared down into the ruins and then leaned forward, shocked out of her melancholy reflections. Someone was down there—a girl had just darted inside, a gaunt, dirty creature carrying a big bundle of rags. She stared about her like some hunted beast, and then, whirling about, she sped toward the tower, disappearing through the broken doorway.

Alicia looked after her in stunned amazement. The girl had seemed terribly frightened of . . . What or whom? Obviously she had been fleeing. Thrusting open the window, Alicia leaned out, looking in the direction from which she had come, and shivered as the cold air penetrated her nightshift. She did not see anyone. She shifted her gaze to the tower, but the girl did not emerge again, and if she had been pursued, she had not been followed into the ruins.

And who was she? A gypsy perhaps? But she had not been dark. Possibly, she was a village girl. Not possibly, probably, and from whom had she been running? She had been barefoot, Alicia recalled, and she had been wearing an old gown without even a shawl to warm her. Impulsively Alicia went to her armoire and took out a morning gown. She dressed hurriedly, and then threw her cloak about her and put another cloak over her arm. She came out of her chamber and, reaching the head of the stairs, paused. A moment later, satisfied that no one was stirring in that sleep-bound house, she went quietly down the steps. It was not until she was outside and at the entrance to the ruins that she wondered whether she ought to have brought Effie with her. The girl had obviously been badly frightened, and frightened creatures often struck out, even at those who offered protection. However, she doubted that she could have much to fear from one who had been so painfully thin—actually emaciated, now that she came to think of it.

Coming to the doorway, she did hesitate, but hearing

nothing, she moved inside. Staring about her in the dimness, she saw nothing. Had the girl slipped out while she was dressing? She tensed, hearing a little mewling cry overhead. It sounded like a kitten or . . . a child? Alicia suddenly remembered the bundle of rags the girl had been carrying. Had it been merely rags or an infant? Another louder cry reached her and there was no mistaking it for anything but the wail of a child.

Alicia hesitated no longer. She hurried to the winding stair, negotiating it as quietly as she could, glad that the treads were of stone rather than a creaking wood. In a few moments she had reached the top and could see across the shadowy floor to where the girl sat holding her baby against her thin bosom and whispering to it. Then, looking up, she gasped and shrank back, clutching her baby tightly, her eyes wide with fear.

"Please," Alicia said as gently as she could, "I mean you no harm. I saw you come in here. I have brought you a cloak. 'Tis such a cold morning." She moved a step nearer and the girl shrank back still further. She had begun to tremble. "Please," Alicia continued soothingly, "I want only to help you. Sure, you cannot remain up here in the cold, you and the poor little baby." She held out the cloak. "At least wrap this about you."

The girl's eyes widened. "They—they—they might have followed you."

"No one followed me or you, my dear. I saw you from my window."

"From the window? You live in the abbey?"

Alicia nodded. "Yes, I am Lady Morley."

"Lady Morley?" the girl repeated. "I—I did not know there was a Lady Morley."

Alicia regarded her with considerable surprise. Despite her tattered garments, her dirty face, and unbound hair, she had an educated voice. "I have been here only a few months," she exclaimed.

"They said there—there were lights in the abbey. They were angry," the girl said incomprehensibly. The child moaned and she kissed the top of its head, "There, there, little love."

"Please take this cloak," Alicia urged, moving a step closer.

The girl tensed. "How—how do I know you are not one of them?" she breathed. "There are some around here, give them shelter. Lucian Morley was to wed Barbara Barrington, so I was told. You are not she."

"No," Alicia winced. "But I am yet wed to Lucian Morley. And you, you are from this district?"

The girl hung her head. "No," she said in a constricted tone of voice. "I am from nowhere, and am nobody. Hush!" she added almost fiercely as the baby wailed again. Then she lifted him in her arms and covered his face with kisses. "He is hungry, poor lamb."

"He must have milk," Alicia said compassionately. "You'd best come with me to the kitchens."

"No," the girl exclaimed loudly. "You are a stranger here, Lady Morley, else you'd not want me in any part of your house. And neither would you want him." She kissed the top of her baby's head. "He and I are outcasts, vagrants, beggars, because, you see, I chose to live rather than to die." There was defiance in her tone now. "I should have found a way to die at once but I was young and I wanted to live even afterwards . . ." She shuddered, then continued, "Again, I should have found a way to end my life when I felt the stirring in my womb. I prayed I might die bearing him, but when they put my son into my arms, I could not bring myself to kill myself . . . or him. I did not know that I should love him so much when I hated his father with all my being, but to hold him was to love him, poor little nameless waif that he is."

Alicia stared at her. It had grown lighter in the tower and now she saw that the girl's hair was long and fair, and despite the dirt on her face and garments, it looked new-washed. Her hair was, in fact, beautiful, almost silvery, and suddenly she remembered Tilda's description of hair that had also been silvery. She said, "Juliet!"

"Yes?" the girl answered, and stared at her wide-eyed. "How did you know?"

"I know Dr. Hepworth," Alicia blurted.

"Oh, God, James!" The girl put her thin hands over her face, "But he—he is no longer here; he cannot be. He has gone to London, has he not?"

In that moment Alicia made a quick decision. "Yes," she said. "He has gone. He went in late September."

"Ah . . ." Juliet whispered. "I thought he must have been long gone, but I am glad he is not here. He must never find out about me."

"He will not, but you, you must come into the house if only for the child's sake. As you love your son, you cannot let him remain here in the cold."

"You are uncommon kind," Juliet murmured. "Does . . . can it mean nothing to you, what I have told you? I am very sure that your husband—"

"For the child," Alicia repeated firmly, and almost as if he knew what she was saying, the baby loosed a fretful cry.

"Very well," Juliet agreed reluctantly. "But I am positive that your husband would not—"

Alicia hesitated and then said more brusquely than she had intended, "My husband will know nothing. We sleep on opposite sides of the house." She flushed and looked down as she met the girl's surprised glance, but she continued determinedly, "My rooms are the only ones in that wing that are presently occupied."

"But I—I am dirty," Juliet protested. "I have been running and hiding, anywhere I might. My . . . my man was killed and there was another wanted me. A week ago he tried to take me, but I was able to escape him. I thought I saw them on the road this morning, the three of them, which is why I came here. But I have been hiding out in stables and even in ditches. Look at me!''

''No matter, you will soon be bathed. My abigail will see to you, and since we are much of a size, I think you can wear one of my gowns. And you must rest.'' As she anticipated another protest, she added quickly, ''For the sake of your child.''

''You are uncommon kind.'' Juliet's voice broke, but a second later she had managed to regain her equilibrium.

''Come,'' Alicia repeated, carefully expelling any hint of sympathy from her tone. The fragile girl of eighteen had, in two years of untold misery and horror, gained a strength she admired. She would not try to undermine it with pity.

Dr. Hepworth lived in a large old house on the edge of town. Alicia had Tilda to thank for having once pointed it out to her. She had found it again easily enough, but now, as she dismounted from Bess, the mare Lucian had provided for her use, she found herself very nervous. She almost regretted the impulse that had brought here here, immediately after she had left Juliet with a bemused Effie. John, the groom who had saddled her horse, had looked at her as if she were mad, riding unaccompanied to an unknown destination. She had not tried to shed any light on his confusion. She had been too much in a hurry to see the doctor, but now, in the very act of reaching for the knocker that centered his front door, she hesitated, wondering what he would think or, rather, what he must feel in view of what had passed between them. But that could not matter, not when she told him about Juliet. Yet, what would he feel on hearing, as she herself had once heard, that the person he had believed lost forever was found?

Yet, though the two instances had a definite kinship, they were not the same. Juliet had not wanted to see the doctor again, but her reasons did not match Lucian's. They were predicated on shame, a shame for which she was not responsible. But what would he think? It was too late to dwell on that. She lifted the knocker and let it fall.

The door was opened by a tousled-haired servant who gaped at her and in answer to her query grumbled, " 'E's not up yet. 'E's been out most the night."

"You will have to rouse him, then," Alicia said firmly, and knew in that moment that she was doing the right thing. Yet, a second later, admitted to his parlor, she was once more unsure.

"Alicia . . . Lady Morley," Dr. Hepworth, clad in a long brocade dressing robe, came hastily into the room. With a dismissive nod to the servant, he waited until the man had left the room and then strode to her, seizing her hands. "My dearest, what has brought you here at this hour? What is amiss?"

She flushed, thinking of their meeting in front of Madame de la Tour's house and unaccountably feeling something she had not expected to experience: a definite regret. But it was far too late to decry the impulse that had brought her here. She said steadily, "She is with me. I have told her nothing, but though she does not want you to know, I thought you must be told."

"What?" Still holding her hands, he stared at her blankly. "I do not understand."

She felt her cheeks grow warmer yet. "I am not making myself clear. I am speaking about Juliet."

He turned white. "Juliet?" he whispered, releasing her and moving backward. "What do you know about Juliet?"

"I was told . . . But never mind, suffice to say that I do know, and she is alive. There is a child . . ." She saw him blench and added quickly, "From all she has told me, I have the feeling that she was ravished."

"Where is she?" he demanded huskily.

"With me, in the abbey. I told her you were away, in London, because I did not know what you would say or whether you would want to see her. She is much changed, I would think. But I believe you should see her."

"I want to see her," he said chokingly. "Will you wait until I am dressed? Then I will come with you."

"Yes, I will wait, I . . ." But he had not lingered to hear what else she might have said. He had left the room. She stared after him, knowing what he must feel and hoping against hope that for both their sakes she had done the right thing.

In a very short time, the doctor returned. "Let us be on our way," he said tersely. He was composed now, but his face was unnaturally pale. As they came out of his house, she saw that his man was waiting with the horses, but it was Dr. Hepworth who lifted her into her saddle and swiftly flung himself upon his own mount. Seconds later, they were off through streets that were just beginning to fill with carts of produce. Fortunately, that traffic was not as dense as it would be later in the morning. Still, by the time they had reached the abbey grounds, Dr. Hepworth's impatience was almost palpable.

Looking at him, Alicia had an all-too-vivid memory of the day she had received Lady Octavia's letter. And what would he think when he saw the battered waif, the changeling who had taken the place of the radiant young girl he had loved and lost? She would soon know, for they had reached the end of the carriageway and he had already leapt from his saddle, hurriedly tying his horse to a post and turning back in her direction with ill-concealed impatience. She had been about to dismount, but suddenly filled with trepidation, she let him help her from the saddle. Her concern increased as they arrived at the door. Juliet probably would not thank her for fetching him, but it was too late to consider her feelings now. She pushed at the door; it did not budge. She had left it on the latch, but someone had closed it. She reached for the knocker, but Dr. Hepworth was before her, slamming it against its plate.

A few minutes later, the butler, looking sleepy and vaguely resentful, pulled it open, moving back hastily as Dr. Hepworth strode inside. "Milady . . ." he began and paused in consternation as the doctor moved toward the stairs.

"Where is she?" he demanded brusquely.

"Come," Alicia said. She glanced back at Church. " 'Tis all right," she murmured, and started up the stairs with the doctor immediately behind her. As they had reached her chamber door, she pointed to it. "She's in there," she said softly.

For a moment he hesitated, staring blindly into space, and then he turned the handle and, opening it, went inside. In the act of closing the door, Alicia heard a cry, almost a scream, and in that same moment he, too, cried out, "Juliet!"

Alicia shut the door quickly. Feeling weak and drained, she sank down in an adjacent chair, staring at the sunbeams that were filtering through a crack in the corners to dance on the walls of the sitting room. Then, she tensed as she heard footsteps approaching. Looking up, she saw Lucian framed in the doorway. He said shortly, "Who is this woman you have brought into my house?" Before she could respond, he added coldly, "And where have you been at this time of the morning?"

She got slowly to her feet. "I went to fetch the doctor," she responded in a tone as cold as his own.

"You . . . alone?"

"I, alone," she corroborated. "But you must have known that, since you are aware that I was away. I presume one of the servants was your informant. The groom, perhaps?"

He regarded her with increasing anger. "I know very little about you," he said, biting off each word. "But I had come to the conclusion that you possessed some sense of what is right and proper. Yet, I am told by my housekeeper that you brought into your chambers a vagrant from off the roads and her brat. I am also told that, without any explanation, you rode off alone—God knows where!"

Still defiantly, she glared back at him. "And now you know my destination. I went to fetch Dr. Hepworth, and as for the woman I brought into the house, she might be a vagrant, but she does have a name. It is Juliet Cotterel.''

"And am I supposed to know who that is?" he demanded coldly.

"No, you were not here when it happened. She was kidnapped two years ago, when she and her fiancé, Dr. Hepworth, were set upon by highwaymen. She has lived a dog's life ever since, ravished and got with child by one of them. He is dead, and pursued by another, she ran into the ruins. I saw her. I brought the doctor here because I was told that he has lived in the vain hope of finding her. He gave up preferment, a London living, because he prayed he might hear something of her. Can you not guess what it means to him to know that she is alive and not lying rotting on the battlefield beneath a pile of bodies and . . .'' She paused in consternation, realizing what she had just said, "I mean . . .'' She choked and turned away, trying vainly not to allow the tears that were swelling her eyelids to fall.

"Alicia!" Lucian came to her side. His anger had faded. "Oh, my dear, I am sorry . . .''

She was still trying to stem her tears, but to no avail. They came seeping through her fingers. She was hardly aware of her husband's arms closing about her or that it was upon his shoulder that she sobbed out all the pain and anguish with which she had been living for months.

∽ 12 ∾

Informed that Dr. Hepworth had called to see her, Alicia wished that Lucian were with her, but he was out, she did not know where. Four days had passed since the doctor had insisted on taking Juliet back to his house, and in that time Alicia had been of two minds as to the wisdom of bringing them together. Again she was comparing her situation to the doctor's. There was no gainsaying the fact that the lovers of two years previously were not the same individuals anymore. Even if Juliet had not lost her memory, her life with a quartet of highwaymen and their occasional hangers-on must needs have toughened and coarsened her. That the delicate, fairy-like creature Tilda had described was gone, went without saying. Even bathed and garbed in one of Alicia's gowns, there had been something wary and wild about the girl who had left in the company of Dr. Hepworth, and she had looked far older than her twenty years. As for Hepworth, he had still appeared dazed, and though he had been carrying the infant, it had seemed to Alicia that he had looked upon the poor mite with something less than affection. But as Lucian had said, the doctor would undoubtedly have trouble summoning up any tender feelings for the by-blow of the miscreant who had been shot by the late coachman of the Duke of Pryde on the night of Tilda's ball.

She had agreed with him, and remembering a conversation

she had had with Tilda the day before yesterday, she winced. That outspoken lady had said frankly, "I can only hope that Dr. Hepworth can find a good home for the poor woman and her brat."

"You do not believe that he will take Juliet back?"

"He could not take her back and remain here—or in London, either," Tilda had said. "Though nothing of what has happened to her was her fault, she would never be able to lift up her head again. Hewes, alas, is a case in point. If he has said it once, he has said it at least twenty times that he cannot imagine that a young man of Dr. Hepworth's cut, with all his life before him, would be willing to take as his bride the ex-doxy of a highwayman and his misbegotten whelp besides."

"He said that?"

"As I have just told you, and furthermore, he is of the opinion that rather than having suffered the degradation of the past two years, Juliet should have found some means by which to kill herself."

"I told you that she had intended—"

"And I conveyed that information to Hewes. He said 'twas a pity she had not the courage to abide by those intentions. And I will tell you, my dear, that I have heard that same opinion voiced by half my friends. The other half, excluding only yourself, have remained silent on the subject, though of course everyone fears his departure. In view of the circumstances, they believe that he might put sentiment above common sense."

And now, Alicia thought unhappily, she would soon know his decision. The butler opened the door. "Dr. Hepworth, milady," he said.

"Thank you, Church."

James came in quickly, and Alicia, seeing his pale set face, felt her heart begin to pound heavily in her chest. He crossed the space between them in two strides and bent over her outstretched hand. What would he tell her? Releasing her hand, he straightened and faced her. "I am going away," he said bluntly.

"Must you?" she questioned, knowing that she had expected such an announcement, but at the same time she was still shocked by it.

He regarded her gravely. "I have no alternative. I love you, Alicia, but there's no hope for me, is there?"

Her heart seemed to be pounding in her throat. She ought to have been affronted by this forthright admission, but she was not. She regarded him regretfully. He had spoken hopelessly, but she suspected that he might still cherish a tendril of hope. Almost imperceptibly, she shook her head. "I wish . . . But no, James, I love Lucian. I expect that no matter what happens, I always will."

He nodded, and from his expression she could read an acceptance of a truth he must have known before he uttered those words. "I know that you will continue to wait and hope," he said huskily. "And 'tis such a waste. God, I do not know why he cannot realize that you are worth twenty, nay, a hundred and twenty Barbara Barringtons! I cannot understand why, memory or no memory, he, living in the same house with you, seeing you each day . . . The man is a fool. But be that as it may, I cannot stay here and . . . there is Juliet."

"Did I do the right thing?" she asked tremulously.

"Yes, you did," he assured her hastily. "There was nothing else you could have done, knowing you. And also 'twas an action that made my last question only a wish, rather than anything more concrete. I think I can help her. I do care for her still, not as much as I once did. I am sorry for that, but there it is. And also she has the child, *his* child." His brows drew together. "She cherishes the boy."

"Could she do anything else? He is flesh of her flesh," Alicia cried.

"I know, but the blood—"

"You are a doctor. Can you believe that the so-called sins of the father will be visited up this child?"

He sighed. "My common sense tells me no, but—"

"Heed your common sense, James," she begged. "Juliet is his mother."

"Yes, that is true, and though she has changed, I still see traces of the girl I knew. Perhaps in time and with care—"

"And love," Alicia added quickly. She gave him a long look. "Do you know, I think you might have been drawn to me because I reminded you of her."

He was silent a moment. Then, he said slowly, "In the beginning, perhaps. I know I've not seen you very often"—he took a step toward her—"but you are quite unique and 'tis a great pity that . . . But I'll not torment you by repeating what we both know. As I once told you, there is the hope that your husband will regain his memory. And possibly that incident at the ball is significant. For my own paltry reasons, I fear I did not want you to build your hopes on it." He sighed. "I am saying too much that is beside the point. I came to tell you that I have made arrangements to go to Canada."

"Canada," she cried.

He nodded. "A man I knew in Glasgow, Dr. Angus Malcolm, is practicing in Nova Scotia, where there is a great need for qualified medical men. He has written to me often and I—*we* will join him there."

" 'Tis so far away," she could not help protesting.

"But there no one will know that my son,"—he swallowed—"is not my son. Juliet is willing, poor child, and I do still have a place for her in my heart, but—"

"I am glad, then." Alicia interrupted. "And once you are away . . ."

He smiled mirthlessly. "I expect you are trying to tell me that absence will not make the heart grow fonder."

"It must not," she said firmly.

"I expect you are right." His eyes lingered on her face. "And I do thank you for that kindness that is such an integral part of your nature. Juliet is also very grateful. She wants me to tell you that until she met you, she thought every hand would be raised against her. You have helped restore her faith in her fellow man and . . ." He frowned. "There is something else she wanted me to tell you. She says that on two occasions she and her companions came here to your cellars. They had been hiding in another abandoned house, but that one burned down. They were not here often, for shortly after they came, word reached them that your husband was expected home. They did make an effort to frighten you off by reviving that old tale of the phantom monks and chanting one night in the midst of a storm, but their, er, acting debut appeared to fool no one, and it being mighty uncomfortable in the ruins, they decided against any more 'appearances.' However, they still have an eye on this house, for what reason I do not know, nor does she. She warns that you must hire more keepers."

"I will tell Lucian," Alicia said.

"Do," he urged. "I would not like to think of you or yours in danger. I had best go now." He paused and stared at her. "That day I met you in town, I hope you'll not think ill of me for that. Being with you . . . Oh, God, Alicia." He bowed his head.

"I do not think ill of you," she told him quickly. "I was as much to blame as you. We must both forget what happened, my dear."

"I will never forget it," he said huskily, and cleared his throat. Moving to her, he took her hand and once more pressed it to his lips.

"Fare you well, Alicia."

"And you, my dear James. Let me know that all is well with you."

"I will," he said, and bowing once again, he hurried out.

Tilda Hewes, looking a trifle wan, was resting on the crocodile-headed sofa in the parlor, a place of jackal-shaped incense jars, cobra-based tables, and other equally exotic furnishings collected by Lord Hewes' mother at a time when

THE FORGOTTEN MARRIAGE 193

all England was celebrating Nelson's Egyptian victories. Having refused to obey her husband's earnest request that she banish these exhibits to the attic, Tilda received only her most intimate friends there.

Smiling at Alicia, who was about to take her leave, she said half-accusingly, "I must tell you, my love, that I do miss Dr. Hepworth. He officiated at my last lying-in and I only hope that Dr. Withstanley proves as competent. I shall be seeing him later this afternoon."

Alicia returned her rueful glance with one of her own. "I need not say that I am also sorry he is gone. But I must agree with his decision."

"I, too. Poor Juliet would never have been received here, as I believe I told you."

"Yes. 'Tis a pity. I am sure he will do well in Canada, however."

"I agree. James Hepworth would do well anywhere," Tilda said positively. "And mark my words, now that Juliet is removed from her past, she will probably become a lady of high degree. She has the birth and the breeding."

"And the courage," Alicia said softly.

"True." Tilda nodded. "She has more than I ever dreamed she possessed, poor creature. God, the life she must have led these two years past. Damn those villains, I wish the rest of them might have joined her ravisher in hell."

"As do I," Alicia said feelingly.

"And meanwhile . . ." Tilda scanned Alicia's face. "You do look happier, my dear."

"I am happier," Alicia said softly.

"And deserve to be even happier," Tilda said pointedly. "And will be," she added.

Alicia smiled and blew her a kiss. "I must be going."

"Swear that you will come again soon. I can see that this is going to be a difficult period for me—full of megrims! I shall need a shoulder to weep upon."

"I promise I will come again as soon as I may," Alicia told her.

Because the weather had been uncertain when she had started out, Alicia had not taken Bess as was her wont. She had come in the post-chaise. Now, as the coachman drove her toward the abbey, she was thinking of Tilda's comments. In the fortnight that had passed since the departure of Dr. Hepworth, she had been happy, but as to whether she would be happier, she was still not sure. Lucian's attitude had undergone considerable change. He was kinder and, on occasion, even affectionate. He had also insisted that she move from her chamber into the wing he occupied. She guessed that her outburst on the day she had brought Juliet into the house had precipitated that decision.

She grimaced. She had been settled in the suite of rooms generally occupied by the mistress of the house, and though Lucian had taken to accompanying her there each night and though he kissed her before going to his own chambers, he had as yet made no other overtures. Yet, that he was becoming fonder of her she had no doubt. Fondness, however, was not love. Still, many marriages among the *ton* had been contracted for reasons other than love, and very often they did not even have the alleviating factor of fondness.

"If only . . ." she murmured, and sighed deeply, not wishing to pursue that thought any further. But it was impossible not to remember the days and nights they had spent together before the fateful Battle of Waterloo! Thinking about them, she felt a warmth on her cheeks and a telltale throbbing at the base of her throat. There were other sensations as well. Having drunk from the cup of passion, it was hard, indeed, to forget the excitement that heady draft had brought her.

"You must be patient," Dr. Hepworth had told her on that afternoon he had paid her a last, unexpected visit. It had been the day before he and his new bride had taken the coach for Liverpool. "I can see a change in your husband already and 'tis my belief that he will regain his memory, my dear Alicia."

"Let him be right," she prayed silently as the post-chaise passed between the gateposts at the abbey.

Coming into the front hall, Alicia was amazed to find a portmanteau at the foot of the stairs. Nearby was Lucian's many-caped overcoat. And in another second, Lucian himself, dressed for traveling, came hurrying down the stairs. Seeing her, he frowned and said coldly, "I was hoping that you would return before I left."

Alicia tensed, surprised as much by his manner as by his comment. "Where are you going?" she demanded.

"I have had a communication from my man of business. I must leave for London immediately," he said curtly.

"Oh, must you go so far . . . in this weather?" she protested.

"This weather?" he repeated. "I see nothing untoward about the weather." He spoke, she thought, almost challengingly, and he was still regarding her so strangely, almost suspiciously, she decided.

"It is passing cold. The snows cannot be far off."

"You forget that I am Yorkshire-born. And I have been subjected to rougher climates."

"I hope you will be taking the traveling coach."

"That is my intent." He nodded.

"How long will you be away?"

"That will depend upon what he has to tell me," Lucian said cryptically.

Again she read suspicion in his gaze, suspicion intermingled with anger, an anger that appeared to be directed at her. She said, "It must be something very important to take you such a long distance."

"I consider it thus."

"Might I know what it is?" she asked.

She received a smoldering glance. "You will be informed in due course, Alicia." He paused and looked upward as Effie's plaintive voice reached them.

"An' 'ow long will ye be gone, then, Jacob?"

"There's no sayin'," the valet answered in equally unhappy tones. Dressed for traveling, Jacob came slowly down the stairs.

Lucian said crisply, "See if the coach is waiting, Jacob."

"Yes, my Lord." He went out.

Lucian looked at Alicia. "You may tell your abigail that I will be back in something over a week."

"I see," she said. "I hope you are taking outriders with you."

"I am."

Jacob returned. "The coach is waiting, my Lord."

"Good." He bent a stern look on Alicia. "I will bid you farewell, then."

"I wish you a safe journey, Lucian."

"I thank you," he responded curtly, and with a brief bow he strode out, followed by his valet. Alicia moved to the door and, opening it, saw him get into the coach. He did not look back.

Coming out onto the porch, Alicia watched the coach until it rounded a bend in the driveway and was lost to sight. A gust of wind stirred the trees and sent a shower of yellowed leaves to the ground. She shivered. It was a cold wind, but no colder than the man she called husband. Why was he going to London, and on such short notice? Obviously because he had received some urgent news . . . About what? What or who required his presence in the city?

Barbara.

The name had lost some of its potency in the last weeks, but now it loomed large in her consciousness, and into her mind floated the phrase "Journeys end in lover's meetings." And was he going to meet Barbara rather than his man of business? Was that the message that had spurred him into action? She was suddenly positive that it had been. Why else would there have been this drastic change in his attitude? Why else . . . She paused in her thinking, overcome by a great lassitude. It occurred to her that she was weary of trying to fathom the workings of Lucian's mind, weary of trying to compete against the potent charms of the Honorable and Incomparable Barbara Barrington! Evidently, she would always stand between them. She had only to lift a beckoning finger and he would be off!

The wind tore at Alicia's hair and sent another shower of leaves raining down. She felt lonely and, worse yet, defeated. A conclusion she had of late put behind her arose once more, and this time she faced it squarely. She ought not to have pressed her claim on this man, who had once but now no longer loved her. Even if he remained with her, he would always yearn for his lost Barbara. Alicia thought longingly of her father and brother. She had heard from them only sporadically in the past months. Timothy, contrary to expectations, had not remained in London to pursue his writing career. He had returned to Brussels. He and Papa had both told her how much they missed her and how they longed to see her again. And she wanted to see them. She even longed for Brussels. She had never been entirely happy in that city, but despite that and despite their straitened circumstances, she had been loved.

As she came into the house, it seemed to her that the chill walked with her. Staring about the cavernous hall with its two armored figures, she felt even more lonely, and in that moment she made a decision. When Lucian came back from his mysterious visit to London, he would not find her. He had taken the coach, but the post-chaise remained, and as soon as she could put the house in order, she would shake the dust of Yorkshire from her feet forever and go home.

It was raining in London and consequently the streets were even more cluttered than usual. Lucian's coachman, his equipage halted by an enormous dray, was uttering words that reached his passenger only as angry mutters. Lucian sympathized with him. The city had never seemed more drab or uninviting. Of course, he reasoned, he was tired—tired and depressed, which was odd, for he ought to have been exultant. Barbara's letter had contained the news that must free him from the so-called bonds of matrimony. Five sentences from that missive ran though his mind as the coach finally moved forward toward the turn that must bring them onto Clarges Street and the Barrington mansion:

> You are not and have never been wed to her. The license is a fraud. By rights she should be transported to New South Wales for forgery. And fortunately, my dear, I can prove these allegations. The time is not far off when we can be married—as planned.

Lucian moved restively. His leg ached and he was weary. The trip had been arduous. They had covered a distance of nearly two hundred miles in three rather than four days, mainly because he had insisted they drive by night as well as by day—with his outriders prepared to shoot if they were troubled by highwaymen.

Rather than staying in his own house, shut for the season, he had gone to Grillons Hotel, coming to that hostelry at the hour of eleven last night. Being overtired, he had not slept well. Indeed, he had spent a good part of the night thinking and trying to reconcile the young woman he had come to admire, if not to love, with the "abandoned creature," as Barbara had termed her in her letter. Oddly enough, it had been Alicia's image that had haunted the dreams that had visited him in his brief and troubled sleep. One of these images had been particularly strange. He had seen her bearing a great number of bundles and standing on the steps of an old house he was sure he had never viewed before, and he certainly had never known Alicia to be so loaded down with heavy bundles. Yet, she had not seemed to mind being so encumbered. In fact, she had been laughing. To his knowledge, he had also never seen her look so young, so carefree, and at the same time, so very beguiling. She *was* very pretty—more than merely pretty, actually. Of late her looks had improved, and really, she was quite lovely. In fact, in her way she was every bit as beautiful as Barbara, and she appeared to love his old home, something he knew Barbara did not.

Alicia had made great improvements in the house. Furthermore, she had proved to be an excellent hostess. She had appeared to be aware of her guests' wants even before they mentioned them. Several of his friends had privately praised her. Sir Anthony Fothringale had called him a "most fortunate man," adding that if Alicia were an example of what was to be found in Brussels, he would be visiting that city in the near future.

Also, of late Lucian had found himself looking at the door that divided their apartments and wondering what it would be like were he to exchange more than a mere good-night kiss with the woman he was having much less trouble referring to as his wife . . . But, according to Barbara, she had never been his wife. According to Barbara, Alicia was a "scheming harpy," a "cold-blooded adventuress" who had cunningly deceived him. It was very difficult to match the young woman he had been seeing every day for the past few months with Barbara's contemptuous description.

Inadvertently, he found himself thinking of Dr. Hepworth. There had been a time when he had thought Alicia attracted to the physician. He had been wrong about that, and though he had not refined too much upon it, he had greatly admired his wife's courage in bringing Hepworth together with the poor girl she had found in the ruins. Barbara, he knew, would not have done that. She would have wasted no time in remanding the girl to the authorities as a vagrant. She would have been absolutely horrified at the idea of foisting a "ruined" woman on a man she had come to call friend. He frowned. Had Alicia's attitude been based on something more than mere compassion? Had there been an empathy between her and the disgraced Juliet Cotterel, an empathy predicated on their similar circumstances?

Lucian winced and then stiffened. The coach was slowing down. A glance out the window showed him the familiar facade of Barbara's house. As the footman opened the door of the vehicle, it occurred to him that he was most reluctant to descend the three steps to the street, even more reluctant to enter the house. He did not want to hear what Barbara had to tell him concerning his wife. Into his mind flashed an image of Alicia's surprised and troubled face as he had bade her a chill farewell. As the coach had rolled away from the house, he had been unable to resist a backward glance and had seen her standing there on the porch—a small and, he had thought, lonely figure. He had been conscious of wanting to instruct his coachman to stop and turn around. But he had not surrendered to that impulse and he would not surrender to this one either.

As he walked up the steps of the Barrington house, he was surprised to find the curtains closed. Upon ringing, the elderly caretaker, not the butler, admitted him. The hall was darker than usual, lighted only by a pair of candelabra standing on the marble-topped consul table. "Miss Barbara'll be comin' soon. Sit ye down, my Lord," the caretaker advised.

Lucian did not avail himself of this invitation. Instead, he stared about him with increasing surprise. He could see the drawing room from here and it, too, was dark, the shades and curtains drawn. It occurred to him that neither the staff nor Barbara's mother was in residence. While he was speculating on the reasons for that, Barbara came swiftly down the stairs

"Lucian," she cried. "Oh, my dearest, at last, at last!" She flung her arms around him.

Surprised and more taken aback than excited, Lucian kissed her on the cheek but, meeting her astonished and hurt look, hastily remedied his error by kissing her on the lips.

"My dearest"—Barbara loosed a gusty sigh—"you are too, too bold and I should never allow such liberties, but I have missed you so dreadfully."

"I have missed you, too," he responded automatically, and much to his secret amazement, he wondered if that were entirely true. He had missed her from time to time, perhaps, but now . . . He looked around the hall. "Where is your mother, my dear?"

"She is in the country." She gave him a conspiratorial glance. "The house, as you must have guessed, is officially closed and I am ostensibly staying in Wiltshire with a friend. That is what Mama believes, and I beg you'll not betray me. 'Twas in your interest that I came here."

"Was that not a chancy thing to do?" He frowned.

"Entirely"—she flung out her hands—"but I had no choice. Once the runner came to me with his discoveries, I had to follow his advice! Pray excuse me for a moment, my love. You can go into the drawing room. There is a fire laid on."

Considerably mystified by her manner and by the fact that her mother was absent, Lucian came into the drawing room, which, as Barbara had said, was much warmer. Sitting down on a brocade settee near the fire, he stared into the flames. They were only a few shades lighter than Barbara's hair, he thought. She was looking very well, but for some odd reason his heart had not leapt at the sight of her. In fact . . . Before he had time to pursue that thought any further, she had joined him.

"There," she said with some satisfaction. "I have sent for her."

"For whom?" Lucian demanded.

"Madame Tasnier. She is from Brussels and she has some very interesting information for you. But first, let me show you what *I* have!" She moved to a table and, opening a small drawer, took out a folded paper. "The runner procured this in Brussels. Oh, Lucian, I was never so shocked as when he told me all that he had discovered."

"The runner?" Lucian repeated. "Would you be meaning that you hired a Bow Street runner?"

"Exactly, my love. He is a Mr. Blount, a dreadful little man with a vile accent that absolutely grated on my ears—but *clever*. I told him all about that creature who calls herself your wife, and, Lucian, he immediately left for Brussels!"

With an air of triumph, Barbara handed Lucian the folded paper. "This, my dearest," she continued, "is a copy of the marriage register in the church, where you were supposedly married. According to your, er, bride, that wedding took place on June eleventh. This is an exact copy of the church register for that day. Do you see your name on it or hers? I do not."

Unfolding the paper with fingers that were trembling slightly, Lucian scanned it. "No, 'tis not here," he corroborated, and was surprised at the wave of disappointment that washed over him.

"Of course it is not there," she said joyfully. "I never doubted it for a minute. I knew you could not have betrayed me—not you, Lucian. Oh, my poor love, you have been most hardly used."

He put the paper down on an adjacent table. "So it seems," he said heavily.

"However, we will unmask the culprit together," Barbara said happily. "In my estimation she ought to be clapped into Newgate prison, but, of course, there would be the most dreadful scandal. 'Twould be better to send her away. I expect you will have to give her money—quite a sum, I fear, if you are to rid yourself of her."

"She does not seem grasping," he felt it incumbent upon him to protest.

Barbara's eyes narrowed. "Have you become her champion, then? Or perhaps her lover?"

Annoyance flooded through him, though he was not sure why, because naturally Barbara, loving him as she did, would be hurt and suspicious by what she must consider a possible defense. He said quickly, "I am neither. Yet she has not asked me for monies. Quite the contrary, she even wanted to make her own clothes—"

"And you did not want that?" Without giving him a chance to reply, she rushed on, "But I understand your thinking, my own. Servants talk and you did not want to be accused of being penny-pinching, as well she knew. She is very clever. You will see how very clever she has been when you meet Madame Tasnier. She will tell you the real truth about the woman you have mistakenly believed to be your wife." Barbara sighed. "Oh, dear, it is all so ugly and unpleasant, but enough! You are looking very well, my dearest, and how is your poor leg?"

" 'Tis better," he said.

"Oh, that is good. And as I have told you, you are certainly looking more fit. Lucian, my angel, I have missed you dreadfully, as I have said. I am so glad this wretched business will soon be concluded and that strumpet out of your life!"

Much to his surprise, Lucian found himself actually indignant at Barbara's use of that particular term. "I do not think—" he began.

"And," Barbara interrupted, "I am glad that we have a real reason to be rid of her. I thought my suggestion of frightening her from the house a good one. I was the tiniest bit annoyed that you decided against it."

"It would have done no good. She does not believe in ghosts."

"Well, it little matters now . . ." she said, and paused at a knock on the door. "Ah, finally she has arrived," she continued thankfully. There was a touch of triumph in her tone. "Madame Tasnier will tell you everything!"

Madame Tasnier was small, thin, and dressed in the black favored by most lodging-housekeepers. She had a narrow face and beady eyes. Her mouth was thin and her nose was slightly hooked. Her complexion was yellow. To Lucian, she breathed of battered old houses on mean streets, of dark halls, steep stairways, and attic bedrooms. The thought of Alicia dwelling in such a place did not sit well with him, which again filled him with surprise. The woman was, he noted, looking at him with some concern. Bobbing a slight curtsy, she said, "I do not believe that me you remember, *monsieur*?"

"No," he said. "My memory—"

"*Oui*," she interrupted. "Mademoiselle Barrington, she 'as tol' me. It is a sadness that . . . and *très difficile*."

"Yes, it does have its difficulties," he acknowledged. "I am told that you are acquainted with my wife?"

"She is acquainted with the woman who calls herself your wife," Barbara corrected quickly. "We are, as you must know, Madame Tasnier, speaking of one Alicia Delacre."

"Ah, *oui*, that one." Madame Tasnier nodded. "She and the one who call 'imself 'er brother. They in my 'ouse live a short time."

Lucian leaned forward. "He calls himself her brother? Mr. Delacre?"

"Ah, *oui*, that one who is, 'ow you say, an ivory turner."

"An ivory turner!" Lucian exclaimed.

" 'E 'as that reputation." Madame Tasnier nodded.

"I cannot believe that Lucian is interested in his, er, profession, Madame. Tell him about his, er, relations with the woman, known hereabouts as his sister."

"Eh, *bien*. These two . . . they are *très* friendly for a brother and 'is sister. I 'ave seen them . . ." She shook her head. "But I do not like to tell what I 'ave seen."

"Please, for the sake of my poor friend, you must," Barbara prompted. "Please."

"Ah, *non*, I cannot. Suffice to say only that I 'appen to know that these two . . . they are not related."

"How do you know that?" Lucian rasped.

"My dear, you sound as if you did not believe Madame Tasnier." Barbara stared at him in consternation. "There is not much of a family resemblance between them . . . if you will remember."

"No, but—"

"Ah, *mon pauvre monsieur*, I speak the truth." Madame Tasnier sighed. "Rooms they share, but they come at different times and in my 'ouse they meet *pour la première fois*."

"The first time, Lucian, the first time," Barbara said triumphantly.

"Yes, I understood what she meant," he said more sharply than he had intended. He continued, "Would you, Madame Tasnier, would you say that to my wife's face?"

"Lucian," Barbara exclaimed. "Are you once more implying that Madame Tasnier is not telling the truth?"

"C'est vrai." Madame Tasnier drew herself up. *"Monsieur,* me, I speak true, and, *oui, oui, oui,* I would say the same to 'er."

"Then, say it you shall," Lucian exclaimed. "I want you to come with me to Richmond."

"Richmond?" Madame Tasnier looked blank. "Where is this Richmond?"

"It is in Yorkshire, nearly two hundred miles from here," Barbara explained. She looked at Lucian. "My love, you have the register and you have Madame Tasnier's sworn statement. Can it be that you still require more proof?"

"I would like to hear what my . . . what she says when confronted with this woman," Lucian replied. He was surprised at the doubts that were assailing him, surprised because he would not see Alicia in any house over which this creature presided. Yet, coupled with his incipient disbelief was a fear that, after all, she might be telling the truth. He looked at Barbara and, for once, received no pleasure from his contemplation of that beautiful and, he thought for the first time, cold, proud face. She reminded him of the statue of some avenging angel while Alicia, who was every bit as beautiful, exuded warmth and love. It was with something closely akin to pain that he mulled over Barbara's accusations. He fixed his eyes on Madame Tasnier, whom he disliked more each time he looked at her. "Will you come with me to Richmond?" he repeated.

"If you are willing to go, Madame Tasnier, I will accompany you," Barbara said determinedly. "I am sure we will be able to make the journey in your coach, Lucian?"

"Yes," he agreed.

Madame Tasnier visited a sharp look upon Lucian's face.

"Me, I do not like the idea that I am not believed, particularly when it comes to that *salope*. But I will go."

Lucian winced. He was aware of a sinking feeling. He had been trying to test her veracity and she had accepted that test or challenge, as the case might be. "Very well," he said. "I hope that you will be able to start first thing tomorrow morning?"

"Ah, *oui*." Madame Tasnier nodded.

Staring at her unprepossessing countenance, Lucian thought she bore a close resemblance to a bird of prey. He pitied anyone who had had the misfortune to stay in her lodging house and the thought of Alicia being under that roof was particularly horrible to him. And if she had been, he would not blame her for trying any device to be free of it. He did not want to think of her possible connection with the man she had introduced as her brother.

He glanced at Barbara. She was smiling triumphantly and it occurred to him that he would not relish the idea of being closeted with either her or Madame Tasnier in the confines of his coach. He hoped that the weather would permit him to ride on horseback most if not all the way.

❧ 13 ❧

In spite of a well-sprung coach and comfortable inns, Barbara and Madame Tasnier pronounced the journey hectic. Miss Barrington also castigated Lucian on his decision to ride outside most of the way, angrily refuting his excuse that he did not want her to feel crowded. She pointed out that his coach was commodious and that, furthermore, *she* would never have been discommoded by *his* presence. When they finally reached the Barrington estate, both ladies shrank from the thought of five extra miles and Lucian managed to anger Barbara still more by refusing her invitation to remain with them.

" 'Twould not be seemly without your mother in residence," he had said. "I think I must return to the abbey."

"You will not say anything to that woman, will you?" Barbara demanded. "Forewarned is forearmed, you know, and she is very clever."

"I will say nothing," he assured her. His horse being weary, he borrowed a mount from the Barrington stables, and accompanied by Martin, one of his outriders, and Jacob, he set off for the abbey.

It was growing dark by the time Lucian and his companions arrived at the abbey gates. That the gatekeeper did not come out to greet them failed to surprise him. He was old and crochety and a glance through his window would suffice, but it occurred to Lucian that it was time and past that the man be pensioned off. He had done very little about the servants. He had also failed to hire more keepers. And that he should have done, given Juliet Cotterel's warning. He had been remiss all around, letting Alicia get along with what could be called a skeleton staff, at least compared to the retinue of retainers in most country houses. She had not complained and she had managed very well.

He frowned. It was amazing how his initial prejudice had dissipated, and without his even knowing it. No, that was not entirely true. Somewhere in the depths of his mind, he had known it, had desired her as much, if he were absolutely frank with himself, as much as he had once desired Barbara. It was well that Barbara could not see into his mind.

During the past four days, he had been trying to deal with the possibility that once the situation with Alicia was resolved, he would be able to wed Barbara, who, when they had put up at the various inns to be found along the Great North Road, had said more than once that she hated Yorkshire in general and the abbey in particular.

She had begun several sentences with the observation, "Were it not for you, dearest Lucian, I would never set foot in this part of the country again. I hated it as a child, with its freezing winds and its bleak moors. Indeed, I wonder that that creature who has had the temerity to call herself your wife had the fortitude to stand it."

Upon his answering that Alicia had seemed to like the abbey, she had attributed that to her oft-mentioned "duplicity," adding that obviously there were no ends to which she would not go in order to retain her hold over him.

Thinking of Barbara's contentions, it was still difficult for him to match them with the young woman he had come to know. Alicia had seemed to love the abbey and she certainly had labored long and hard to rearrange the rooms. She was liked by his friends, and generally they could tell the true from the false. The servants respected her and they were even more discerning than their masters. If only there was not this blackness in his mind . . .

Riding around a bend in the road, he was surprised and shocked to find that the house was dark. Usually, by this hour, the windows were ablaze with candlelight. He glanced over his shoulder at Martin and Jacob. "There does not seem to be anyone at home," he remarked uneasily.

"No, my Lord," Martin said.

"An' where be Effie?" Jacob sounded equally uneasy.

Lucian spurred his horse forward, and reaching the entrance to the house, he leapt down and secured his mount at a nearby post. Martin and Jacob would have ridden to the stables, but something prompted Lucian to say quickly, "No, stay with me."

A few seconds later, coming up on the porch, a most unwelcome suspicion was forming in Lucian's mind. Had Alicia taken advantage of his absence to flee? Had she, being as clever as Madame Tasnier and Barbara insisted, guessed that his hasty decision to leave for London was based on the fact that her perfidy had come to light? It was a suspicion he must needs entertain, and yet, at the same time, he deeply regretted that necessity. In spite of all Madame Tasnier had had to say in London and during the course of their journey, her presence had continued to revolt him; oddly enough, the idea of Alicia spending as much as a moment under her roof had continued to disgust and anger him. However, he remembered unhappily, the woman had not deviated from her story one iota and there was the further evidence of the marriage register.

Reaching the door, he saw that the curtains of the small windows on either side of the door were not even drawn. Was the house empty, then? He slammed the knocker against its plate and then there were cries behind him. He whirled in time to see Martin stagger and fall beside Jacob, who lay at

the bottom of the steps. A dark shape with something in its
hand sprang toward him. He moved aside but could not avoid
a blow to the head. It sent sparks dancing before his eyes and
was followed by a blotting out of everything.

The cannon boomed and there was the clash of steel on
steel. On every side of him came grunts and groans and cries
of mortal agony. He lay on the ground, his face pressed
against the earth. His head ached fiercely and there was a
pounding at his temples. He had been struck down, he realized, while fighting hand to hand with a French officer. The
man's visage had been splotched with blood. He was weaken-
ing, and then, from behind, someone else had come and
struck the blow that had felled him. His leg hurt him, too. He
was in considerable pain, but at least he was alive. He was
glad of that. If he had died, he would never see his love
again, and even if he went to heaven, it would be hell without
Alicia.

Rough voices were in his ears and a woman's cry . . . A
woman on the battlefield? Some officers' wives had traveled
with them, but could not have ventured into the thick of the
fighting. The guns had suddenly stopped booming and now
he no longer felt the rubble of the field beneath his cheek.
No, there was a floor . . . A floor? Yes, he could not be
mistaken in that . . . a wooden floor. Had he been pulled
into one of the little houses that he had seen on his way
here?

"Do not touch me," someone cried. It had been a woman's voice, a voice he knew. Lucian opened his eyes and saw
furniture legs. And beyond them, on the wall, flickering
shadows cast there by candle flames. And across the floor he
now saw feet, small feet in neat black slippers. He tensed.
Those feet were bound together by a rope and above them
was the edge of a gown, a golden-brown material that he
knew from somewhere . . . and there was a sound in his ears,
footsteps, heavy footsteps coming down a flight of stairs.

"Damn'n blast, I cannot find 'em," a man growled.

"Damn ye for a blasted simpleton. I told ye where to look," rasped another equally rough voice.

"But 'tis all every which way . . . wasn't where we left'm. Somebody's been at them trunks."

"Ah, an' would you be knowin' about that, my pretty?" demanded his companion.

"I do not know what you mean," came the answer, delivered in a small, unsteady voice.

"Alicia," Lucian mouthed, and started to raise his throbbing head, but thought better of it. He closed his eyes as memories parted from his mind for so long a time rolled over him like the waves of an ocean, shutting out all other sounds but bringing with them realization, at last. And with it came a lifting of the black curtain that concealed so many, many secrets. Yet, he could not dwell on these; he must try to understand what had happened: why Alicia, his dearest love, his wife, was bound to a chair in the great hall of the abbey, by thieves, two of them, unless he were deeply mistaken. No, more than two, he decided as another set of footsteps clumped heavily across the floor.

"Wot's all this?" demanded the newcomer. "Where's the swag?"

" 'E can't find it," returned Voice Number Two.

"Wot's this? 'Ave ye in yer mind to gammon me?"

There were strong protests from the other two men and then the third man said contemptuously, "The two o' ye couldn't find yer own noses'n them attached to yer ugly faces. I tol' you where 'twas. Ye come wi' me'n ye'll find it right enough."

"Wot? 'N leave 'im on the floor wi'out bindin' 'im up?"

"Nah, look at 'im. Ain't stirred an inch since I laid 'im out," said the second man. Footsteps approached Lucian. His head was lifted by the hair and let drop; pain shot through him, but resolutely he did not stir. "You see . . . 'e's as cold as a trout an' if yer not sure look at this."

Lucian had expected it and braced himself, but when the

kick to his ribs was administered, a groan escaped him.
Fortunately, it was covered by Alicia's scream.

"Let him alone," she wailed. "Can you not see—" There
was another cry, followed by rough laughter.

"Let 'er be," Voice Number Three exclaimed. "Ye can
buss 'er later'n to yer 'eart's content. She be a pretty piece,
I'll tell you'n a fair exchange for the one wot got away, wot
d'ye say to that, my lass? 'Twas you took in our Juliet, were
it not? An' you'll 'oo'll go in 'er place, one wench is very
like the next."

"I'd rather die," she cried.

" 'Twas wot she said, but she didn't, 'n didn't even try.
She were 'appy enough'n ye'll be 'appy too. Let me gi' ye a
taste o' wot she got'n see if you don't agree, lovey."

There was another cry from Alicia. Lucian bit back a
groan. He was hard put not to stir, not to leap to his feet and
choke the life from her tormentor. However, in his present
weakened condition, he could do very little against the three
of them. He would have to wait.

"Bide ye there, Mark," one of the men growled.

"Aye, I don't mind," the other responded.

In another few minutes only Mark remained in the hall,
striding back and forth. Lucian, daring to open his eyes,
could see the glint of his spurs on his mud-caked boots.
Suddenly he strode to Alicia's chair and now his thick legs
shut it from Lucian's vision. Tensing, he cautiously lifted his
head. A wave of dizziness coursed through him and Mark
growled, "Eh, but yer a pretty piece. I'll 'ave a taste o' ye
myself. Share'n share alike's wot I say."

"Keep away from me," Alicia cried furiously. "You
. . ." Her words were muffled, and listening to those strangled sounds, Lucian could bear it no longer. Rising swiftly
but silently, he saw the suit of armor with the mace caught in
its mailed fist. As a child, he had once pulled it out and tried
to swing it around him, but to no avail and an eventual
beating from his father. Yet, it had come from that hand

easily enough, he remembered; it had only been resting there. Hoping against hope, he reached for it and pulled it out, but this time the figure rocked dangerously and crashed to the floor. Caught off guard, the man called Mark turned with a cry and Lucian swung the mace, catching his would-be assailant in the chest. With a strangled groan, he stood staring wide-eyed at Lucian and then, clutching his chest, fell forward, lying very still. Shooting a look at the stairs, Lucian stepped to them and stood there for a moment, his ears straining for sounds, but there were none. Moving back, he said to Alicia, "Are there more than three of them?"

"I do not believe so. I am not sure," she said weakly. She looked up at him in concern. "Your head . . . and he kicked you."

"Never mind that, my very dearest," he said. Moving behind her chair, he winced, seeing that the ropes that bound her wrists were pulled so tight that even in the wavering light in the hall her hands looked unnaturally white. Kneeling, he started to yank at the knots.

"You must not," she hissed. "They may return. That man had a pistol. You must get it," she urged.

"Yes, you are right." Lucian rose, and bending over the fallen man, he started to turn him over and stopped as he saw the blood oozing from his crushed chest. The pistol was thrust into his belt. He swiftly wrenched it out, pushing him down and hoping that Alicia had not seen the terrible wound. As he straightened up, he heard a footstep and shot a look at the stairs, but realized in that same moment that the sound was behind him.

"The door, Lucian," Alicia gasped.

Turning, he saw the door opening. He cocked the pistol, and putting his finger on the trigger, he stepped forward and then stopped as Martin entered. He looked pale and his jaw was swollen, but his expression was grim and determined. "Thank God, ye be all right, my Lord," he muttered.

"And you, man?" Lucian demanded.

"I be fit as a fiddle'n Jacob, 'e's gone to fetch 'elp."

"Good." Lucian thrust the pistol at Martin. "The other two villains will be coming down. Keep this trained on the stairs and shoot if need be. I must see to my wife." Lucian stepped back to Alicia's chair and would have started with the knots had he not remembered the pocket knife he always carried with him. Pulling it out, he cut through the ropes that bound her and then knelt to free her feet.

"Lucian," she whispered urgently, "had you not better—"

"This will take but a moment, my angel," he assured her huskily.

"My Lord . . ." Martin said in a low voice.

Lucian cut the last of the ropes and rose. "Do you . . ." he whispered, and then, looking in the direction of the stairs, he stiffened as he heard descending footsteps. From the sound he guessed they were on the third-floor landing. "Alicia . . ." He turned back to her, and pulling her to her feet, he half-carried her to the door and pushed her onto the porch. "Stay here," he whispered, and hurried back. Bending down, he seized the mace, crossed to Martin's side, and muttered, "Shoot, but not to kill."

"Damn ye for a thick-witted cove. Did I not tell ye them necklaces was there? It wanted only a bit o' lookin'."

"Wasn't where we put'm," came the sullen reply. "Damned stupid to 'ave 'em 'idden in the 'ouse in the first place."

" 'Ow was I to know when they'd be back. Ain't nobody been 'ere for twelve year, save 'im wot's on the gate'n deaf as a post."

They were nearing the first landing now. Lucian clutched the mace and Martin raised the pistol. And then the pair were in sight. There was a loud shot followed by a yell of agony as one of the men staggered into view and fell on the landing. The other dashed for the balustrade and was trying to leap over it when Lucian threw the mace, striking him in the leg. With a hoarse scream, he crumpled on the floor and lay next to his companion, writhing and groaning.

"Lucian!" Alicia ran to his side.

He put an arm around her. "Did I not tell you to stay outside?" he tried to speak sternly.

"I could not." She stared at the fallen rogues and shuddered. "I—I was afraid they might kill you."

He looked down at her and drew her closer. "But I could not die, my own not when I had just begun to live. Oh, Alicia," —tears clouded his eyes— "can you ever forgive me? All I can say in my own defense is that I could not remember."

"Oh, my love." She reached up to touch his cheek. "There's naught to forgive, now that you are here with me again . . . really here."

Unmindful of Martin, unmindful of his groaning and disabled prisoners, Lucian gathered his wife in his arms and covered her face with kisses.

It was not until several minutes later that he thought to ask, "Where are the other servants?"

Alicia regarded him gravely. "I gave them leave to take the next three days off. You see, I did not want them to tell you where I had gone. And I had it in mind to leave Effie here, for I knew she would want to be with Jacob. They will be married, you see. Consequently, I suggested that she go with Mary, but if I had been thinking clearly, I would not have been that foolish. I should have left someone in the house, but my thoughts were in such a turmoil . . . you see . . ."

He put his arms around her. "You need not give me any more explanations, my love. I know that I was the reason for that turmoil, but I swear I will make it up to you now and for the rest of my life." He kissed her once again.

"Barbara!"

In the middle of the night, the name burst from Lucian's lips, awakening Alicia.

"Barbara?" she murmured.

She was considerably startled when her husband began to laugh loudly. It was a moment before he was able to say, "Good God, in all the uproar and with the constable here, I completely forgot that she and your, er, landlady are anxiously awaiting me—or rather us."

"My landlady, love?" Alicia demanded confusedly.

He flushed. "I did have trouble believing it," he said defensively. "Damn Barbara, is there no end to her perfidy or, rather, I ought to say, her blasted pride?"

"What can you mean, Lucian?"

Reluctantly, between kisses and apologies, he produced his explanation, adding grimly, "But, my love, I think we must play this comedy to its conclusion, do you not agree?"

It was a moment before Alicia completely understood his purpose, but when she did, she laughed delightedly. "In other circumstances, I might take pity on her, but on this occasion I am content to obey my husband."

The news of the death of one and the capture and arrest of the two other highwaymen who had been terrorizing the county for the last decade spread quickly. The tale had reached Barbara's house before Lucian and Alicia arrived. Consequently, the caretaker greeted them with a broad smile. He went as far as to say, "It were bang up wot you done, my Lord," and having delivered himself of this praise, he quickly ushered them into the drawing room.

A fire was glowing on the hearth beneath a massive marble fireplace, but there was a chill in the room and general mustiness suggesting that it had not been aired in some time. The furnishings were old and heavy. Looking about her, Alicia could well understand why Barbara preferred the city. Her thoughts were scattered by the entrance of her hostess and Madame Tasnier, whom Lucian, she discovered, had described to perfection. Furthermore, there was something about the woman that made Alicia shiver. She cast a side glance at Lucian and saw that once more he was looking very grim. Fortunately, his expression went well with the part he was determined to play. He had risen as the Incomparable Barbara and her guest entered, and now he lifted Barbara's hand to his lips.

"My dearest." Barbara looked well in a gown of her favorite green. She kept her eyes on Lucian to the exclusion of Alicia, whose presence she had not deigned to acknowledge. "What is this I hear about your heroics at the abbey? Did you indeed capture those rogues single-handedly?"

"No, that is an exaggeration, Barbara. I had the help of my outrider, Martin."

"As always, you are too modest, my dearest love." Barbara's green glance took in and again dismissed Alicia. "And I hear that Lady Harvey's long-lost pearl and diamond necklace was discovered in an attic trunk as well as other jewelry. Is that true?"

"Quite true, Barbara. There was quite a little cache of jewels. They are now in the custody of the constable, but be that as it may. As you can see, I have brought my wife."

"Your . . . wife?" Barbara said so contemptuously that Alicia longed to hit her. "You are using that title out of habit, I presume."

"Yes," he said meaningfully. "Out of habit."

Barbara turned to Alicia, saying coldly, "I presume you must recognize Madame Tasnier?"

"No, I . . . do not," Alicia faltered, hoping that she sounded as nervous as Lucian had instructed her to be.

"Ah, *mais moi*, I recognize you," Madame Tasnier said, her small eyes boring into Alicia's face.

"You do?" Alicia gazed at her in well-feigned amazement. "But I am sure we have never met."

"Ah, do you so soon forget your old friends, then, *mademoiselle*?" Madame Tasnier inquired.

"Do you, Alicia?" Lucian asked.

"But we have never met," Alicia cried.

"Doxy!" Barbara snapped. "And she your landlady for at least five years."

"Five years . . ." Alicia faltered. "I do not understand. My father and my brother—"

"Your brother! Do tell us about your brother, *Lady* Morley," Barbara said contemptuously. "If, indeed, you have one."

"But I do," Alicia exclaimed, her eyes wide and her expression confused. "His name is Timothy and you yourself have met him."

"I?" Barbara questioned a slight smile playing about her mouth. "I did meet a man with you, but I put it to you, Lady Morley, that he whom you called brother was, in effect, no other relation to you than—"

"Enough," Lucian suddenly exclaimed. "I do not wish to continue this travesty. It is wrong to subject my wife to such ugliness—even though she, as well as myself, knows that 'tis all a lie. My apologies, my dearest love." He moved to Alicia and put an arm around her. "Suffice to say, Barbara, that I have good cause to thank the rogues who invaded our house, for I suffered a blow on my head that restored my memory. You say that there is no record of my marriage? I find that very odd, considering that we were married in Brussels at the Church of St. Stephen on June eleventh, 1815. And I think that the record must remain in the register that you were clever enough to copy or to have copied—perhaps by the enterprising Mr. Blount, if, indeed, there is such a person. From what I have heard about Bow Street runners, they would scorn to provide anyone with such patently false information. As for you, Madame Tasnier . . ." He paused and was pleased to see the woman dart a terrified glance at Barbara's frozen face.

"I—I—" she began.

"I expect," Lucian continued inexorably, "that you are some manner of actress. 'Twas my original intent to have you prisoned, but my wife has talked me out of it. As for you, my dear Barbara, I believe that you remember well enough what you said to me on the occasion of my leaving for Brussels? I am flattered, indeed, by your change of heart, but as you see, I am married, and very happily. And now, we will bid you good morning." He turned to Alicia, adding softly, "Come, my angel, my good angel, let us go home and commence our life together."

✺ L'envoi ✺

Alicia was sitting on a little stool not far from the broken tower in the abbey ruins. Propped on an easel before her was a half-finished canvas. She was adding a touch of gray to a depiction of the tower roof when she heard her name called. She looked up with a smile. "Tilda!"

"Ah." Her visitor surged forward, holding up the voluminous skirts of her riding habit. Coming to Alicia's side, she stared at the work. "Ah, that is something I like. You will have to give me one of your pictures, or rather, I shall commission you to paint our gardens. They are just coming into bloom and the tulips are magnificent, all yellow and purple and pink. But should we wait until the roses come out? How are you feeling, my love?"

"Very well indeed," Alicia assured her.

"And how is dear Lucian feeling?"

"Calmer than the first time, though he does have periods of nervousness."

"Did I not tell you that is the way of it? They are like hens on a hot griddle, the first time, but wonderfully calm by the second lying-in, at least that was true of Hewes. And how is the son and heir?"

"Sleeping after a most rambunctious morning. Lucian took him to the east meadow and he came back babbling of tadpoles and minnows, both of which he wants to keep in his room, much to Effie's horror."

"She ought to be used to the ways of boys. Her lad is the same age as little Lucian."

"Oh, she is." Alicia smiled.

"And you might tell her that my Margaret is the same way, but her preference is for beetles, if you can believe it. I have tried in vain to get her to turn her attention to butterflies, but as yet, to no avail. The boys are no help, for they will encourage her. Mrs. Simpson, the governess, has threatened to leave and you know how difficult it is to get anyone to come here . . . But enough! I have news for you."

"And what news would that be?" Lucian suddenly emerged from behind a broken wall.

Tilda jumped. "You did startle me," she cried accusingly. "Have you been there all this while?"

"No." He grinned. "Ought my ears to be burning?"

"Not in the least." Alicia smiled up at him fondly. "We were talking about Tilda's beetles."

"Not my beetles," Tilda corrected, "Margaret's beetles. But I must tell you that Barbara is finally getting married, and high time. Her mama is ecstatic. She was sure that Barbara must remain at her side—and several disappointments have not sweetened my dearest cousin's temper. Imagine, she actually cast out lures for your brother, Timothy, Alicia!"

"For Timothy! I never heard that," Alicia exclaimed.

"Oh, did I not tell you? But I do not think I have seen you in the last fortnight. Her mama told me that when Timothy's latest book was on display at Hatchard's, Barbara met him and did not make the connection. She invited him to a soiree at her house."

"He did not come, surely," Alicia exclaimed. "But, of course, he would not—he would have let me know."

"I think, my love, that he did go and left early. Barbara, I understand, was furious."

"Oh, dear, he ought to have resisted that particular temptation," Alicia sighed.

"I do not agree." Lucian grinned. "But for Timothy's

sake, I am glad he did not have a lapse of memory. Who would Barbara be marrying, Tilda?''

"A Mr. Hope from America, whom she met in London. I expect he was impressed by her background—so that he did not mind her age."

"But she is not very old," Alicia said kindly.

"She will be twenty-seven in August and looks much older," Tilda said with some satisfaction. "I never saw anyone fade so quickly, but no matter. She and her bride-groom will be settling in America, a place called Charleston, wherever that is. I only hope she likes it."

"She would never give up hope," Lucian said wickedly.

"I am sure she never will!" Tilda laughed. "For 'tis the first time that anyone has come up to scratch. I wonder if she will meet Dr. Hepworth and his wife over there?"

"Nova Scotia is a goodly distance from Charleston, I think," Alicia said.

"Oh, is it?" Tilda spoke vaguely. "I know so little about the New World, but have you heard from the doctor recently? I hope that when you last wrote to him, you told him that we still miss him, though I do think Dr. Kennard is a worthy replacement but certainly not so handsome. He is doing well, is he not? I think you told me that he was. Dr. Hepworth, I mean."

"Very well, indeed." Alicia nodded. "He has bought a new house and Juliet has given birth to twin girls."

"Oh, lovely, then they have four or five children?"

"Four," Alicia said. "She had another son two years ago."

"Oh, that's right. I would love to have twin girls myself and dress them alike . . . But I must go. I came only to tell you about sweet Barbara, and do not forget, Alicia, you must paint our gardens. I will let you know when. June, I think, or perhaps July."

"Not July," Lucian protested.

"Really? Why not?" Tilda regarded him in some surprise.

"Have you forgotten that my wife is breeding?" he demanded sternly.

"But not until October, I thought. I mean, 'tis expected then, is it not?"

"Still . . ." He frowned.

"Goodness." Tilda regarded him amazedly and then grinned at Alicia. "I thought you told me . . ." She shook her head. "Well, perhaps by the third." With a wave of her hand, she was off.

"And what did she mean by that, my love?" Lucian demanded.

Alicia smiled up at him. "I think she believes you overconcerned, and I fear I must agree with her. 'Tis six months away, my dearest."

"In July, 'twill be four months only, my precious. I'll not have it said that I do not care for my own."

"No one could ever say that," she murmured happily.

He knelt beside her. "And can you blame me?" he demanded. "Sometimes, I wonder what I have done to deserve you." he slipped his arms around her.

"Everything anybody could possibly do," she managed to say lovingly before he silenced her with his kiss.